DON'T TELL

A PSYCHOLOGICAL THRILLER

MARY STONE
MATT GIEGERICH

MARY
STONE
PUBLISHING

Copyright © 2024 by Mary Stone Publishing

All rights reserved.

No part of this book may be reproduced in any form or by any electronic or mechanical means, including information storage and retrieval systems, without written permission from the author, except for the use of brief quotations in a book review.

❧ Created with Vellum

Mary Stone
To my three boys, who understand the thrill of a twist and share my love for the darker corners of storytelling. This journey into the mind is for you.

Matt Giegerich
Dedicated to therapists and mental health workers everywhere. Thank you for caring.

DESCRIPTION

I don't trust anyone. Not after my dad's abandonment. Not after the toxic affair with my high school teacher. Not after the attack that nearly killed me.
And definitely not after the lies I've told—to myself and others.

For twelve years, I've buried my secrets, trying to live the perfect suburban life. I'm married to a wonderful man, and I have a rewarding career at Camp Wildfire—a sanctuary for troubled teens nestled on the edge of a sprawling forest. Life looks good on the surface, but one crack and it could all fall apart.

Turns out, that crack has a name. Amanda.

Her arrival rips open old wounds, forcing me to confront the past I've kept hidden from everyone, including my husband. The secrets I've buried are threatening to destroy me—and I've recently learned that I'm not the only one hiding something big.

A camper has gone missing, echoing a tragic disappearance from years ago. As I learn more about the girl, I'm forced to question everything. My marriage. My memories. And my own sanity.

Because some monsters are real. Especially the ones inside us.

From bestselling author Mary Stone and Matt Giegerich, Don't Tell is a pulse-pounding psychological thriller that will captivate fans of The Perfect Marriage, Behind Closed Doors, and The Wife Between Us. Get ready for a twisty, unputdownable journey into the darkness that lurks behind the perfect facade.

CHAPTER
ONE

They say secrets keep you young. I call bullshit.

The woman sitting across from me—knitted brow, lips thinned by worry—looks like she'd agree. Her manicured nails tap an impatient rhythm on my desk, a subtle reminder of her status.

Queen Bitch.

This is Carol Holland, the mother of a prospective resident at Camp Wildfire and my total opposite. While her polished appearance speaks of wealth and power, I sit here with clipped fingernails, a loose ponytail, and cheeks sun-kissed from too much time by the lake.

It's clear in the set of Carol's shoulders and the tilt of her chin. She doesn't like being questioned, especially by people she considers beneath her station. Too bad for her that in this office, *my* office, power sits on my side of the desk.

"Have you asked Amanda who the father is?"

She glares at me like I'm a bug in her chardonnay. "Of course I've asked my daughter who the father is. At least a hundred times. But she's fourteen years old. She won't look me in the eye on her best day. Won't let me within a thousand feet of all this chaos."

I twist my wedding ring, but my focus doesn't waver from hers. "Is there a reason you use the word 'chaos?'"

"Don't you dare therapize me." Carol slams her four-shot soy Starbucks cappuccino down, sending a spray of beige foam across my desk. "There are plenty of camps for troubled teens around here. If you're going to waste my time, I'll take my daughter and my checkbook somewhere else."

I blink a few times but keep a blank face otherwise. No mother of a prospective camper has ever been this aggressive. "I was under the impression you'd researched the options and chosen Camp Wildfire for a reason."

She huffs, and her frown lines deepen. "Yes, naturally, I did my research. My daughter did too. Camp Wildfire was her top pick." She picks up her coffee but doesn't drink it. "I need you to find out the name of the man who impregnated my daughter."

The hair on the back of my neck lifts. "Man? This wasn't a boy from school?"

If an older man impregnated Amanda, that changes everything.

"I don't know who it was. That's what I'm saying." Carol picks at the order label on her coffee cup, eyes tearing. "Everything's been impossible with her, ever since this condition began."

That word—*condition*—is so demeaning. Part of me wants to tell this uppity mother about my life as a teenage girl. I want her to comprehend a fraction of the confusion and shame her daughter is experiencing. And I want her to understand that this "condition" is not the end of anyone's life.

But that kind of self-disclosure is inappropriate. And I

don't want to do anything that will risk her pulling Amanda from my care.

"I'm confident we'll be able to help Amanda while she's here at Camp Wildfire." I make unblinking eye contact and keep my voice steady.

"Good." Carol crumples the label in her fist. "You have to keep her safe."

"This camp is a refuge."

"And the nearby town—"

"A sleepy little village. Two stoplights. One gas station. No real crime in a decade or more." My left eyelid twitches at the word "crime," and I secretly admonish it.

I can cite the amount of time, exactly, since my personal experience with violent crime in this area. Eleven years and eleven months ago, almost to the day.

"A young woman suffered a brutal beating by two men who left her for dead."

Carol sizes me up, and I square my shoulders. The people pleaser in me wants to make a joke, somehow draw a smile from her. But I force myself to sit through the tension, projecting as much calm confidence as I can.

It works.

Carol Holland dabs at a tear at the corner of her eye, motioning for me to hand her a pen from the cup on my desk. When I select one and pass it over, she takes the pen with trembling fingers and scans the paperwork one last time.

Amanda will stay here for eight weeks. I have permission to record all my sessions with her. And she'll receive three square meals a day along with enough time in nature to make every office-bound adult on the Eastern Seaboard burn with jealousy.

But Camp Wildfire is a good place. A home for troubled girls or those whose parents think they're troubled. We're always at full capacity, housing 100 girls year-round, and there's no shame in sending a child here. Nonetheless, Carol avoids my eyes as she signs the papers and hands them back to me, clinging to the shred of pride she walked in with.

A few moments later, I lead Carol out to the lobby. Her daughter waits on a padded bench, crowded by an oversize spider plant on the end table.

Like her mother, Amanda has shoulder-length blond hair with a featherlight presence that's at once delicate and formidable. She shares the defiant look evident in her mother's blue eyes that says they know the world treats them differently because they're beautiful, and they don't trust it for a second.

I know it well.

This defiance is also evident in the faded blue streaks in Amanda's hair, a remnant of teenage rebellion that will likely remain when her due date rolls around in a few months.

Carol looms over her daughter and reaches out to touch her, though her hand hovers a few inches short of the girl's shoulder.

Who does she think will break if the two connect? Her daughter or herself?

"Okay, Mandy. I'm leaving you here with Ms. Silva. We're all set."

My maiden name rolls off Carol's tongue. At this point, I hear it more than my married name, though technically everyone outside the camp knows me as Mrs. Lizette Yuen.

Amanda balances her phone on her generous baby bump, shifting in her seat but not looking away from the colorful game she's playing.

With a clenched jaw, Carol manages a strained "okay, then" and leans in for an awkward hug. Amanda recoils, her sudden motion knocking the spider plant off the end table.

Well...that answers that question.

"Oops." Amanda glances at the toppled-over plant and the splayed-out soil with flat indifference.

"Amanda. Don't tell me you're just going to sit there and look at the plant you knocked over."

She turns back to the game on her phone with a casual shrug. "It's not my fault it's in a stupid place."

Carol uses the tip of her suede pump to gather the dirt into a small pile, casting a look in my direction. "I'm sorry. Seems I forgot my daughter is secretly a royal princess." She sends a glare in Amanda's direction, but the girl is glued to her game again.

I bet Mr. and Mrs. Holland employed the electronic babysitter more often than they'd admit. Not that I can judge them for it.

"It's fine, Carol." I put my hand on her shoulder. "I'll have the maintenance staff take care of this."

Carol mutters a quick thank-you, scraping the toe of her shoe against the bench leg to clear off the dirt. "I guess I didn't need to dig my favorite pumps into potting soil."

Amanda snickers, running a hand through her hair. "Oh no. Not the Jimmy Choos."

"Amanda, please." Carol locks eyes with her daughter for a long moment. At last, she cracks, pulling Amanda into a tight embrace that the young woman does not reciprocate in the slightest.

I've seen hundreds of goodbyes like this at Camp Wildfire. Carol wants to appear loving, but she's done and said so many horrible things over the preceding months, there's no way she can buy it back with one heartfelt goodbye.

Amanda wants to appear tough and independent, but she's wearing the Tiffany charm bracelet that was likely a gift from her high-powered dad. And it'll be a long time, if ever, before she cuts those purse strings.

It's clear from talking to the Holland women that secrets don't keep us young. They simply *keep* us. Afraid. Contained. Smaller than any person should be.

Amanda Holland stands stone-faced by her twin bed, her expression unchanging as I point out the cabin's perks—no spiders, intact windows, fresh linens—with the most optimism I can muster. "It's one of the nicer accommodations at Wildfire," I tell her, though her scowl suggests she's hardly impressed.

As I finish laying out her schedule—individual therapy once a day, group therapy three times a week—I reach into my bag with a smile. "Almost forgot. I have a present for you."

A flicker of excitement lights up her eyes before she covers it up with her standard mask of teenage disdain. "I don't want any presents."

"You sure?" I slip a plastic container of peanut butter fudge from my backpack and extend it to her. "Got this from the shop in town."

Amanda takes the treat, rolling her eyes. "You're not going to win me over with fudge."

"I can take it back if you don't want it." I reach toward the container.

She pulls the sweet treat close to her body before shoving it into the top drawer of her dresser.

"Great. Now, let's go. I'll show you the forest out back. Perfect spot for meditating, journaling, or secretly eating peanut butter fudge."

I stride with purpose as Amanda hustles to follow me out to the trails behind the cabin. She doesn't know it, but her intake interview has begun.

A gentle breeze plays with my long brown hair as we approach the woods. I catch Amanda's gaze drifting. It's a reluctant concession to the scene's beauty, and I'll take it. But there's a stark energy shift as we set foot inside the forest.

The canopy is so rich that the forest floor is dark despite

the sun shining high overhead. A moist, piney scent hangs in the air. And before we've made it ten feet past the tree line, swarms of buzzing mosquitoes close in from every side.

Amanda swipes at the mosquitoes like she's swinging an axe. "Get away from me, asshole bugs!" But the swarm is so dense, the swiping does nothing.

Ignoring the cursing, I speed up. "Five more minutes, and we'll be at the lake. You're gonna love it."

"Saw pictures online." Amanda splats a bug against her arm, panting as she works to keep pace. "More of a pond than a lake. I bet it's only there for 'troubled teens' to drown themselves in."

I burst out laughing. I had not expected the gallows humor, though given Amanda's attitude, maybe I should have. "Sorry. Note to self." I tap my temple with a finger. "Jokes about drowning teens are not funny."

"Wasn't a joke." Amanda glances sideways at me.

"We try not to use terms like 'troubled teen' here at Camp Wildfire anyway." I step on a series of rocks, crossing a small stream toward the lake. "We prefer 'wasted youth,' or just 'degenerates.' 'Tiny little psychopaths' also works."

This time, Amanda cracks a grin. "You can't say stuff like that."

"I was a total 'degenerate' as a teenager, so I'm allowed." I stop and pull a pair of ice-cold water bottles from my bag and hold one out to her.

Amanda shakes her head. "I'm just counting the years until I'm finally legal." Her fingers trace the rough texture of the tree bark beside us. "Less than four left."

I take a long drink of water and can't stop from examining her pregnant belly. Carol mentioned that Amanda's six months along, but given the size of her stomach, she looks seven or more. I cap the water and stash it in my bag. "What happens then?"

"I can leave my parents' house and move in with the love of my life." Her face softens, and her eyes mist over as her lips stretch into a warm smile.

Look at that. Her smile muscles are fully functioning.

When I offer her a tissue, she dabs at her eyes. "He's so sweet. Nothing like the boys at school. The last time he saw me, he just couldn't stop telling me how beautiful I am, how much I glow, and how happy he is that I'm going to be the mother of his child."

"Must be hard to be away from someone like that." I walk along the path through a bramble, holding the branches back so Amanda can follow unscathed. I'm treading carefully, both literally and figuratively, with this conversation. "This guy…he's older? Has his own place?"

"I didn't say that." Amanda turns sideways to squeeze through the brush, and we continue.

Knowing the risks of pushing too hard, I backpedal a bit. "Sorry, you'd said he wasn't like the boys at school, so I assumed."

She's quiet for a while as we walk. "We have a secure attachment style, so we're fine when we're away from each other. Lots of days, we don't even need to talk."

Attachment style, noun
The nature of an individual's emotional bonds with those closest to them, typically formed in childhood and manifested in adult romantic relationships. Three out of four attachment styles are essentially toxic. Often leads to a push-pull dynamic in which one partner pursues and the other becomes cold and aloof. See also: the lyrics to most love songs ever written.

. . .

My heart sinks as her words confirm my worst fears. Teenagers don't use clinical terms like "secure attachment style." Psychological jargon, probably lifted from a textbook, is a telltale sign of grooming. And there's no way Amanda and her groomer don't have an "anxious-avoidant" dynamic.

I can hear my own groomer's voice in my head. *"You're so mature. You're wise beyond your years."*

As if reading my thoughts, Amanda continues, her voice gentle. "Sometimes I get kind of anxious, but he always tells me when I'm being crazy. We all need that, don't you think?" She rubs a hand over her belly. "We're going to raise the baby together, like a real family." Her tone drips with dreamy optimism about her future with her baby's father.

Frustration sears through me as I fight the urge to shake Amanda into reality. I take a deep breath to center myself before rejoining the conversation, intent on discovering the identity of Amanda's mysterious lover.

But she's caressing her belly, lost in the miracle of life, and this moment of tenderness pulls me back from my anger, reminding me of her delicate situation.

Amanda starts rattling off baby names, asking the kid inside her to give a little kick when they hear one they like.

I offer the obligatory smile and words of support. Any adult would've recognized my smile as sad, regretful even. But this teenage girl, pregnant and deluded by some fairy-tale future, doesn't catch it.

We soon arrive at the lake, and I step aside to let her take it in. We're in the sun again. The indigo water shimmers. I turn to Amanda and smile widely, covering up the embers of envy burning a hole through my chest.

CHAPTER
TWO

Every woman is familiar with the chameleon qualities of the male predators among us. Amanda Holland is about to gain this knowledge firsthand.

As storm clouds darken the afternoon sky, I sit in my office and cycle through memories of the men who've changed my life forever.

First, Mr. Blessed towers over me with gorgeous, wavy hair and a shining smile. His checkered shirt hugs lean muscles, as do his just-right khaki pants. And the hint of a drawl in his voice is so clear, it feels like I spoke with him just yesterday.

Then there's the linebacker I dated my sophomore year at Colorado State. I caught the guy cheating three times before I found the courage to end the relationship.

The last time I saw a picture of him, he hadn't aged well. Smile lines were etched into bloated, alcoholic cheeks. His eyes —blue like a North Carolina sky—had been hollowed by resignation. And veins bulged along his neck, rising like buckled sidewalks.

Lost in those haunting thoughts, I'm startled by a knock at my office door. A little yelp escapes my throat.

My boss, Jonathan Gary, enters. Jonathan is the senior Licensed Clinical Social Worker at Wildfire, and he greets me with a self-effacing laugh. "Why do women always spook when I approach?"

"Probably because you sneak around like a ninja mouse."

Jonathan's smile shows off his annoyingly perfect teeth. "I can't let my degree from the rodent dojo go to waste."

I cross the room and give him a quick, professional hug, shaking off the memories of my monsters. "You're back early."

"You know what they say about the Grand Canyon." He sits in the armchair across from my desk. "It's kinda meh."

I roll my eyes. "Admit it. You thought you needed two weeks off, but after five days, you were desperate for those Camp Wildfire collard greens."

"Close, but not quite. Annabelle needed to get back to Beaufort for work." Jonathan mimes striking a ball with a putter. "Plus, I wanted to lose more rounds of golf to your husband and his brother."

I always mean to ask after Jonathan's wife, a marine biologist who spends summers in South Carolina studying sea turtles, but somehow the conversation never flows that way. This time, I open my mouth, intent on inquiring about her, but fall silent when Jonathan hands me a small gift bag.

"We got you guys something." He presents a bag on an outstretched palm with a playful flourish. "It's hot sauce. Because you and Artie seem to think stomach lining is optional."

Laughing, I pull a bright-red bottle of *Canyon Killer* hot sauce from the bag. The label depicts a howling ghost glaring at me, face haloed by a ring of fire, breathing fire, floating over a pit of fire.

I appreciate the gag gift. It's nice that my boss and my husband are good friends. Jonathan is much easier to stomach than Arthur's twin brother, Will. I could take or leave that guy, but the trio's long-standing friendship makes the world feel small, in a comforting way.

I try to keep a light energy as I thank Jonathan, but I feel him tracking me as I stow the hot sauce in my purse.

"You doing okay this morning?" His voice is neutral, like the one he'd use in a therapy session.

"What? Yeah." My gaze drifts across the room, landing on my fiddle-leaf fig plant. I cross over and kneel to assess the wilted brown leaves that need pruning.

"You sure?" The chair squeaks as he swivels. "Because you seem like you're dissociating over there."

I grab my scissors and hit them with rubbing alcohol to prep for pruning. "Just thinking about Amanda Holland, I guess. I think there's an older man involved."

"Didn't we expect that?"

"Don't be flip." I place the scissors down before stepping back to survey the plant again. "I'm almost positive this girl's a victim."

The facts race through my mind. Fifteen. That's the age of consent in Virginia. Any sexual activity between an adult and someone younger than that is illegal, even if both parties swear it's true love. Charges range from a Class Four misdemeanor to a Class Six felony.

As they should.

"Has she specifically said, 'this guy is older than me?'"

"No, but it's obvious." I roll my head to stretch the tight muscles in my neck. "The signs are all there. Love-bombing, future-faking, gaslighting. He's textbook."

"Lizette..."

The Zanzibar gem catches my eye next. Thin stalks stretch up from the pot, each decorated with deep-green oval leaves in a herringbone pattern. I'd fed the plant a new fertilizer last week, and now I can't help but admire the impressive new growth.

The plant is a testament to what proper care can achieve, and the parallels in my life are not lost on me.

"I just need to be methodical with Amanda, you know? Try various approaches until I find something that works. I need her to see him for who he really is."

Jonathan nods. "Times like these, I bet you wish you had a close colleague who specializes in complex PTSD."

He wants to take over, like he's done before. And I can't deny he's a good therapist. Under Jonathan's supervision, Camp Wildfire has evolved into a place where girls can reset their nervous systems through daily therapy, wilderness experiences, and wholesome socialization. He's helped hundreds of campers heal deep traumas.

But Amanda's situation cuts too close. It picks at scabs I've spent years trying to heal or hide, and I can't hand this case over. Not when it feels so personal, so raw.

"I'm not giving you the case." I rub a Zanzibar leaf between my thumb and forefinger. "I need to do this."

If not for Amanda, then for me.

"But—"

"Jonathan. I've got this." I leave my little green friend and hoist my messenger bag onto the desk to pack up for the day. "By the end of summer, she'll be ready to face the truth about this guy. Ready to start healing."

"Okay." Jonathan heads toward the door. "Careful not to press too hard, though. Not on her future plans. Not on the identity of the father. Not—"

"We both know I'm better than that." I laugh, trying to project nonchalant confidence. "I'm not some crazy plant lady who gets too caught up in the lives of her campers."

Jonathan smiles with a mix of amusement and concern before exiting.

Locking up my office, I head out. In the hallway, the clamor of the day has dwindled to a soft murmur, leaving a haunting quiet that echoes with the faint sounds of doors closing and subdued conversations. And the main building, housing the cafeteria, activity rooms, and both mine and Jonathan's offices, feels eerie in its stillness.

I slide into the driver's seat of my car and insert the key in the ignition, ready to leave the day behind. The engine sputters, groans, then falls silent. I try again, frustration mounting as my older-than-sin Mitsubishi Outlander refuses to start.

I curse like a drunk frat boy as I bang the steering wheel with the heel of my hand.

"Stupid dome light. Needs to turn off on its own, not kill my damn battery."

This is the third time my battery's died this month. And in this case, the third time is not "a charm" by any means.

Just then, I notice Jonathan standing a few feet away, observing the whole situation with what appears to be delight.

Soon enough, he's got jumper cables hooked up between our vehicles, and my engine starts purring. I thank Jonathan, and he casts a playful look in my direction.

"Next time this happens, I'm charging you a fee."

"Wow." I laugh. "It's like that, then."

"Yeah, jumping your car seems like a lucrative side hustle." Jonathan grins as he removes the jumper cables. "Plus, I'm saving up for Fiji."

"Really?"

"I dunno. I could be."

I give his arm a light punch. "It's not my fault the dome light doesn't turn off when it's supposed to."

"But it's your fault you keep forgetting to get it fixed." Jonathan looks over at me, eyes softening. "Why don't you take tomorrow morning off? Get this issue solved for real."

For a moment, I consider declining. There's always more work to be done at camp, always another girl who needs help.

But the weight of the day sits heavy on my shoulders, and a few hours to myself might be exactly what I need.

I accept Jonathan's offer without protest and climb back into the car. As I head home with my windows down, the late June sunlight filters through the dense forest flanking the road. The warmth of the sun and breeze slicing through my windows feels good. But out there in Putnam Forest, the trees are alive and watchful, as if they know my every secret.

I'm just ten minutes from home—nearing the edge of the woods—when a bobcat darts in front of my car. I slam on the brakes, heart pounding and tires squealing. The acrid smell of burned rubber cuts through the humid air, and I cough, my lungs stinging.

The bobcat stands frozen in the road in front of me for thirty whole seconds, the sheen of its coat glistening in the afternoon sun. Then, apparently bored with our stare-off, the enormous feline bounds into the forest with an effortless leap.

I continue driving, on high alert now, with my windows rolled up and my radio off. Despite the familiarity of the route, today the road home is a journey through uncharted territory, where every turn hides a potential threat.

CHAPTER
THREE

Trust is a rare and beautiful thing.

For most of my life, I thought of trust like Santa Claus or the Easter Bunny or stories that ended with "happily ever after." I didn't believe in the concept, but it was cute that others did. I sometimes even took joy in the naive glimmer of hope in their eyes.

Just because I can't access trust doesn't mean other people shouldn't embrace it. That comfort of trust is the glue that holds relationships, families, and entire societies together—just like the Easter Bunny and Santa Claus hold childhood together for billions of kids each year.

It's just...not for me. But anyone would've developed the same perspective if they'd endured what I have. First, there's my dad, who shattered my sense of security by abandoning our family when I was just eleven. Then there's my disastrous first love at the tender age of seventeen. And finally, the brutal attack less than a year later that cemented my cynicism.

Instead of learning to trust, I spent my twenties mastering Muay Thai. And now, at nearly thirty, I find it's given me much more comfort than a belief in Dasher, Dancer, Donner, and Blitzen ever could.

Many might hear my theories on trust and ask how someone with this perspective could work as an LCSW. They could argue that building trust is essential in a therapeutic environment and question whether someone without this ability could help these lost girls.

To these naysayers, my reply would be simple—it's my lack of trust that makes me good at my job.

I know when people are lying. For most, their first instinct is to lie, and I know how to use those lies to bring them close. To start the healing process.

Lost in these thoughts, the bobcat a distant memory, I open the door to our home. The familiar aroma of dinner pulls me back from the edge of my anxieties and into the comforting presence of my husband.

Arthur is the one exception to my theories on trust. And as I enter to find him at the stove, listening to a boring land-surveying podcast, I'm grateful to have married the one good man I've ever met.

Almost six feet tall with jet-black hair and dark eyes to match, Arthur Yuen is the optimal combination of sexy and boring. That is to say—he's very sexy and very, very boring. Like...the most dangerous thing about him is the gun he's got securely locked in a safe in his closet. And even that was just a hand-me-down from his dad.

When you've led the kind of life I have, when tragedy and loss are part of your body, part of your DNA, you need predictable and reliable just as much as you need oxygen. So Arthur's brand of boring works for me.

As I enter, my husband of four years is so consumed by the task of carrot peeling, he doesn't notice me standing behind him. I tiptoe closer, attacking with a hug from behind.

Arthur jumps, and the peeler clatters to the floor. "Shoot! Darn it, Lizard, you scared me."

I pat his cute butt as he grabs the peeler. Even nicer than when I was a junior at Wildfire High, crushing on the hottest nerd in the senior class.

Laughing, I mock Arthur in my best Urkel imitation. "Did I do that?"

"Laugh it up, Yuen. The more you sneak around, the more dangerous this household becomes. I was weaponized, for Pete's sake!" He places the peeler on the counter and pulls me in for a deep kiss.

My eyes close on reflex. His lips on mine stop time, if only for an instant.

Arthur tightens his arms around me, his fast-twitch muscles tensing like a predator ready to spring. But I am not his prey. I'm a member of his family he'd protect against anything.

Before I know it, he lets go and shoos me toward the table, which is set with a candle and a floral centerpiece.

"Go sit. I made supper." I married the only half-Chinese man—aside from Arthur's twin brother—for a hundred miles with a Southern accent. It's not too thick, but it dances on his tongue every fourth word or so, and I am not mad about it.

"Ooh, you made an Arthur specialty?"

"Take a seat, and you'll find out. C'mon now. I want to serve you."

Doing as I'm told, I wiggle into my chair at our oversize kitchen table. Everything in our home is oversize, as my mother reminds me every time she visits.

"Five bedrooms for two people?"
"Two acres for two people?"
"Three-car garage for two people?!"

If it were up to her, we'd live in the Yuen family cabin deeper into Wildfire. Two small bedrooms, one bathroom, and a tiny kitchen. Not my style, but a great spot for Arthur to focus on work whenever a big project pops up.

No. I'm all about my big, oversize suburban home, surrounded by my little green babies.

My Swiss cheese plant, whom I lovingly refer to as Ringo, sits on a windowsill above the kitchen sink.

Ringo has large, glossy leaves and is dotted with elegant holes every few inches. He gives our place a lush, tropical vibe, and I paired him with a hand-painted vase that complements our boho-chic decor well. Several other plants are gathered around him and on most available surfaces and walls throughout the home.

The therapist in me understands I might have a compulsion to take care of things. But a home is not a home until it's teeming with life, and my plants are always reminding me of the values of resilience, versatility, and drinking plenty of water.

Besides, plants are the only life I can give this home.

Arthur smirks as he approaches with a salad bowl. "Shit, am I interrupting a private moment between you and Ringo?"

"Is it that obvious?"

"Yeah, do you two need the room?"

I laugh as Arthur gives me a heaping serving of salad and sits at the table.

Slivered almonds, freshly sliced strawberries, arugula, and blue cheese—salad of my dreams right here. I narrow my eyes and take a playful bite, allowing my fork to rest in my mouth for an extra second. "This is fancy, even for you."

"I've got pesto pasta for our second course too." Arthur pours himself a glass of white wine and smiles. "It's been a year, you know."

"A year since..." *Shit.* I rack my brain for what I'm forgetting.

"A year since we've started trying to have a baby."

My heart shrivels, and an uncomfortable warmth stings the backs of my eyes. "Oh."

He plucks a strawberry slice from the salad and pops it in his mouth. "I'm talking about the kind of baby that doesn't need fertilizer and natural sunlight to survive, to be clear."

I stab at my salad. "Uh-huh."

Marriage is packed with conversations no one teaches you how to have. At any time, your partner has the power to wrench you from happiness into uncertainty or confusion. That's why you need the kind of transparency Arthur and I have cultivated.

Or so he thinks.

My fork clangs as it hits the plate. "I'm sorry. It's just… trying and failing to have a baby isn't a cause for celebration."

Arthur sips his wine, and I simmer with jealousy. He's been limiting my drinking because it's "bad when you're trying." But I've been working through old bottles any time I've had the house to myself. And I would kill for a glass right about now.

"The doctor said we needed to try 'natural methods' for a year before we could get real help," He sets his glass down. "It's been a fun year of going for it, trust me, but things haven't worked out as we'd hoped." He takes a casual bite of salad, keeping a strong note of optimism in his voice. "And that's okay. That's normal for so many couples."

Something about his optimism conjures my defensiveness. "It's obviously okay."

"What I'm trying to say is…" he lowers his fork and wipes the edge of his mouth with a napkin, "I saved the payout from my last surveying contract with the city, so money isn't an issue. And I've stopped eating soy, and I've been pounding back salmon for months. So I think if we go about this pregnancy the, uh, scientific way…" His expression softens with vulnerability. "I think we're going to have a baby, Lizette."

I do my best to bring a smile to my face. My wonderful, sweet husband expects me to be excited, and for good reason. For the past 365 days, I've led him to believe I saw a future for us with a family and children all our own. But no matter how much salmon he eats, it will never happen.

How did I let it get this far?

When we first discussed getting married, Arthur was adamant about not wanting children. I'd been thrilled with the decision...until 8,760 hours ago, almost to the minute. That's when he sat me down and told me he'd changed his mind.

"I think we should have a baby."

I'd panicked. I'd never told him the full story about my shameful past—what I'd lost in the attack. Thinking about everything that happened was hard enough, let alone talking about it. But as he'd promised me the sun and stars and the moon if I'd agree to give him a child, my mouth had done one of the stupidest things in history. It had smiled and said, *"I want a baby too."*

I'd clung to hope that Arthur would change his mind again. After all, he's always been annoyed by children. They're too loud, too dirty, too clingy or disrespectful or...the list goes on and on.

But for months, he'd tracked my cycle—or thought he did—always insisting on sex during "peak ovulation days." Somehow, his excitement only seemed to grow with each failed attempt. But no matter how perfectly we timed it, month after month, I did not get pregnant.

Made sense to me. Not so much to him.

Eventually, Arthur stopped mentioning my ovulation. I thought he'd given up forever. But when you're married, forever has a way of creeping up on you just when you least expect it.

Now, a year later, I force a smile. "I can't believe we've been trying for twelve whole months."

He leans forward. "So…"

Here I am. Continuing to dig my own grave. "So…let's take the next steps." I swallow hard. "Three cheers for medical intervention."

"Liz. What's wrong?" Arthur takes my hands.

"Nothing."

His voice is insistent. "Lizette."

I bite back tears, and my big, fat, lying mouth produces my first honest sentence of the conversation. "Wanted it to happen naturally, I guess."

"And that's totally valid." His eyes crinkle with kindness. "I know doctors are scary, especially after what you've been through, but—"

"I don't want to talk about doctors." I pull him in. Our foreheads kiss. His breath warms my lips.

A pang of mixed emotions hits me. There's fear and frustration, sure. And plenty of shame. But there's also an undeniable love that seeks solace in his touch.

I press my lips against his. Within seconds, he pulls me to my feet and presses me against the wall.

My words slide out between kisses. "This is much better than talking."

As Arthur leads me to the bedroom, I force myself to stay composed. Once on the bed, he draws me closer, and his strong arms envelop me.

His touch should erase my fears, but it only sharpens the edges of the secret I hold between us. And the teddy bear on our dresser, with its hopeful eyes fixed on an imagined future, mocks me. I feel like a hypocrite and a fraud.

Amid these feelings, a realization dawns. Trust isn't just about believing others won't hurt you. It's about having the courage to be vulnerable and to show your true self, regardless of the outcome.

I don't deserve the faith Arthur shows me, and with the secrets I keep, it's no wonder I have so little faith in myself.

CHAPTER
FOUR

The next morning, I wake to ecstasy.

Before my eyes even crack the seal of sleep to welcome in the summer sun, Arthur is under the covers, pleasuring me.

I grip the covers and arch into his tongue, moaning in approval.

"Yeah?" I love the way he checks in.

I echo his word back in the profound affirmative. "Yes."

The first time Arthur pulled this sweet surprise on me was the summer I turned twenty-three. After dating ever-so-briefly in high school, we parted for over five years. A lot happened in that time. But when we got back together…we more than made up for lost time.

That summer was so hot, and there was no air in my apartment, but we'd spend the entire day moored on the shores of my twin bed with no desire to be anywhere else.

I remember discovering the freckle on his back right shoulder. That same day, we learned together how much I like to be kissed behind my ears. It was July in the South, and our bodies clung to each other like cellophane. We didn't care. We didn't want it any other way.

Arthur kisses his way up my torso. A sound emerges from deep within my core, a cross between a growl and a purr. Finally, he lands a firm kiss on my lips, his tongue swirling with mine. He pulls back when I want more. Teases me. Comes back in, runs his fingertips behind my head and pulls me closer.

My breathing syncs with his, and I enter a meditative state. Remnants of his Old Spice—as basic as it might be—bring me deeper into the zone, so earthy, warm, and masculine. Now it's my turn to pull him in for a deeper kiss, but once our lips meet again, I lose focus.

Our conversation from the previous night was a grand tour of my lies. Calling it anything else is just another attempt to deceive myself, like I deceive everyone else. But that's the thing about being a people pleaser—you can't work your magic on your own psyche. That's why, in the long run, it's unsustainable.

At least, that's what I've been told.

He whispers between kisses. "Let's go to the beach today."

"I can't. I have the morning off, but—"

"Tell Jonathan you want to take the whole day. He went on vacation, and now he's back. It's your turn to have a little fun."

I run my fingers through his soft hair. "Arthur—"

"Come on." He grabs my ass and keeps kissing me. "We could be at Virginia Beach by lunch."

"That sounds amazing. And don't stop kissing me."

"But..."

I take a long pause before I reply. A day at the beach with Arthur means continuing the conversation from last night.

An hour in the car, to Arthur, means an hour planning, dreaming, and scheming. It means I'll be riding shotgun, googling fertility procedures, and reading reviews of doctors while he drums on the steering wheel and gushes about all the progress we're making.

"I can't blow off my afternoon to go to the beach today." I swing my legs out of bed and take a drink of water from the glass on the nightstand. "There's a new camper at Wildfire. She needs me there until she's more settled."

"There's always a new camper." Arthur's voice has lost its seductive, convincing quality. "Jonathan was off on the adventure of a lifetime. You deserve—"

"I have to be there for this girl. It's my job."

Arthur rolls out of bed and trudges toward the bathroom, grumbling about camp and my commitments and my allergy to spontaneous fun.

If I were the one storming off, Arthur would follow me into the bathroom and make sure I was okay. But I stay put and silently rejoice when I hear the shower start running.

I had planned to spend the morning on self-care and car repair, free from my usual commitments. But after this tiff with Arthur, it's clear I have to abandon my morning off and head to work as usual. It's the opposite of what I need, but it feels like the only option.

Avoidance, noun
A coping mechanism in which an individual evades uncomfortable or distressing emotions, conversations, or tasks by distracting themselves with other activities. Often leads to temporary relief but leaves the underlying issue unresolved. Common among stubborn spouses, like myself. See also, why I'm heading to work instead of dealing with my marriage.

As I set the coffee to brew, I try to push the morning's tension out of my mind. But just as I'm about to leave, I notice a pamphlet wedged between the toaster and the microwave. I pull it out and see it's adorned with images of happy couples and babies, titled *Clear River Hospital Family Planning Clinic — Where Miracles Begin*.

So much for pushing the tension out of my mind.

As I flick through the pages, I'm distracted by a close-up photo of a happy baby boy. Looking into the baby's eyes, I'm not sure I feel what women are supposed to feel. There's no primal urge to make a baby just like him. No desire to find that baby and smother him with love. In fact, I might as well be looking at a photo of a pumpkin or a puppy.

Scratch that. A photo of a dog would actually ignite the nurturer in me.

And that's when it hits me—a sudden, intrusive realization. *I'm not sure I'd want a child even if it were possible.*

Shaking my head, I force the thought back down. Seconds later, I'm in my car, and yet again, it won't start.

I shoot Arthur a text. *Taking your truck. Can you have your brother jump the car and then bring it in to have the dome light fixed today?*

For a moment, I sit and focus on the text screen, hoping he'll say something sweet or kind. Hoping he'll do something to smooth over the tension.

The reply comes faster than expected, but it's just a thumbs-up reaction.

I stare at that lone emoji, a digital representation of our morning's disconnect. It's then that I realize I've forgotten to text Jonathan.

Guilt washes over me as I type my pathetic confession.

Arthur's taking care of my dome light. Looks like I'm working this morning after all.

CHAPTER
FIVE

Nestled in a secluded clearing beside Virginia pines, my Friday group sits on the soft, needle-strewn ground surrounding Lake Wildfire.

"All right." I clear my throat, squinting against the sun. "Let's go around the circle and share what's real and honest for us today."

Fifteen blank faces stare back at me. Amanda Holland is among them, one hand on her belly, the other supporting her as she leans back against a tree. I'd hoped she'd jump to share, but the hardness in her eyes tells me that's not likely.

The girls' counselor, Yolanda, had told the girls we were kayaking out to the far shore of the lake for group therapy. And here we are, and they're looking at me like they had no warning whatsoever.

I've learned with teenage girls, and most people, it's beneficial to sit in uncomfortable silence, so I resist the urge to prompt them. Instead, I lean back and watch.

A dark cloud passes over the sun as a strong wind whips across the shore. There's a storm brewing. Not now, but it'll be here soon enough. All at once, the energy shifts, and I'm aware of the dark, tangled forest looming behind me like an unwelcome stranger.

A voice from deep within says, *It's not safe here*. I swallow hard to clear the bad energy. *Someone could be watching you. Anyone.*

I've experienced paranoia like this before. Dr. Whitlock says it's natural, considering what I've gone through, considering the police never found the men who attacked me. Despite her reassurances, my fears feel unreasonable, and they embarrass me.

Of all people, in all professions, I should be able to control the voices in my head.

I know I shouldn't *should* on myself. But it would sure be nice to shut them down forever.

Of course, don't most therapists become counselors in the hopes of curing their fucked-up selves?

"I guess I could share." Brita Flynn looks at me. Her serious eyes have a chilling quality, like she sees right into your soul. Like those eyes have been here before.

"Thank you, Brita. Go ahead." I train my focus on her. A few of the girls shift positions to get a better view as Brita talks. A Carolina wren takes flight from a piece of driftwood, heading back toward camp.

"Today I've been thinking a lot about, like, being a loser." Brita chews on the inside of her cheek. "All through middle school, none of the popular girls wanted to talk to me. None of the boys wanted anything to do with me."

Amanda pulls at her shirt and adjusts the way she's sitting, keeping her attention on Brita.

"I was just some weirdo people thought was, like, named after a water filter." A self-deprecating laugh escapes Brita's lips. "Then, freshman year, boys started talking to me and wanting to be around me. I guess I liked it."

I know where this is going, and I have a hunch the

campers do too. Brita cringes and lowers her head, pushing through the curtain of shame.

"Once I had their attention, I did pretty much anything I could to keep it." She swallows hard. "The boys gave me beer, so I drank beer. Cigarettes. Weed. Whatever. I wanted to hang with them so bad, so I tried to be whatever everyone else wanted me to be. I totally forgot how to be myself. And that sucks. That's my share, I guess. That's what's 'real and honest.'"

"Thank you, Brita. That was brave of you. It takes a lot of self-awareness to understand the thoughts that drive our behaviors. And, to quote Eckart Tolle, which I don't love to do, but it's relevant. 'Awareness is the greatest agent for change.'"

I try to catch Amanda's eye. She won't turn in my direction.

"Has anyone else found themselves changing their behavior to fit in at school, with friends, or to get or keep someone's attention?" Silence. I lean forward a few inches. "Amanda. Do you relate?"

She locks eyes with me. "Actually, Ms. Silva, I have a question."

I pick up a pebble and roll it between my fingers. "Questions are good."

"One of the girls here, I'm not saying who, told me I should never go into the woods by myself." She does her best to maintain focus on me, but I don't miss when her gaze flicks toward Madeline Miller, one of the more inscrutable campers in attendance this year.

Amanda continues. "She said a camper went missing a long time ago. Said the cops found her locket in the woods, but they never found her."

A ripple of hushed conversation converges on the girls like a swarm of bees. A headache forms at the base of my skull.

Every few years, the girls get ahold of this story, and it's never fun.

Madeline's voice, deeper than the others and more commanding, cuts through the excitement. "It's true. The girl was sixteen years old, and her name was Regina Smith."

The murmurs evolve quickly into high-pitched panic. I raise my hand for quiet. "Everyone, calm down. I'll address this, but we need to be respectful."

Once the girls settle, I take a deep breath. "I was actually finishing high school in Colorado when Regina disappeared. Still, I know how deeply it affected the town. There are many theories about what happened, but it's important to remember these are unconfirmed rumors."

Madeline raises her hand. I ignore her.

Choosing my words carefully, I go on. "Some believe Regina ran away from camp and started a new life elsewhere. Personally, that's what I think. But others have darker theories. Some say she'd fallen in with a bad group of guys. She was with one of them when things got a little rough. The kid panicked and buried her out in Putnam Forest."

Suppressing a shudder, I remember when my mom accosted me at breakfast, insisting Wildfire was overrun with murderous, drug-addicted teenage boys.

The rumor had hit especially close to home after what had happened to me the summer after junior year. That incident led to Mom moving us away, insisting I finish high school elsewhere. But the dark cloud of its aftermath had followed me to my new school.

The girls' eyes are wide. They begin to talk amongst themselves, but Yolanda quiets them down.

I consider stopping, but Madeline's going to share every theory, if she hasn't already, so they might as well hear them from me. "The most extreme rumors suggest Regina was kidnapped by an older man she was having a relationship with.

They had a disagreement, and he...he brought her out to the forest and ended her life."

Even after all these years, part of me can't help but wonder what the truth really is. These aren't campfire tales—Regina Smith's disappearance is real—and the looming question mark brings my focus to the tree line, scanning for danger. I force myself to turn back to the girls, their faces a mix of horror and fascination.

"While what happened to Regina Smith is anybody's guess, these stories highlight the importance of looking out for each other and recognizing potentially dangerous situations. It's crucial to be aware of the risks around us, to not blame victims, and to empower ourselves and protect one another."

The girls glance at each other. Some are still wide-eyed. Some offer a supportive little grin.

I make eye contact with several of them in turn, settling on Amanda. "Our choices can have unforeseen consequences, and it's important to trust your instincts if something doesn't feel right. If you ever feel uncomfortable or unsafe, please reach out to me, Yolanda, Mr. Gary, or any of the staff. We're here to support and protect you."

The girls exchange glances again, some nodding thoughtfully, others looking skeptical. Before I can gauge their full reactions, Madeline pipes up. "Tell them about Myer Whitley."

"Madeline. I—"

"That's the guy who murdered Regina." She scans her audience. "He lured her away from camp and killed her in the woods. They say the dude still lives in town. The chief of police knew Whitley killed Regina, but they didn't have enough evidence to convict."

I try to break into Madeline's speech, but as her septum ring and choppy bangs might suggest, the girl is not one to be interrupted, especially not by figures of authority.

She bulldozes me without missing a syllable. "I'm telling y'all. The cops know she was killed. And the guy who did it is wandering around town twenty minutes from here, free as that fucking bluebird right there, waiting to strike again."

"Are you done, Madeline?"

She shrugs. I'm tempted to remind her about the rules around language but decide now's not the time.

"I have two points to make," I say.

"Whatever." She shoves her hands in her pockets and looks away.

"One, that's not a bluebird. It's a wren."

"It's not even blue," one of the campers chimes in. Madeline shoots her a glare.

"Two, Myer Whitley is not wandering Wildfire. He's in prison. Been there for years, not getting out anytime soon."

"Not what I heard," says Madeline.

"Well, you heard wrong." I fix her with my most authoritative look. "Myer Whitley was a year ahead of me at Wildfire High." I clear my throat. "He was off committing another crime when Regina went missing. That's not why he's in jail now. Got locked up for something else years later."

Madeline opens her mouth, but I cut her off.

"Bottom line, the guy had nothing to do with what happened to Regina Smith. Everyone who was here back then knows the whole story, and everything else is gossip."

Madeline snorts, but I ignore her again.

I soften my voice. "Regina's disappearance was a tragedy. It's all anyone talked about for months. But it doesn't serve anyone to rehash those tragedies or to use them to scare fellow campers." I let my words sink in for a moment before speaking again. "There is nothing to be afraid of. Not here and not in town."

Yolanda and I take a few questions from the girls, my shoulders dropping as their panic subsides. Just when I'm about to redirect us back to the real and honest, one of the younger campers points at my feet and shrieks. "Snake! Ms. Silva, snake!"

Sure enough, a copperhead slithers over my scuffed sneakers. The snake is rust-colored with brown markings, and it's perfectly camouflaged in the Virginia wilderness. Its tail brushes through a patch of dried leaves, and the crackling sound tightens my stomach.

My heart thuds. Copperheads are usually nocturnal this time of year. But here's this silent killer in broad daylight, close enough to bite me. I look around the circle. This is my chance to prove to the girls that I understand predators in the Virginia wilds. Snakes, men, and everything in between.

"Interesting. A little copperhead." The girls gasp as I catch the snake behind its head—like I've done a million times. Though I'm sure professional snake handlers know safer ways to avoid the copperhead's venomous bite, this method's always worked for me.

Still freaks me out though.

With forced calm, I get up from the circle and release the reptile back into the woods, far away from group therapy.

My hands are shaking, but that's something the campers don't need to know.

As soon as I emerge from the trees and return to the circle, I warn the girls not to try that at home, but they cheer and lavish me with praise, awed by my calm under pressure.

Even Yolanda's got her eyebrows raised, and she's seen it all out in the wilderness.

Madeline does not cheer along with the other girls, though. She sits back, her arms folded. I wonder where she got her information about Myer Whitley. Wonder if there are more dark theories where those came from.

CHAPTER
SIX

Dark clouds let loose sheets of rain as we arrive back at camp, along with a wave of memories I'd rather keep suppressed.

But talking about Regina Smith's disappearance has transported me to my days at Wildfire High, and the more I try to shake those thoughts, the harder they hold me.

As I race through the deluge toward my office, my mind swims with thoughts of my AP Psychology teacher, Mr. Blessed. The man who taught me so much, who prepared me for my career.

The man who groomed me.

Vivid flashes of Mr. Blessed's too-wide smile that, ironically, never quite reached his eyes. The way his hand would linger a moment too long when handing back my papers. The slight tremor in his voice when we were alone.

I can almost smell the mixture of chalk dust and cologne that clung to him, and I swear I can hear the soft click of his loafers on the linoleum floor of his classroom, the last on the left in the junior hallway.

If my dad hadn't left for the Appalachian wilderness, trying to escape his own struggles, would things have been different? Was his absence why I sought comfort in Mr. Blessed's embrace?

And more importantly, was that why Mr. Blessed had selected me? Had he been able to smell my vulnerability?

Opening the door to my office, I'm startled to find Jonathan with his feet on my desk, engrossed in a thick therapy manual. "Oh, hi."

"Um…hi." He bookmarks the page, closes it, and flashes me a grin. "I'm a sucker for fast-moving plots." His ease contrasts sharply with the heaviness of my thoughts.

I hang up my raincoat and run my hands through my dampened hair. "Find anything interesting in there?"

He taps the cover of the book. "Actually, yes. Did you know up to four percent of adults have antisocial personality disorder?"

I play along.

"That means one in twenty people is a psychopath." I cross to the Keurig, inserting a dark roast pod. "Seems low."

His laughter smacks me right in the back and makes me giggle too. There's an undercurrent of something unspoken between us. The hint of a spark that remains dormant most of the time. Today, though, maybe because of the rain or the unsettling memories, it sends an unwanted tingle through my legs.

I turn as he stands and stretches, pulling his arms up over his head and twisting to the side. "Your hubby called me today, by the way. He wants to set up a round of golf soon. Me, him, and Will. Though I doubt Officer Yuen can tear himself away from the station for a full eighteen holes." He drops his arms. "Also said it might be good for you to take a vacation. Starting tonight and lasting at least the weekend."

"Arthur said that?" My voice belies a hint of annoyance, despite my efforts to keep my emotions tamped down.

"Technically, it was my idea. I thought the only way to get

you to take an actual day off would be to get you out of town. He agreed, though." Jonathan twists to the opposite side, groaning in satisfaction as his back cracks.

"I can't take off in the middle of the summer."

"Sure you can. I did."

Thunder booms outside. A girl screams theatrically from her cabin, and a chorus of laughter follows. Both sounds root inside my body, upping my tension.

Jonathan's eyes twinkle as he walks over and grabs me by the shoulders. "Lizette Yuen. You're going to the beach. ASAP. And that's an order."

We lock eyes for a long moment, a silent standoff that makes the room too hot. Finally, I cave. "If you take the girls into the forest, you need to be careful. For some reason, our friendly neighborhood snakes are hanging out in broad daylight this year."

CHAPTER

SEVEN

The deluge of the early evening storm fades to a gentle drizzle as I head out to the parking lot. A shroud of mist clings to a sprawling field adjacent to the lot, and the bittersweet smell of wet asphalt mixed with moss hangs in the air.

My mind wanders into the void of information surrounding the disappearance of Regina Smith. Despite my best efforts to redirect my attention, I can't stop thinking about the darker rumors about the young woman.

Was she killed and dragged into the forest? Was it teenage boys? An older man? Could her body be buried out there somewhere, forgotten?

I shake my head, trying to free myself from these grim speculations. There's no telling if Madeline is right about Regina's fate. But as I near Arthur's F-150, my breath quickens.

Anyone could be lurking in that forest. Anyone could be waiting to strike.

I remind myself that I know these woods better than most. Hidden trails wind through the dense forest, connecting Camp Wildfire to my home out in the suburbs.

I've walked those paths countless times over the years, finding solace in the quiet of nature and the familiarity of the route. It's a secret passage between my two worlds—home and work—that I've come to cherish. But tonight, even that comforting knowledge does little to quell my unease.

Just as I reach for the truck door, craving the sanctuary of its familiar interior and a break from my racing thoughts, my phone rings. I hesitate before answering with a breathless, "Hey, honey."

"We're going to the beach!" Arthur's voice erupts through the phone, bursting with enthusiasm.

His cheerfulness catches me off guard, but despite my mood, a laugh escapes me as I climb into the truck. "Are you trying to leave for this trip tonight?"

"I'm thinking tomorrow morning. Breakfast on the road. Toes in the sand by eleven." He lets out an enthusiastic "woo hoo!" and it reminds me how much I love his *joie de vivre*.

Arthur isn't going to force me to answer questions about ovulation while I'm buying soft serve from an ice cream truck. He wants to have fun. That's it. Everything else is me projecting.

"Will came over and gave you a jump, by the way. It looked so cool, his police cruiser hooked up to the old Outlander with jumper cables."

I laugh. *Sometimes boys are impressed by the simplest things.*

"We got it into the shop so they could check on the dome light. Mechanic said it was just a loose wire, probably chewed up by a squirrel." Arthur's smile dances in his voice, doing a happy little cha-cha over every word he speaks. "It's cool. I'm a manly man who can fix things and start cars and stuff. If my big brother helps in his big, fancy cop car, that is."

Will is Arthur's older brother by all of four minutes, and I smile indulgently at the old, familiar joke. Suddenly, I'm one of the teenagers, flirting with my boyfriend like I've got all the time in the world. "When you put it like that, it's such a turn-on."

"Nothing better than turning your wife on right just in time for sex on the beach."

My breath catches. Is Arthur still trying for a natural conception? Or does he just want to have a little fun, forget about our failed pregnancy attempts for a couple days?

Shaking off my paranoia, I decide on the latter, and we make a few more jokes before hanging up. Then I climb behind the wheel and start Arthur's truck. But the earlier storm splashed mud across the windshield, and he's all out of wiper fluid. Of course.

Lucky for me, my super-nerd husband keeps extra fluids in a bin in the cab. I grab the gallon of purple windshield wiper fluid, pop the hood, and hop out.

"Arthur Yuen isn't the only one who can fix things and start cars and stuff." I twist the cap off the container. "Just wait 'til I tell him about this. Helpless little Lizette added wiper fluid all…by…her…"

Well, hell.

I stare at the labyrinthine engine bay. "What the shit is all this shitting shit?" Leaning forward to get a closer look, I suddenly can't recall the last time I looked under the hood of an automobile, or if I ever have.

Sweeping my gaze over the engine bay, I let out a laugh. The wiper fluid is clearly labeled next to the battery.

When I tug on the reservoir cap, I notice a small plastic box tucked beside it. Something about the box looks…off. I give it a pull, and it comes loose in my hand.

My stomach drops as I step away from the truck.

What did I just do? I broke Arthur's truck. I broke his damn truck. The one possession he has any affinity for, and I had to go and mess with it.

My hands shake as I turn the box over, searching for any

clue as to what it might be. *Hopefully not the starter*, I think, even though that means next to nothing to me. Should I try to put it back? What if I break something else? I'm totally helpless here, and Arthur's not going to be happy.

As panic bubbles up, I notice it's heavy and it's scuffed in a way that suggests it's fallen a lot.

There's a tiny lip on it, so I grab hold and pry it open. Inside, I find a smartphone.

My mouth goes dry.

The phone is powered on. Passcode protected.

Shit, shit, shit. I just found a phone hidden under the hood of my husband's pickup.

That sounds like the lyrics in a sad country tune, or the first sentence a broken woman utters when she places a call to a divorce lawyer.

But I'm not supposed to be that woman.

Thunder booms above me, the sky opens, and I'm soaked within seconds. Hurrying to seal the phone back in the plastic case, I grab the bottle of wiper fluid, rush back inside the truck, and slam the door. Barely looking, I toss the little black box onto the passenger seat.

At least the rain has cleaned off my muddy windshield.

My stomach churns. Once again, I have the sense someone is watching. It's the same sensation I had out on the lakeshore earlier, like there are secrets in the forest, snaking toward me.

Just last night, I had reassured myself with the belief that the only real threats were the secrets I'm hiding from the people I care about, and that nothing else was out to get me.

But now, I'm starting to think I was mistaken.

CHAPTER
EIGHT

I try to guess the code three times, sitting out there in the Camp Wildfire parking lot. My birthday. Arthur's birthday. Our anniversary.

Wrong, wrong, wrong.

I groan. "Why would the passcode to my husband's secret phone be related to me, of all people?"

As I set the phone on the armrest, a sudden thought strikes me. Jonathan could emerge from the main building at any second and find me there trying to hack into a mysterious phone I found stashed in my husband's engine compartment.

Just like that, I throw the truck in drive and pull out, checking the rearview to make sure Jonathan doesn't catch me making my escape.

Every second of the drive home is torturous. The rain on the windshield falls hard and fast as the world around me morphs into a Manet on acid. All I see are the vague shapes of approaching cars, their amber headlights flickering dimly in the gray light of the storm.

My thoughts are equally disorienting.

One second, I tell myself Arthur will have a simple explanation for the secret phone.

The next, my paranoia takes over, and I tell myself he must be cheating on me. It's been going on for years. He loves her, he has a family with her, and he's leaving me so he can be with her for real and raise their three adorable children.

Then reason tries to assert itself, to swing the pendulum back.

Arthur could never do that to me.

But isn't that what every woman thinks, moments before she realizes she's married to a cheater?

Before long, my anxiety's so high, my mind detaches from my body. I have little awareness of my actions, the truck, or the road. Shallow breaths, in and out through my nose, stop an inch into my lungs. My eyes grow wider but focus less. The truck must be driving itself.

A phone rings. In one quick motion, my head swivels to the secret phone on the passenger seat. Lifeless and dark. It's not that phone. Another ring. It's Arthur calling my cell.

I forward the call to voicemail. My phone rings again. I flick on the silencer.

Minutes later, I'm parked down the block from my house, holding the secret phone in my trembling hands.

The device awakens and prompts me for the passcode. Like an idiot, my fingers type in my own birthday for the second time. I delete the numbers as soon as I type them. My brain is ground turkey.

C'mon, Liz, think.

I'd have better luck typing in his lover's birthday. Or the anniversary of the day they met. Or the address of the hotel where they rendezvous for Thai food and a quickie.

Stop it.

Shaking my head, I place the secret phone beside me and pick up mine, because he's calling me, yet again. I ignore it, shove the phone in my purse, and cruise the rest of the block home.

As I pull into the driveway, he's standing on the porch, waiting.

In the dim porchlight, set against the angry gray weather, there's a darkness in his smile I've never noticed. More than that, our modern Colonial has taken on a suburban familiarity that doesn't sit well with me.

The plantation shutters, the pristine green lawn with the little security sign, the wraparound porch...the perfection of it all settles in my stomach like rotten fish, as if I'm looking at a movie set for a melodramatic story of infidelity that'll end up on some women's channel.

What is perfection, if not a mask worn to hide the ugliness beneath the surface?

Arthur heaves a packed duffel bag above his head in triumph. That's when I notice he's wearing his favorite flamingo board shorts and he's got sunglasses perched on his forehead, despite the rain. It's his *I'm excited for vacation* statement. On a good day, I'd laugh and point out he's ridiculous for wearing board shorts the day before we head to the beach.

But today is not a good day.

I snap the secret phone into its box, shove the box in my purse, and hurry out. The brutal rain is still falling hard. I stomp through a puddle at the base of our walkway and make eye contact with my husband.

He meets me on the steps, keeping that big, dumb smile plastered on his face. "Come on! Get out of the rain. I've got a bottle of merlot uncorked inside." Arthur steps into the house, but I hesitate, letting the rain drench my shoulders and trickle down my back. He realizes I'm not behind him and turns back in the open door. "Liz?"

"Yeah, I'm coming." The floorboards creak as I follow him

inside. Jimmy Buffet drifts out from the smart speaker in the kitchen. Again, the sameness of it all puts me off.

Arthur hands me a glass and sips from his own.

"To Virginia Beach," he says.

My hands tremble as I set the glass down. "I thought you didn't want me to drink while we're trying."

I immediately hate myself for the flippant response.

He responds with a light joviality. "Like I said. Special occasion."

I'd love to return his happy energy, but I can't. It's time for me to reveal what I've found, and I'm frozen. I try to speak but only manage to croak out a few dry syllables.

Arthur swallows. "Liz. What's wrong?"

Saying nothing, I open my purse and set the secret phone on the granite counter. It took weeks to select that exact slab of granite. Green with flecks of white. At the time, it had felt so unique, so special.

Arthur eyes the phone, mouth open and eyes unblinking.

I wonder how many other couples have chosen identical countertops, and how many of those marriages have survived.

CHAPTER
NINE

"What's this?" Arthur turns the phone over like he's an alien who's never conceived of this technology. Yet the device fits perfectly in the palm of his hand.

I press on the counter with so much force I might push the slab off the cabinetry below. "You tell me."

He straightens the wine glass so it's in line with the bottle, centering each on the granite. Jimmy Buffet belts a line about coconut shrimp or some other dumb shit in the background.

"Alexa, turn off the music." I bark the order, almost feeling bad for dear Alexa. The room is silent except for the sound of my husband's deep sigh.

"First of all, I'm sorry." He keeps fussing with the wine bottle, twisting it a hair this way and then that.

"Stop with the wine and look at me."

He takes a sip and then sets his glass down, the wine gurgling from his mouth to the pit of his stomach. When he looks at me, his nearly black eyes are red, and his cheeks are flushed.

"The phone belongs to my brother. Kind of. Vicky doesn't want him taking on dangerous cases." He mumbles the words, looking like a school kid in the principal's office. "You remember that, right?"

My firm, angry stare is all he needs to keep going.

"My asswipe of a brother didn't listen. He volunteered to help some guy in witness protection, even though Vicky warned him it was too dangerous. Then it kind of just... spiraled out of control."

"How does this all lead to *you* having a secret phone hidden in the engine of your truck?" I emphasize the word *you* to make my skepticism clear. Despite that, I crave the relief that comes with forgiveness. So much of me wants to sweep this under the rug.

"Will didn't give me the phone to use. I held it for him. Then we'd sometimes meet up in town, and he'd use it to call the guy in witness protection. He wanted to be sure Vicky never overheard the calls or found the phone, I guess." The veins in Arthur's hands tighten as he reaches out to adjust the wine bottle again.

I pull the bottle toward me so it's out of reach. "How long ago was this?"

"A few months."

"So it's over now?" Arthur nods. I slide the phone toward him. "It has a full charge."

Arthur takes the device. "Where's the box?"

"It's in my purse."

"Well, that's what keeps it charged. The box snaps into the electronics in the truck, so whenever the engine's running, the phone is charging. It's honestly kind of—"

"Arthur, I swear, if you are about to describe any feature on your secret phone as *cool*..."

He fusses with the drawstring on his stupid, tiny, ridiculous, bright-pink board shorts. Watching him, the molecules of an infinitesimal laugh form in my throat. I don't let it out, but it's at that moment that I believe Arthur is telling the truth.

This man loves me, and he loves his brother. And he's never given me a single reason to doubt him, so I'm not going to start now.

Right?

Nope. I need to see more.

"Can I see the messages and call log?" I hold out my hand, ready to begin my investigation into the device. I know how my mind works. This is going to nag at me until every puzzle piece is in its rightful place.

His face falls. "I don't have the access code. It's not my phone, remember?"

My brain and heart go to war as I study his face. I'm very familiar with body language and the nuances of micro-expressions. Unless he's more skilled of an actor than I thought, he's telling the truth.

Right?

Dammit to hell.

Instead of pushing, I back off. For now.

"You can't be getting involved in Will's job like this. He chose to be a cop. You chose to be a land surveyor. I don't want that kind of danger and risk anywhere around you, or us."

He lowers his gaze. "I know."

"What if this witness was caught up in something dangerous? That phone was on. Someone could be tracking it. Criminals could've showed up here, at our house, looking for him. Killers, even."

"I know."

"There could've been a shoot-out in our front yard."

I debate throwing in a comment about the insanity of considering raising a child in that kind of environment but manage to bite it back. No need to go there when I've got the upper hand.

Our eyes meet, and I place my hand on Arthur's. "You get why I was suspicious, right?"

He nods. "Yeah, I get it."

"I'm sorry, I guess." Guilt makes the back of my neck itch. "For how I approached this."

"I'm lucky you didn't kill me." A smile forms at the outermost edge of his lips. "Many husbands have died for less."

The laugh I'd resisted earlier pops out. And it's relaxing. Arthur joins me, then pulls me in for a kiss. His soft lips and warm embrace send a calming wave of energy up my spine.

The sound of a ringing phone pulls our lips apart. My head jerks toward the device on the counter. Arthur takes his iPhone from his pocket.

"Relax, honey." He checks the caller ID. "It's work."

I can't help but notice Arthur pocket the burner as he heads to his basement office.

My life would be so much easier if I'd just commit to taking Arthur at his word right now and every day for the rest of my life. But nothing sickens me more than the thought of adding my name to the list of women scorned while "Margaritaville" played unassumingly in the background. So cliché.

The floorboards creak as I tiptoe to the top of the basement stairs. Arthur's talking about red-cockaded woodpeckers on state land—of course—and the burner phone is sitting on his desk in plain sight.

Arthur only grabbed the phone so he could return it to his brother. He and Will both forgot about it after the investigation closed, and now Arthur figures it's time to end their secret alliance.

That's what I tell myself, at least.

But I've pulled the wool over my eyes so many times in the past simply because I didn't want to see the truth. I must never make that mistake again, so I'm going to find out for sure that Arthur is being honest.

He sits at his desk and pours himself a nip of whiskey. The way he sips takes me back to childhood, to the first man who left me alone to cut myself on the sharp edges of my broken heart.

My memories of my dad are like rings left on a coffee table. I know he was there because I can still see the evidence. But his presence only made things worse. And once he was gone, there was no way to wash away the stains he left behind.

The story is like so many that play out in American homes. Drank too much. Yelled too much. Wasn't around other than for the drinking and the yelling. Dear old dad disappeared for adventure in the great outdoors when I was eleven and left my mom alone to raise me and my sister.

The story gets a little more interesting in the next part. Dad cleaned up his act in a matter of months. Met a new wife out on the Appalachian Trail. Made a big show of doting on his new step-kids in a way he never did me or my older sister.

This all leads to what we LCSWs call abandonment wounds.

Abandonment wound, noun

A deep emotional injury stemming from experiences of being left behind, neglected, or rejected, especially during formative years. These wounds can result from actual physical abandonment by a parent or caregiver or emotional abandonment where physical presence is not coupled with emotional connectedness. See also, Lizette's dumbass dad.

. . .

When Mr. Blessed made an appearance in my life, I must have subconsciously hoped he'd heal this deep emotional injury. But it's hard to fix daddy issues with romantic partners, especially as a teenage girl. And my doomed relationship with my teacher poured salt, acid, and volcanic lava into the open wounds from my formative years.

My father, Mr. Blessed, my cheating linebacker boyfriend from college, and two men in masks. All the men who've ever hurt me in my life, and I can't even put names or faces to the final two.

Images of the attack strike like lightning in my mind.

Two men in ski masks. My bedroom. A broken window. The smell of stale cigarettes on the hands of the bigger man. My stomach on fire from where they were beating me with a bat. Blood pooling beneath me as they drag me from my room. Thinking I could still save myself, even as they threw me down the stairs.

One man wanted to kill me, but the other stopped him. If it wasn't for that second man—

In his office, Arthur lets out a big, uproarious laugh, mutters a few words about "pesky woodpeckers," and laughs again. I stop myself from thinking more about the attack or Mr. Blessed and instead slip out to the porch with my phone in hand.

This is my only chance to talk to Will before Arthur has a chance to tell him I've discovered the secret phone. And talking to Will might be the only way I'll be able to put my mind at rest—despite his objectively obnoxious qualities—so I tap the screen and scroll to his name.

It's cooler than I expected outside, but the rain's stopped, and the scent of a distant bonfire carries in the wind. Our street, though populated by twenty or so cookie-cutter suburban homes, is protected by miles of farmland or forest in every direction. Despite this, I'm overwhelmed by the sensation that I'm being watched.

I call Will, and as the phone rings, I rehearse how I think the conversation will go.

He's going to sound groggy. He'll deny he was sleeping, but we'll both know he was passed out on the couch after one of Vicky's heavy meals.

There will be a moment of sarcastic quips. Light with an antagonistic twist. And eventually, we'll get into the meat of the conversation. I'll ask about the phone. And I'll get quiet as he listens.

Will's recorded voice interrupts my thoughts.

I was not prepared to leave a message, and I scramble, trying to think of what to say. There's no way I can record anything specific about the secret phone on his voicemail. And I need to deliver the information in real time, so I can color the story and gauge his reaction.

The machine beeps, and I stumble into an awkward message. "Hey, Will. Uh. It's Lizette. Just...had a quick question for you. Yep! Okay. Byeee."

My finger shakes as I end the call and shove the phone into my back pocket. I stumble back as Arthur opens the front door with a creak.

"Hey."

I somehow manage a quick smile. "Hi."

He remains in the threshold, one foot inside and another on the porch. "I'd still love to hit the beach tomorrow, if you want."

I shake my head. It's not the right time. Nothing makes that clearer than the mystery of this burner phone.

CHAPTER
TEN

Few things on earth are more rare or more powerful than a truly confident teenage girl.

This truth weighs on my mind as I settle into the dreary Monday morning. The weekend passed in a haze of rain and restlessness—my plans for a rejuvenating beach trip replaced by hours of half-hearted work and a strange, forced friendliness between me and Arthur.

As I adjust the pens on my desk for the third time, my office door swings open. Amanda Holland enters, and immediately I'm struck by how utterly unaffected she seems by the Monday gloom that hangs over me. Unlike the other young women in my care, Amanda carries herself with her shoulders back, radiating a confidence that seems almost out of place in a teenager.

She makes herself comfortable in one of the armchairs in my talk zone, looking fresh as ever—as if she's returning from the sunny beach weekend I missed out on. She scans the room before her eyes settle on me.

"Believe it or not, this is not my first therapy session ever."

I straighten in my chair, willing my mind to match her clarity. "I believe it."

Morning light streams into the office between the leaves of two hanging pothos plants, their yellow-and-white variegation cascading over the pots.

"Think you've got enough plants in here?"

"They improve air quality and are great for our physical and mental health." I round my desk and sit in an overstuffed armchair across from Amanda. My digital recorder clacks against the coffee table as I set it between us. "Just a reminder that I record these sessions. It's camp policy, meant to keep both you and me protected."

"Protected from what?"

"That answer is too long and boring to get into now. But the short version is that recording our sessions helps ensure our discussions are accurately captured." I adjust the recorder's position on the table. "I review these recordings before and after our sessions to best help you. This is also a way to maintain transparency and accountability in—"

"This is the short version?" Amanda presses record on the device. She clears her throat in a very dramatic *I'm about to start singing opera* way and leans toward the recorder. "Greetings, whoever. This is Amanda Holland, coming to you live from the office of Virginia's most accomplished plant hoarder."

I smile. It's not hard for me to see how Amanda's unique brand of confidence and attitude might've attracted attention from guys of all ages.

"You seem much more comfortable this morning than when you arrived on Thursday."

"I never stay in a bad mood long. It's bad for my skin." She touches the skin next to her eyes, as if worried wrinkles might already be settling in. "And I try to make the best of shitty situations, which, no offense, this is."

I brush a strand of my long dark hair behind my ear as I consider whether I ever had the bravado Amanda is displaying now.

Is that kind of confidence what drew Mr. Blessed's eye to me?

No. I was much more of a blushing rose. Someone who responded to all outside attention with demure detachment. It's much more likely my lack of confidence attracted Mr. Blessed.

And that makes what happened between us much more sinister.

"You want the info dump I give to all my new shrinks, or would you prefer I get more creative?" Amanda shifts in her seat then looks at me with raised eyebrows.

I mirror her expression. "Let's get creative. Might as well have fun in here, right?"

"Second thought, I'm not in the mood. I'll just give you the boring facts."

She's testing me. I know it. And I also know the only way I fail is if she thinks it bothers me, which it doesn't.

"Rich, powerful lawyer dad. Mom who stays home. Their relationship is a disaster. It's like she works for him. It's pathetic. What I have with my guy is nothing like that." A little self-satisfied smile plays at her lips. "Let's see, what else? I've smoked weed, and I've drank, but not in forever, obviously." She gestures to her abdomen. "I don't know. For the most part, I've always been an outsider."

"No friends?"

"None that I like." The sardonic laugh she pairs with the retort stings my heart. This is a girl who uses her personality and sense of humor to keep people from getting too close. I suspect she's using those same defenses to keep from truly knowing herself. But that's not a conversation for today.

My priority this morning is making sure she's safe. Finding

out about the father of her baby. Assisting her if he's the toxic manipulator I suspect he is.

"Do you like your baby's father?"

"Love of my life. I already told you." Amanda shifts in her chair, tucking a foot under her thigh. "Why are we even talking like this? I'm sure my mom caught you up on the situation."

"I don't think your mom knows the whole situation." I take a sip of my water. "She doesn't know who the father is, for instance. Doesn't know anything about him."

"He's gonna take care of me and the baby, if that's what everyone's worried about. He even gave me money when we found out. Said he's going to be there for me every step of the way." A full smile lights Amanda's face. "He's amazing."

"Have you considered telling your parents all that?"

"They wanted me to get rid of the baby." Amanda's face reddens. "I don't know. Maybe if I told them my guy is older, they'd support it more? Like...he can take care of the kid. He can take care of me too."

Nausea sweeps my body. My worst fears for Amanda have been confirmed. She's being groomed by an older man. And he's setting her up for a very, very hard life.

"Then why don't you tell them that?"

She stares at me for the span of a hundred heartbeats. I let the silence fill the void between us, refusing to be the one to break first.

Her nostrils flare. "Because Virginia's laws have no concept of actual love."

Bingo.

She knows her lover will be tossed headfirst into jail.

Before I have a chance to reply, Amanda gets to her feet and crosses to the far window. "Nice pothos, by the way. It's looking healthy. Your snake plant is dehydrated, though." She reaches toward my watering pot. "Is it okay if..."

I nod. "Of course."

Amanda waters the snake plant and then circles the room, tending to others. "You've got a green thumb." She strokes my monstera with gentle attention. "I got tired of watching my mom kill her plants, so I took over. And they thrived. Every single one of them."

She's speaking with causal nonchalance, but her shoulders are tight, her movements stiff. I badly want to ask her a question, but I stay quiet to make room for whatever's brewing inside her.

When Amanda looks back at me, her expression has hardened. "Do you know how many ridiculous precautions I've had to take, solely because the man I love is older than me?"

I relax into the question. "Tell me."

She turns back to the plants, more edge finding its way into her voice. "Sneaking around. Lying. Not telling anyone about this amazing guy, no matter how bad I want to."

"Sounds hard." I do my best to send her calming validation. The more she shares, the better the prognosis for our time together. "How does it feel to carry that secret and not be able to share it with anyone?"

"It feels like shit." She throws her hands upward. "He even had to get a secret cell phone like a drug dealer to hide me from his ugly wife."

My nostrils flare. My heart beats so prominently in my throat, I move my hair to cover it. "I'm sorry, what? A secret...a secret what?"

She repeats the line about her lover's secret cell phone and ugly wife verbatim.

Intellectually, I know this has nothing to do with me. It'd be surprising if Amanda's older, secret boyfriend didn't have a wife and a burner phone. But this specific detail hits way too close to home.

"Maybe you shouldn't be so hard on the guy's wife." The words spill out before I consider them. "She's innocent in all this."

"Hardly." Amanda sniffs. "She's been withdrawing from him for years. Stopped doing all the stuff they liked to do together. Got obsessed with her job."

"In situations like these, the man often wants his mistress to turn against his wife." I need to stop talking. This is way too personal, and I need to detach myself. But, dammit, I can't. I need this young woman to not be the fool I once was. "He and the younger woman unite against her. It keeps the younger woman from seeing his behavior for what it is. Helps him hide the truth of his actions."

Amanda turns to me with a look of disgust. "I thought you're just supposed to listen."

Her reprimand snaps me back to reality. "Um. Right. You're right. Please. Tell me more."

Amanda brushes off my distracted apology and concludes the session with twenty more minutes split evenly between bragging about her conquest and disparaging her lover's "harpy shrew" of a wife.

As she speaks, my mind once again detaches from my body. How did I think it was a good idea to leap to the defense of this guy's wife? I was so unprofessional. It was borderline unhinged.

But seriously, what the hell is going on with Arthur's secret phone? Was he holding it for Will like he said? Or does he have an Amanda somewhere, complaining to her about his workaholic wife?

Once the session ends, I rush into the bathroom and let out a shaky breath. My hair is a mess. I must've been running my hands through it absentmindedly. Tears hover on the surface of my olive-colored eyes. I barely recognize myself.

I consider splashing water on my face, but that'll make the

whole situation worse. Reaching into my purse for a hairbrush, I instead grab my phone.

Will has not called me back.

I call again, leave another voice message, and wait... desperate for the truth to finally break free.

CHAPTER
ELEVEN

Every day, Jonathan and I share our lunch at a picnic table beneath the sweeping branches of my favorite tree at camp—a weeping willow nestled beside a babbling brook.

Usually, before I even unpack my food, I find myself drawn to the soothing sounds of the running water. Today, I can't hear the water over the session with Amanda that's been replaying on a loop inside my mind.

Out of the corner of my eye, I watch Jonathan tilting his head so that one ear faces the sun. He has a huge smile on his face.

"I have a theory that getting sunlight directly into the ear canal elevates mood and releases serotonin in the brain."

I snort. "And this theory is based on..."

"Every time I get sun in my ears, I'm walking on clouds for the rest of the day."

I pull my bagged lunch out of my purse. It's leftover pasta from the dinner Arthur cooked. Too bad I don't have any wine to pair with it.

"Not a sunny-ear kind of day for me." I force open the lid

on the pasta. The freshness of the pesto zests the air. I squelch a tomato with the tines of my fork and stir.

Jonathan pops open the lid on his lunch. When Annabelle is in town, his meals are varied and often delicious. When she's gone, it's the same thing every day. Turkey burgers and a side salad. "Does this have anything to do with the reason you didn't take advantage of your morning off?"

"No." I give the pasta a second lackadaisical stir. Work Husband is not privy to the juicy details of my rare struggles with Real Husband, and I'm going to keep it that way. "But it has a lot to do with Amanda Holland."

He takes a bite of salad. "Say more."

Jonathan is part of Amanda's therapeutic team at the camp. He's not only allowed to know the details of my conversations with her, camp policy requires it, so I hold nothing back as I recount the session.

The more I speak, the more aggressively Jonathan spears his lettuce. After a while, he drops his fork and focuses all his attention on me, shaking his head with disdain. "Let me make sure I have this right." He pushes his food away. "Statutory rapist. Controls her with misused therapy terms. Tells her he supports the baby but stays with his wife."

I answer with a sigh, finally taking my first bite of pasta. I'm mad at Arthur for being a better cook than me, and I'm even more angry that my anxiety is keeping me from appreciating the food.

"This poor kid. I'm sure he's gaslighting her every time they talk. Telling her she's wrong to doubt him when she's got every reason in the world to hate the guy."

As Jonathan's words hang in the air, a cardinal takes flight nearby, interrupting the quiet between us. His gaze lingers on the bird for a long moment before the cardinal vanishes into the forest.

Finally, he turns to me. "I've told you about my biggest failure, right?"

I take a sip from my tumbler of lukewarm coffee. There's a bitter aftertaste that makes me cough. "That's quite the statement."

"Yeah, well..." He looks away with a distracted sadness in his eyes. "There was this camper here, years ago. Long before you showed up."

I turn my full attention to him. "What happened?"

"She arrived on her first day much more open than girls typically are. Talking a mile a minute about everything going on in her life. And it wasn't surface-level stuff either. Not like 'my mom's a bitch' or 'school's pointless' or any of that. There was a measure of self-awareness that was, frankly, incredible."

"Sounds dangerous."

"Right." Jonathan rolls his tongue around his cheek, and his jaw gets tight. "This is not a happy story."

"The word 'failure' gave that away." I'd hoped my attempt at humor would break the tension. All I get is a sad afterthought of a smile from Jonathan before he looks down and stays silent for a long minute.

It's like he's fighting back tears...or more.

In the distance, a camper shrieks with laughter. The sound sends a ripple of corresponding shrieks into the air, gradually dying off.

I know what happened without him saying anything more. A chill runs through me as the reality of the situation sinks in. Another girl, another predator. Another life destroyed.

"The guy she was with was a master of emotional manipulation. Got into her head. You know how they do."

I stab my pasta with my fork. "They walk into the minds of vulnerable people like they own the place and start rearranging furniture."

Jonathan audibly breathes out through his nose, an acknowledgment of the dark sense of humor the universe often has. When he speaks again, his voice is barely above a whisper.

"She was raped. Not by the manipulator, but by another guy, someone she thought was a friend. Then the toxic boyfriend, the one who'd been manipulating her…he found out about the rape and turned it around on her."

"I'm so sorry."

Though I try to catch Jonathan's eye, he's too caught up picking a splinter off the picnic table. "She killed herself. The boyfriend talked her into it."

I close my eyes. "We can't let that happen to Amanda or any of our girls."

Jonathan keeps working on that splinter. I've been where he is. The self-blame keeps you up nights. Thoughts of what you could've said, what you could've done differently, ways you could've prevented the inevitable.

This is a moment for camaraderie, and I need to offer a nugget of vulnerability in return. He'll never know just how deep I dig to help him feel less alone.

I force myself to speak. "A similar thing happened to me once."

He looks up. To say his eyes are hopeful wouldn't be accurate, but they welcome my olive branch of vulnerability.

What I'm about to say, I've told so few people. For a moment, I consider pulling back. But then I catch his eyes again—seeking, almost pleading—and find the strength to stumble forward.

"A girl, um…a girl I knew in high school…had an affair with her teacher when she was sixteen. She thought this guy was a gift from God."

If "gift from God" could ever be an understatement, this is that rare moment.

"A couple times, this girl...she tried to end it. He'd unleash such unspeakable rage on her. She thought she was the one at fault, like she was the evil one."

I press my fingertips together to keep them from shaking. It's so sad how the most manipulative people always manage to find those among us who are easiest to manipulate.

Jonathan swallowed. "Did she...is she alive still?"

I nod. "She got out of it. But she did not escape unscathed."

Jonathan puts his hand over mine. We take a deep breath together. After a moment, I slide my hand away and return to my meal. Jonathan does the same, the silent companionship recalibrating my frayed nerves.

If only he knew the whole truth about that sad teenage girl.

CHAPTER

TWELVE

I pull into my driveway after work, fixating once again on thoughts of Arthur's secret phone. When I left camp, Will still hadn't called me back. By this point, I'm sure Arthur has fully briefed his brother. Nonetheless, I'm about to check for Will's return call for the thousandth time when I'm distracted by our picture-perfect home.

I'll never forget how much I loved the place the first time I saw it. With its white shutters, crisp lawn, and striking red door, the place seemed torn from the pages of a magazine.

Among the many charming details, my favorite has always been the brick chimney. Covered in gorgeous English ivy, it looks like something straight out of a storybook. Back when we'd bought the house, the chimney alone had justified my insistence on submitting an offer over asking, and I've never regretted it for a moment.

Not even when the chimney sweep informed us just a few weeks ago that the English ivy has worked its way into the structure and might destroy it from the inside out.

I volunteered to remove the ivy myself—insisted, in fact—and then put it off for weeks. But today, tearing out greenery is just the task I need to distract myself from Arthur, and Will, and the mystery of the hidden phone.

With renewed determination, I head to the chimney, grab a vine, and pull. A long strand of ivy comes off, but still more clings to the brick. I try to pry it up with my fingernails but fail. Then come the garden shears and a pool of sweat at the small of my back. And the ivy's days are numbered.

After more than two hours of this uncomfortable nonsense, only the thick growth at the base of the chimney remains, twisted and knotted into itself.

I pull. It doesn't budge. I pull harder. Nothing. The shears call to me, but I want to defeat this final boss on my own.

With both hands, I grab ahold of the vines. One deep breath later, and I'm in the middle of the toughest tug-o-war match of my life. Finally, the ivy gives way, sending me flying on my ass.

Laughing, I look back at the ivy I've vanquished.

Staring back at me is a large copperhead, coiled and glaring. I crab-crawl backward and climb to my feet. The snake hisses, and I stumble back another step.

For a moment, I consider running away. Then I remember who I am.

Gathering my courage, I grab it behind the head, just like I'd grabbed the snake at Camp Wildfire. This one wriggles more, and for a second, I wish I'd used the snake hook from the garage. But it's too late for that, so I keep my grip firm and deposit the varmint twenty steps into the woods.

"And don't come back!" I shout as the snake slithers away, grimacing like Clint Eastwood in pretty much any Clint Eastwood movie.

"You're getting pretty good at defeating enemy snakes, Mrs. Yuen."

Arthur emerges from the house holding two drinks in fancy glasses.

The sight of my husband stirs my anxiety. I want to grill him on the story he told me about the secret phone—*Do the details line up? Does his face twitch when he recounts the facts?* —but I decide on a more tactful approach instead. "When did you get home?"

"Few minutes ago." He hands me one of the glasses. "Lychee Martini Mocktail."

Ugh. Arthur thinks I love his mocktails, but they're just another way I've been humoring him through my lies. I accept the drink with a small smile and choke down a sip.

Too sweet. Needs booze.

I wonder if he's been using the drinks to humor me through his lies as well.

In a flash, I imagine laying my suspicions on the table then and there. Instead, I lock eyes with Arthur as I take my second sip.

"So I found a clinic in Richmond that's supposed to be world class." He slurps the lychee out of his drink. "Think you might want to check it out?"

The cognitive dissonance is so severe, I get a brain zap like I'm going through opioid withdrawal. My husband, who might be cheating, won't stop pushing the idea of having a baby with me. Meanwhile, I couldn't possibly have a baby, not if my life depended on it.

The prospect of going to a facility in Richmond to initiate the IVF process is enough to send me screaming into the forest, snakes and all. A doctor can't be the one to tell my husband the truth about my broken body. I've gone to extremes for the last year to draw out this lie, but that is a line I can't let myself cross.

"I've been thinking about that..." I lower my drink.

Arthur lowers his too. "Liz—"

"No, hear me out." The drink is cold in my hand, and the ice clinks against the glass as my lying mouth opens to speak.

"It's just...my whole life I've dreamed of becoming a mother. I don't want to do it through a test tube. If there's any way we might get pregnant naturally—"

"You told me we could get help after a year."

Arthur's breathing quickens as I bullshit some ideas about motherhood being a natural and sacred experience, about how much it all means to me. "Being pregnant, being a mother isn't something I want to do with doctors poking at me and 'making' my body work." The more I talk, the more his face contorts.

Once I get the whole spiel out, he stands silent for a long moment. Finally, he crosses back toward the porch, taking slow and careful steps.

I trail a few feet behind him. "Arthur?"

He places his drink on the porch rail and turns back to me. His expression is softer than I'd expected, more compassionate. "I know something else might be going on, Liz. After what you went through...it wouldn't surprise me if it left you unable to conceive."

Two men. A baseball bat to the stomach. A long fall down the stairs.

He takes my hand in his. I flinch and pull away. Though it seems like Arthur has created an opening for me to tell the truth, I can't take it. The weight of my lies—about my infertility, about Mr. Blessed—feels heavier than ever.

Shame, and its deadly weight, keep my mouth closed.

Our history flashes through my mind. Arthur and I first dated when I was a junior in high school. He was a senior then. My first "older man." Our three-month relationship teetered on the edge of serious, filled with intense emotions and stolen kisses, but never crossed into truly physical territory. It ended abruptly when I got involved with Mr. Blessed...a man who redefined my concept of *older*.

I'd ruined things with Arthur for Mr. Blessed's lies, and

even now, years later, Arthur doesn't know about that relationship.

Guilt shortens my breath. Self-hatred floods my body. *How dare I attack Arthur with my suspicions when I've been hiding so much for so long?*

If he's cheating, I deserve it. I was a liar as a teenager, and I haven't changed. The box of tampons in the bathroom, the heating pillow I curl up with once a month. Tears flow down my face. This time, when Arthur takes my hand in his, I don't pull away.

"Liz. If you can't…if it's not in the plans for us…that's okay. I'm going to love you no matter what. We can use a surrogate or adopt. There are so many kids out there. So many options."

He pulls me into his arms. Just like that, years of carefully held control slip away. He whispers consolations I can barely hear over the sobs racking my body.

The smell of his Old Spice takes me back to that summer we met, over a decade ago. So much has changed since then, but the essence of this man, the goodness…that will always remain.

I hope.

CHAPTER
THIRTEEN

I'm not someone who falls asleep easily. It takes two episodes of a boring podcast on a good night. Even then, I usually wake up when the stupid music plays over the credits, and I've got to roll over and start again.

So it doesn't surprise me that I can't fall asleep after talking to Arthur about our fertility struggles.

Anxiety attacks me on every front. At home, my husband has a secret cell phone, and his brother won't call me back to confirm the story. At work, I have a pregnant teenage girl who's been fooled into thinking her assailant will be there for her baby. And the lies about my ability to conceive a child add to the mess, creating turmoil even the most dramatic woman wouldn't envy.

Though Arthur and I had gotten close to the truth on the fertility issue, there's so much he doesn't know. The deception is so deep that I'm not sure how I can ever come clean.

The microwave shows 1:17 a.m. when I remove my mug of chamomile tea and head out to the garden. As I step outside, a wave of cool air hits me, and I pull my robe tight. A ceramic frog looks up at me from the bed of roses, his big, silly grin menacing in the moonlight.

My brain plays Russian roulette with my worries and lands on Amanda Holland. I think back to her description of her lover's wife, a "harpy shrew." I doubt she knows what either word means, but she'd said them with such hatred that it doesn't matter.

When I replay the part of the conversation where I snapped at Amanda, my stomach churns like it's eating itself.

My lack of professionalism mortifies me. But my self-hatred is rooted much, much deeper than I want to admit. I dug that well of contempt way back when I was Amanda's age, and my conversation with her brought old, murky waters to the surface.

Like her, I was in love with an older man. During my torrential affair with Mr. Blessed, I took such great pleasure in hating his wife. I crammed entire journals with hate mail I wrote to her and never sent. Pages upon pages were dedicated just to calling her names. And every entry in between gushed about my deep connection with Mr. Blessed and the future we'd share together once he left his wife behind.

I'll never forget my nickname for her—the Rat.

Even though she was gorgeous, I'd felt so clever, giving her that name.

Reflecting on it now, I cringe at the irony. I was in a toxic, manipulative relationship with my AP Psychology teacher. And the tactics he used were all too calculated, like a sinister curriculum he'd devised just for me.

Manipulation. Emotional coercion. Strategic inconsistency.

He employed all these methods expertly, each one crafted to make me believe we had a future, even as he went home each night to his happy suburban life.

Every girl in school wanted to be in my position. They

wanted his halogen smile pointed at them. They dreamed of the kind of special attention I got. And I loved being the beneficiary of his laser focus.

It didn't happen like in the movies, though.

He didn't keep me after class and slip me a worn copy of his favorite book to read. Instead, it all began over email. He'd send articles following up on comments I'd made in class, but always from his personal account.

There'd be small compliments in every message. First about my brain, then about my clothes, then about my body. Eventually, those emails became text messages, from a phone I soon learned was his burner.

I know I didn't deserve what happened to me. But no matter how hard I try, no matter how many seminars I lead on the topic, I can't release myself from the guilt and shame.

That's why it all came spilling out on Amanda in my office. She doesn't deserve what's happening to her either. And neither did the girl Jonathan told me about. That poor girl, manipulated into suicide.

It could've been me. And it could easily be Amanda if I don't give her the help she needs.

That menacing frog catches my eye for a second time, and the roulette wheel in my mind spins and lands on Arthur and his stupid secret phone.

"It's possible he was telling the truth." I speak the words out loud, but neither the tree frogs nor the ceramic frog respond. So much of my body wants to believe my husband. Every fiber of my being needs him to have been telling the truth.

My mind spends the next few minutes wrestling the temptation to call Will for the third time in the last twenty-four hours. I bet he'll confirm Arthur's story. But he might slip up and confuse an important detail or stumble in another telling way. Will can be an idiot like that. And I'm sure talking to him will help, even if it's painful.

Cognitive behavioral therapists would call what I'm doing "fortune-telling," and they would warn me not to waste time predicting events when I can't know the future. But the pull is so strong, I can't ignore it.

Fortune-telling, noun

A cognitive distortion wherein a person predicts negative outcomes without actual evidence, often assuming the worst-case scenario will happen. Common side effects include unnecessary stress and convincing oneself of impending doom. See also, why I'm trying to predict the future instead of staying in the present like a rational person.

I'm not sure if it's seconds or minutes later, but soon enough, I'm back on Mr. Blessed. Ever since Arthur and I married, I've kept the details of that damaging affair compartmentalized, protecting myself from the pain of those intrusive thoughts. But I've got no discipline tonight.

And I'm seventeen again and standing at his front door like prey outside a predator's lair.

The first time I'd visited him there, he'd worn a University of Virginia t-shirt over blue jeans. It was the first time I'd seen him out of the khakis and button-ups he wore to school. The look was so casual—so sexy—I'd almost melted.

"Come in, come in."

I hadn't seen it then, but the way he'd urged me inside dripped with paranoia. He must've been afraid a neighbor would see a student at his home. Then again, only a sociopath would arrange a rendezvous there in the first place.

Fragments of that night and many others like it stick in my brain like throwing stars embedded in a cottonwood target.

"You're so beautiful."

"So mature, so wise beyond your years."

"I'll take care of you. I'll leave her. I promise."

"No one can know about us. Not yet."

We spent hours gazing into one another's eyes that night. I don't think we blinked a dozen times between us. It was one of the first times we were alone together for that long. My fate was sealed then, and I'd had no idea how far things would go.

Memories of the pregnancy sicken me. In my naivete, I'd rejoiced at carrying his child.

He'd acted so happy at the news. "We're going to make a beautiful family, Lizette. All grade A students, like you."

The smile I'd unleashed at those words was so big, I swear it wrapped all the way around to the back of my head. My unplanned pregnancy meant Mr. Blessed would have to leave his wife within the next nine months, and nothing could've made me happier.

"I was so stupid."

The shame is evident in my voice as I look back at the sinister frog and shake my head. I'm not wearing any shoes, but I walk out toward the forest anyway. It's like I'm trying to escape my past.

I have no compassion for who I was then. Yes, I was groomed. But I wasn't a little kid. I was seventeen. I'd already taken the PSAT and scored a 1350. I was too smart to be taken in by charming smiles and the lies behind them.

"I was pathetic."

Am I still? Is Arthur lying to me?

A snapping twig startles me. I'm barefoot a hundred yards into the forest. Spinning around, I barely make out my house in the dark. My feet are wet and covered in grass clippings and leaves. The sound of tree frogs and crickets surrounds me.

I'm terrified Arthur will find me out here and think I'm losing my mind.

Am I losing my mind?

I hustle back home. The door creaks as I sneak inside. I wipe the grass off my feet with a paper towel and bury it in the trash. I fill a mason jar with water and drink it fast, wiping my mouth with a used kitchen towel.

When I enter the bedroom, the smell of Arthur's soap drifts from his freshly showered body on the bed. My feet relax into the plush carpet. Arthur's rhythmic breath moves in and out with the hint of a snore after every exhale.

What happens next was not part of the plan.

Arthur's phone rests on the nightstand, inches from his head. I hesitate. I've never snooped in Arthur's stuff, and this is a big line to cross. But if there's a small chance looking at his phone can help ease my mind, it's a chance I'm willing to take.

Tiptoeing over, I swipe it and pad into the bathroom.

I close the bathroom door, keeping my eyes on Arthur until he's out of sight. Perched on the toilet, I kick a box of maxi pads under the sink—just a prop in my unthinkable deception—and unlock his phone. He's shared the pin code with me before. Has he changed it since then?

It's our anniversary.

Typing in the date, I'm relieved when the device opens. And just like that, I'm that woman, searching for secrets buried in her sleeping husband's phone.

CHAPTER
FOURTEEN

The threat of Arthur waking up pulses through me as I search his phone.

It's an older device, so the messages app takes an extra second to open. I think I hear something in the bedroom and clutch the phone to my chest. The moment passes. When I look back to the phone, the app has opened to every conversation Arthur has ever logged on the device.

That he hasn't deleted, at least.

Shaking off the thought, I notice that his only two pinned contacts are me and his mother. I read at double speed as I scroll through the rest of his conversations, looking for something suspicious.

There's a thread with Jonathan and Will about golfing soon, filled with shit-talking and one-upmanship. Separate from that is another conversation, just between Arthur and Will—a side conversation about the golf game, talking about which of them will beat Jonathan by more. There's no mention of the secret burner phone or me.

I check the recent call logs. In the past two days, Arthur

has made and received calls to and from me, work, and his mom, but he hasn't contacted Will once.

"That's weird. Arthur didn't text or call his brother after I found the hidden phone?"

Unless that's the kind of conversation you'd never have on your main phone. Or Arthur texted Will ASAP and deleted it.

A loud snore erupts from the bedroom. Edging over to the door, I open it a fraction of an inch and peer through. Arthur rolls over, letting out another loud snore before settling into sleep again.

I can't spend all night hiding in the bathroom, but searching the phone is an out-of-body experience, and I can't seem to stop what I've started. My thumbs fly through one inane conversation after another. Each time, I tell myself this is the last one I'll read, but then I click another, and another.

A car rattles past our house, thumping hip-hop so loud, I hear the chassis shake. Another peek at the bedroom tells me Arthur remains sound asleep.

I seal myself back inside the bathroom and turn back to the phone. My fingers shake as I search the device for hidden messaging apps, dating apps, or mysterious social media behavior.

I seem to be confirming what I already know...

Arthur's the most boring man in the world. There are no questionable apps, his listening history is filled with audiobooks about literal rocks, and most of his internet searches are about birds, nature, or topographical anomalies.

The last app I search is Facebook, still expecting to turn up a skeleton in one of my husband's digital closets. Finding his activity log, I learn he hasn't sent a message in the last two years, not since he used Marketplace to look for an antique coffee table as a birthday gift for me.

Arthur lets out another loud snore. Checking the time on

the phone, I realize I've been lost down this toxic rabbit hole for over an hour.

I'm about to slip out of the bathroom when Arthur calls my name. Shit. I've pushed it too far, and he's noticed the missing phone.

"Are you okay in there?" He sounds half asleep.

"Yeah. Just finishing up." My heart freezes as he mumbles something. I exhale, flush the toilet, and run the sink.

That was way too close for comfort, and I need to get a grip.

I spend most of the next workday trying to avoid thinking about my invasion of Arthur's privacy. But the intrusive thoughts are a heavyweight boxer, and I'm far outmatched in the center of the ring.

The guilt is a strong right hook to the flank.

How could I have betrayed my husband like that?

The confusion is an uppercut taken on the chin.

But aren't I right to have suspicions?

The shame and stupidity are the knockout combination.

Of course you didn't find anything on his phone. That's why he has two.

The inability to think clearly about the situation bothers me more than anything else. It's not like me to flip-flop between extreme emotions. Then again, it's not like me to lose trust in my husband either.

Camp Wildfire—and the mountain of paperwork waiting for me there—is the only distraction available, and I manage to use it as an emotional blinder for the day. But by the time four o'clock rolls around, I'm all out of willpower, and Amanda's face keeps popping up in my mind. Each time it does, my anger at her "perfect partner" grows, and soon enough, I'm having a full-blown conversation with myself.

"This guy doesn't love her. He's a manipulative criminal."

"But why's he still manipulating her when he's going to disappear the moment the baby's born? Does he really need to cling to his power over her for that long?"

"Maybe he's already gone, and the relationship is all in her mind right now."

"No, she talks about him like he's very much still influencing her."

If I can't resolve my issues with Arthur, maybe I can find satisfaction helping Amanda escape her groomer.

I'm about to do a deep internet search on Amanda when I get up, go to the door, and glance around the hallway. Jonathan's nowhere to be seen, and that's great, because I don't need any witnesses to the boundary violations I'm about to commit.

Seconds later, I sit back down and start researching Amanda Holland with the urgency of a heroin addict headed to meet their dealer for a fix. A tiny voice in the back of my mind warns me to stop. I might not like what I find, and there's a strong chance that whatever information's out there will nauseate me.

But I'm determined to help Amanda, and my misguided altruism drives me forward.

I search her name. I search her name in combination with her high school. I search her full name, middle included, with the home address I pull from her file.

Plenty of results populate. But all of Amanda's social media accounts are set to private. And nothing indicates an older man is in her life.

Giving up on Amanda, I search her mother and click around for a few minutes. There are several articles on Carol's philanthropic efforts in Texas, where the family lived until recently. But there's not much else.

The entryway door whooshes from down the hall, and Jonathan sweeps past my door with a, "Howdy!"

I give him a quick wave back, trying to signal that I'm busy. He slips into his office, but he could turn around and pop in on me at any second. It's pretty much his M.O. I pause, my finger frozen on the mouse, ready to exit out of the page if he comes in. But I don't hear any footsteps…

I navigate to an article from *The Washington Post* written about Amanda's father, Peter. The piece describes Peter Holland as a "formidable Commonwealth attorney," and it tells the story of a controversial case he'd recently won on behalf of the state.

The case hinged on the technicalities of land-usage rights, and Peter had locked down the victory by hiring an expert to demonstrate that several important boundary lines were out of date.

The expert brought to help Amanda's father was a land surveyor named Arthur Yuen.

CHAPTER
FIFTEEN

I close my eyes and try to process this new information. My husband has a connection to Amanda's father. Is that a coincidence? Or is there something more?

Amanda's description of her lover's wife blares in my head like an ambulance.

She's been withdrawing from him for years. Stopped doing all the stuff they liked to do together. Got obsessed with her job.

Can those words be applied to me?

I suppose Arthur had complained I'd stopped wanting to go to the arcade with him a few years ago. But that was the stuff we did when we were teenagers. Does it make me a bad wife just because I've developed a preference for wine bars and good conversation?

"Did Arthur…" I can't bring myself to speak my suspicions out loud. They're too ridiculous. There's no way Arthur impregnated a teenage girl he met through his job and hid it from me for so long.

And you've been lying to him for how long?

Silencing my inner voice, I refocus on Amanda. She'd also referenced a secret phone her lover got to hide his relationship with her. And she's repeatedly insulted the man's wife, calling her hideous, and ugly, and all sorts of names I can't even remember. Dumb shrew, was it?

No. Harpy shrew, that was it.

If she thought I was this guy's wife, would she have said that stuff to my face? And I might not be a beauty queen, but I'm not ugly.

Am I?

"Unless she enjoys messing with me. I mean, if she hates this woman so much...why wouldn't she take pleasure in insulting her directly?"

I would've loved to have done the same to Mrs. Blessed.

The entire time I'm processing my conversations with Amanda, I'm cycling back through her private social media accounts, trying to find a way in. Just when I'm about to quit searching, I look her up on Block Party, a short-lived app that was briefly popular with teen girls a few months ago.

Amanda's profile pops up immediately. It's public. From the preview images, I spot several pictures featuring a man who looks suspiciously like Arthur. I'm about to enlarge the photos when there's a quiet knock on my doorframe.

I snap the laptop shut and clear my throat. "Come in."

Jonathan plants both feet inside my office. "I'm headed home in a few. You still at it?"

"Just a couple more hours. Reviewing files, blah blah blah."

Reviewing files and digging into Amanda's abandoned social media account, if you'll kindly GTFO.

"How is it that you always seem to be working later than I do?" Jonathan smiles, but the comment catches me in my stomach.

"*Got obsessed with her job*" echoes in my mind. I'm home every night by seven. But Arthur's home by five, and he's spent plenty of nights eating alone.

My thumb throbs. I look down to see a small trickle of blood where I've been picking at my cuticles without realizing. Shoving the thumb under the desk, I give Jonathan my most polite smile. "I'll be headed home soon. Don't worry. I won't tell anyone you're half-assing it."

Jonathan shoots back a witty retort, whistling as he heads out with a pep in his step. As soon as he's gone, I flip my laptop open and click on Amanda's Block Party profile.

The man in the photos is not Arthur, not even remotely Chinese on closer inspection. It's one of Amanda's uncles. And the account hasn't been updated since before Amanda and her family moved from Texas to Virginia.

Before I go, I type out the important facts in chronological order.

Arthur worked with Peter Holland on that land-usage case. He'd gone out of town for four nights, if I remember correctly, to meet with Peter and draw up the necessary maps. And this all went down almost exactly eight months ago.

Amanda says she's six months pregnant.

Arthur always plans his travels meticulously, booking everything well in advance. This includes our "baby-making sessions," which he schedules around his misguided understanding of my cycle—a misconception I've deliberately fostered.

But his meticulous planning could have a darker side. What if Arthur met Amanda on that first trip and pursued the connection later? With his keen attention to detail, arranging secrets meetings would have been simple. A fake name here, cash payments there. He could've covered his tracks without breaking his routines.

I hate myself for having these thoughts about my husband, but this connection to Amanda's family is too big to ignore.

"Just ask Arthur about it." My tapestry of plants absorbs

my voice. "I would. But last time I did that, I ended up second-guessing myself, thinking I was crazy."

Maybe I am crazy. Maybe I've always been. Maybe I have a thing for men who abuse unsuspecting women and girls.

As I run through my limited options for what to do next, my phone dings with a text. I look down, hoping I've finally heard from Will, but the text is from a private number.

I am not alone.

Regina.

I read the text aloud several times before placing the phone down and looking out the window at the dense forest beyond camp. The only Regina I know is the missing girl from all those years ago. But there's no way the text could be from her.

Then I shoot back a quick reply, my breath trapped at the base of my throat.

Who is this?

CHAPTER
SIXTEEN

The shock of seeing Regina's name quickly morphs into annoyance. I'm positive one of the campers is behind the message. We confiscate all devices on check-in, but that doesn't mean someone couldn't have a secret phone. If that's the case, I'd bet money on Madeline, considering our conversation at the lake.

I'm tempted to round the campers up and demand answers. But that's a bad idea. If Madeline didn't already have the girls on edge, my surprise mandatory assembly definitely would.

I could meet with Madeline alone, but that's clearly what she's vying for. Another confrontation.

Instead, I hurry out to my car, muttering about the immaturity of teenage girls and pushing the more grotesque rumors surrounding Regina Smith out of my mind.

She did not text me from her grave. She did not text me from her kidnapper's phone. She did not text me at all. A camper did. Just to give me a pointless, boring scare.

My keys jangle with my hurried steps as I near my car. A voice from behind stops me.

"Yo!" I turn to find Jonathan following me out, grinning. "Thought you had extra work tonight."

"Um..." *Do I tell Jonathan about the text? Or is that going to make me seem crazy?* "And I thought you already left."

Jonathan narrows his eyes playfully. "Were you pretending to stay late just to make me feel like a slacker?"

I muster a small smile. "Ha. No. As it turns out, sorting files is boring, and I'm tired. The two don't mix."

He nods. "Sounds like you might be hangry. Or hurious? That's hungry mixed with—"

"Furious, I get it." There's no way my impatient tone is getting past Jonathan without an inquisition.

"There's the friendly coworker I know and love." His grin fades as he approaches, adjusting the canvas messenger bag on his shoulder. "You doing okay?"

"Yeah...I'm...I'm doing fine."

Thoughts of Arthur and Amanda flood my mind. I want to tell Jonathan about my suspicions, but I can't get into that. Not now, not ever.

Still, his searching eyes dislodge a buried question, and my voice wavers as I ask it. "If you know someone's lying to you, is it wrong to lie back in order to find out the truth?"

Jonathan's expression is a mix of anticipation and empathy. It's strangely comforting, as if he's been waiting and ready to lend an ear.

"Are you asking for my therapeutic advice, or for my advice as a friend?" He squints at the sun, which is more than halfway down to the horizon, raising a hand to block the light. "Very different answers."

"I know the right thing to say as a therapist. Direct and honest communication is key. Don't be afraid to assert your boundaries or express your needs. Blah blah blah."

"This about Arthur?"

I shake my head. "No. My...my sister. She's being weird

about our Fourth of July plans, and I kinda want to call her out on it. It shouldn't be stressing me like this. But she's involving my mom. And it's...it's driving me crazy."

"I get it." Jonathan shifts so the sun is no longer in his eyes. "I doubt you need to get involved with family drama over holiday plans. But if Mary Beth's jerking you around, she better have a damn good reason."

Actually, my sister's great, and my brother-in-law makes bomb smashburgers. What I want to talk about is my husband and the teenage camper he might've knocked up.

"You sure that's it?" Jonathan takes a step toward me. Now there's only two feet between us. "This seems heavier than your standard patriotic drama."

From this close, I can see specks of brown in his green eyes. My chin quivers as I reply with an almost inaudible, "Yeah."

He probably thinks it's that time of the month. If he only knew.

"You need a hug?"

I really, really do. I nod.

As Jonathan wraps his arms around me, the comforting scent of laundry detergent and fresh-cut grass envelops me.

Taking a step back, I glance toward the forest.

Have those trees witnessed a violent murder? Have they tangled Regina's body in their roots?

Jonathan, once again demonstrating his annoying people-reading skills, cocks his head. "Something else going on?"

"I also got this, uh, weird text."

"From your sister?"

Taking a deep breath, I pull my phone out, open to the Regina message, and hand it to my boss.

The Regina message appears in blue, my reply in green. On my iPhone, this color change suggests the sender didn't receive my message—I'm either blocked or the phone is off.

I start to tell Jonathan the text was probably sent by some

annoying camper. But he holds up his finger, and I quiet down as he recites the text with silent lips. I watch as he reads it repeatedly, his brow furrowing deeper each time. He types something out, and I lean forward to get a better look.

"What are you doing?"

"Forwarding the texts to myself." He sounds annoyed, which is understandable given the situation. "Gotta have all the info if I'm going to figure this out." He hands the phone back. "Now I'm wishing it was just sister stuff."

I start picking at my thumb again. This time, the pain makes me stop, and I shove my hand in my pocket. "It's mostly sister stuff. Our usual stupid family drama. But yeah. Also a mysterious text from someone claiming to be a missing camper."

Jonathan lets out a quiet laugh, exhaling through his nose. We make eye contact. Those brown flecks are even sharper now, brought out by the soft light of the sun.

Breaking the connection, I inform him about Madeline, Amanda, the circulating rumors around camp, and my theory that a camper might've been behind the creepy text.

"But we collect all devices at check in," he reminds me. "And I haven't approved any supervised phone use today."

"Maybe someone smuggled one in. It's happened before."

Jonathan nods. "These kids think they're funny. Or they joke about what might've happened to Regina Smith so they can feel better about it, like they're still invincible teenagers. But it's not right how they make a game out of it. A young woman went missing. She's got a family, and I'm sure some of them are still holding out hope."

Hope. It's the most powerful and complex cognitive process we experience as humans. It can inspire incredible resilience and progress, but it also sets us up for profound disappointment. Hope is not simply an emotion, but a dynamic interplay of goal-setting, agency, and pathways thinking.

"Yeah. Hope is a wonderful and terrible thing."

He inhales sharply. "I was here when she disappeared, you know. What was that, about a decade ago?"

I knew Jonathan lived in town then, but we've never talked about it.

He shakes his head. "It was intense. Whole town turned out to hunt for her. Not like you'd expect, though. No line of people walking hand in hand through the forest. It was more disorganized than that, more emotional."

"Sounds rough."

His shoulders sag. "You should've been there when Regina's mother was screaming her name. She kept searching for days after the team gave up. The sound of it was like someone clawing out your insides."

A pickup roars past on the main road, heavy metal thundering from its speakers, a Confederate flag snapping fiercely in the wind. Any other day, this sight would've drawn a comment from me. Today, it barely registers.

"Is it possible Regina ran away from camp?" I ask. "That's what I told my girls the other day. Told them that's what I heard, at least."

Jonathan shrugs. "It's possible, sure."

"They never caught anyone, right? And they never found her body, so..."

His face contorts, as if he's recalling a gruesome detail.

I lean toward him. "What?"

"Nothing. I don't know. Maybe I don't believe in pointless optimism."

"It's not pointless. They didn't find her body, so she could've just run away. We know that happens with these kids sometimes."

He kicks at the dirt. "We know other things happen sometimes too."

"But the cops never caught anyone." The annoyance in my voice is impossible to conceal. "Unless you think it was Myer Whitley and he's been sitting on the truth."

"Can't have been him. He was assaulting another girl when Regina went missing. Over in Shepstone."

"Right." My stomach flips as I recall Whitley's disturbing alibi. I'd kept things general when talking to Madeline and the other campers—no need to share he'd been attacking another girl—but remembering it now nauseates me. "It's creepy to think you and Arthur were in the same high school class with a violent criminal like that."

"You went to that school too," Jonathan says. "And he was pretty popular. A lot of people liked him."

"Not me." I pin Jonathan with an accusatory look. "Did you like him?"

The question leaves my lips before I can stop it. Why did I ask that? Am I probing for Jonathan's past, or am I unconsciously seeking validation for my own complicated history with "good" men?

Jonathan smooths a patch of gravel with his foot. "I didn't know him that well." He lifts a shoulder. "But I went to a few of his parties."

I shouldn't be surprised, but I am. "You went to Myer Whitley's parties?"

"It's weirder that you didn't."

"I didn't go to any parties in high school. And I left after junior year." I try to catch his eye, but he's looking out toward the horizon. "What were they like?"

When Jonathan turns back to me, the customary twinkle has returned to his eyes. "I only went to a couple. And I left because kids were drinking and smoking weed."

I laugh and kick Jonathan's foot away from the gravel he's still smoothing. "You were an even bigger dork than I was."

"Hey, not my gravel! I just got it all smoothed out."

"You're such a perfectionist," I tease, attempting to restore his little square of gravel. "How did Myer Whitley end up in jail anyway? I know it wasn't for assaulting Kylie, so what was it for?"

"Attempted bank robbery, if you can believe it. Heard he got, like, fifteen years." Jonathan unclasps his watch, then latches it again. "I bet he's exactly the same guy he was in high school."

I cast my eyes downward. If I were still the same person as I was in high school, I'd be caught in a toxic relationship with a manipulative psychopath. And I really, really hope I've grown past that by now.

CHAPTER
SEVENTEEN

As I drive away, Camp Wildfire fades into the distance in my rearview mirror. The intense humidity doesn't register with me until camp has fully disappeared. But when it hits, it's suffocating.

Jamming the buttons on the dash, I turn the AC up to full blast. The air comes out too warm, so I roll the windows down. The rush of air is a brief relief before a sudden downpour begins.

"Shit, shit, shit!" By the time I've got the windows rolled up, my left arm and leg are soaked, the AC has turned cold, and my whole body is freezing.

My muscles clench, and I groan, but the frustration soon turns to a laugh. For a brief, wet moment, I blame myself for letting exasperation take hold. But I quickly remind myself that, like all people, I deserve grace.

What I do at Camp Wildfire is taxing. The campers are dredging up a potential murder. Oh, and there's a slim possibility my husband might have impregnated the most vulnerable among them. An annoyed groan barely captures the extent of my frustrations.

By the time I pull into the driveway, the rain has slowed to a drizzle. As I climb out of my car, I stare at Arthur's truck parked in the garage, my mind swirling with questions and suspicions.

If Arthur's keeping something from me, there's no way he's continued to keep his secrets hidden under the hood of his truck. Yet I'm drawn to the vehicle like a murderer returning to the scene of the crime.

I want to pop the hood a second time. Maybe it's the need for reassurance or the nagging feeling that I missed something the first time. But I can't let Arthur catch me in the act.

Stepping into the mudroom, I scan for Arthur's truck keys on the hook. No luck. The door to the main house creaks as I enter the kitchen. It's dark inside from the storm. As stark and still as a museum at dawn.

I don't see Arthur. But I'm sure he's close. And I cannot let him find me sneaking around my own house like a criminal.

His truck keys are tossed down beside his work laptop on the counter.

As I reach for the cold metal of the key ring, a shiver runs through me. How well do I know the man I share my bed with?

My fingers close around the keys. I hold them tight, so they don't jangle, as I stalk back toward the garage.

Best case, I have a few minutes. Worst case, Arthur sneaks up and catches me in the act. Either way, I need to get another peek inside that truck.

Outside, the summer rain has stopped. Rain often breaks the Virginia humidity, but in this case, the stickiness has already returned, and the air in the garage is thick. Sweat drips from my forehead as I climb behind the driver's seat. The hood pops with a clunk.

Seconds later, I've got a flashlight in my hand, and I'm scrutinizing the engine bay for something suspicious.

The box containing the phone has not been replaced, and a quick scan of the rest of the area reveals little. Just as I'd suspected. Closing the hood as quietly as I can, I return to the cab and give it a thorough search.

There's nothing under the seats. Not even a crumb or an old french fry. Arthur is clean to a fault. But this is odd, even for him.

"I'm sure he cleaned this thing out already."

I wipe my forehead with the back of my arm as I straighten up and climb out of the truck. A quick look back inside the house reveals a still-dark kitchen in a still-quiet house. Reentering the hot garage, I cross to the far corner. Once again, I dial Will's number.

This time, he answers. "Everything all right?"

I pause, the humidity clinging to me like a second skin. "Oh. Uh. Everything's fine. Just checking in."

A long silence follows as Will eats a crunchy snack. "You've called me a bunch of times."

I wince, fighting the urge to gag at the sound of his chomping. "Yeah. I...I know I have. I also know you haven't called me back."

"It's about the phone, right?"

I close my eyes. Arthur and Will have already talked, just as I'd suspected. I squeak out a defeated, "Yeah."

Will sighs. It sounds forced. Practiced, even. "The phone is mine. I started doing some work with a guy in witness protection after Vicky asked me not to, and the phone was part of it. I got scared the wife was gonna find me out, so I asked Artie to stash the phone for me. Ill-advised, I know."

Sweat drips from my face onto the concrete. The humid air, heavy with oil and rain, makes it hard to breathe, and my hands tremble.

Will's narrative, so perfectly aligned with my husband's earlier explanations, doesn't sit right.

He lets out a big, dramatic yawn. "Anyhow, I better get going. We're all good here, right?"

Confusion tightens my voice. "What do you mean, 'we're all good?'"

Why does it feel like he's patting me on the head like a good little girl?

"I mean we're all good." He takes another bite of food and continues with his mouth full. "That actually reminds me... don't share any of this with Vicky, okay? She doesn't need to know."

It's all too convenient, too smooth. And I feel like a pawn in this game now.

"Liz?"

With newfound resolve, I reply, "I won't lie for you, Will."

His voice hardens. "Then you're causing everyone a whole lot of hurt for no reason. Is that what you want?"

Seriously? "Maybe if you get in a little trouble with your wife, you'll stop roping my family into your highly dangerous work."

"Lizette." His tone has a warning in it. "I understand what you're saying. And you're right. But we can't go running to Vicky with this. Please. At least give me some time to tell her myself."

"Whatever." I end the call and slip my phone into my pocket.

When I turn back toward the house, Arthur is standing in the doorway.

CHAPTER
EIGHTEEN

He scrubs a hand over his stubble. "Who were you talking to?"

I lock eyes with my husband. "It was Will."

"So this is about trust." Arthur takes a step back, looking at me like I'm a stranger.

"I don't know." My voice turns icy. "He's singing your tune word for word about the phone."

Arthur looks away with a heavy sigh. "So you're mad because my brother is telling the truth."

"Maybe he's telling the truth. Or maybe you've synced up your lies."

Arthur glances at me. "Really, Liz? After all these years, this is where we're at?"

I lift my hands. *You tell me.*

"Did we not settle this phone stuff Friday?" Arthur throws his hands up. "But I guess you really don't trust me, huh? That's why you're out here rooting around my truck like a criminal."

"I haven't touched your truck." The lie is so thick, it catches in my throat, but I manage to choke it out.

"Yeah, right." Arthur strides over to the F-150, lifts the hood and brings it down with a resounding crash that reverberates through the garage like a judge's gavel. "Next time you pop the hood, make sure it latches closed."

Shit. Shit. Shit.

Although I'm embarrassed by my lies, I refuse to be led off topic. "Are you telling me there's going to be a 'next time' for me to find a hidden phone in your truck?"

"What's going on here, Liz?" Arthur's voice drips with disbelief. "You think I'm cheating on you or something?"

I can't help but imagine a scenario in which Arthur and Amanda are more than acquaintances. A sharp pain grips my chest, making it hard to breathe. "I...I don't know."

"You know what? I can't deal with this." He storms back into the house.

Desperation clings to my voice as I call out to him. "Arthur, wait!"

I follow him inside, my footsteps quickening as I enter the kitchen.

He's at the sink, filling a glass of water. He takes a healthy gulp. "I need space, Lizette."

"Can you blame me for being confused and upset?" My voice cracks, a mix of accusation and vulnerability bleeding through as I plead for some semblance of empathy. "What would you do if you found a secret phone hidden in my car?"

"If there were good reasons, trust wouldn't be an issue." He empties the rest of his glass in one long gulp and refills it, a ritual that appears to momentarily dissolve his frustration.

He offers me the glass. I accept it but place it on the granite countertop, searching his eyes. I want to believe him. He's the best man I've ever known.

So why am I working so hard to turn my suburban utopia into a nightmare?

"It's possible I'm reading too much into this," I admit, my tone softening. "It's just...finding that phone threw me. Trust isn't always easy for me."

"Why? I've always told you the absolute truth."

Arthur has no idea how Mr. Blessed's manipulations laid the foundation of a worldview I've hidden from everyone, especially him.

"You're right. You've always been honest with me."

"And you with me." His eyes are unwavering. "Unless there's a secret family you've kept hidden?" He grins.

I attempt to smile back, but the result feels forced. I teeter on the brink of confession—*I can't have children*—and the words hover on my lips.

Arthur leans in. "Liz, you're not hiding a secret family, are you?"

The weight of his words pulls me back to a memory I've tried to bury. The day after the attack, aside from my mom, Arthur was the first official visitor in my hospital room.

He was a few months into his relationship with his new girlfriend, Hazel. But he showed up—with roses, no less—and in that moment, he became family.

I'd wanted to tell him about the damage to my body, all the way back then. But I was terrified of losing him. Deep down, I believed we'd end up together—and I knew he didn't care about having kids—so I didn't bother mentioning the gruesome details of my injury. What teenagers want to have that conversation anyway? So I kept quiet, believing it wouldn't matter in the long run.

Years passed, and our relationship deepened. Then Arthur changed his mind and decided he wanted kids, and I'd led him to believe I wanted the same. Suddenly, my omission took on a whole new meaning.

Before long, the lie had spread through every crack in our lives, like the English ivy that invaded the chimney. Now the structure of our marriage was threatened, and there was little I could do.

Arthur puts his hand on mine. "Liz?"

I swallow hard, intent on telling him the whole truth. But my mouth sticks to technicalities. "No secret family. Of course not."

CHAPTER
NINETEEN

Two days later, Amanda slouches in the chair across from me, her eyes darting around the room as she avoids my gaze. It's my third session today, and I should be fully engaged, asking probing questions, drawing out her feelings.

Instead, I find myself fighting the urge to lean back and ask that stereotypical therapy question. *"And how does that make you feel?"*

Therapists hate clichés as much as writers do. For this reason—and many more—

it frustrates me to see my marriage reduced to worn-out tropes. For two nights now, the basement couch has been Arthur's makeshift bed. Distance has become my shield. And despite my yearning to repair the relationship, I find myself rejecting Arthur's repeated peace offerings.

It's cliché on top of cliché on top of cliché.

Worst of all, I can't help but compare these hard times with all the good times that came before. I remember our first real date—the homecoming dance, my junior year—and how exciting it was.

There were so many sweet moments in the months after

DON'T TELL

that. Slipping each other love notes in the school hallways. Driving all over the state just to find the perfect donut. But then I'd connected with Mr. Blessed, and he'd supported me in a way Arthur seemed incapable of back then.

Then I got pregnant.

Maybe I'd been just like these girls at Camp Wildfire. Too eager to buy into bullshit promises. Too hungry for a future that was never real to begin with. I have something real now. "So deciding to trust him again should be simple," I blurt.

Amanda stops talking and cocks her head. "I'm sorry, what?"

I refocus, doing my best to cover my tracks. "Um...it sounds like trust is the underlying issue here, doesn't it?"

"With my mom?"

Nodding, I clear my throat. "That's right. Um, continue. I'm sorry."

As Amanda speaks, I do my best to stay focused on her mom drama. But I want—need—to steer the conversation toward her father, the land dispute case, and Arthur.

Over the past two days, memories of Amanda's dad, Peter Holland, have gradually come back to me. He was on the news during the land dispute case. I'd paid extra attention because of Arthur's involvement in the story, and, I'll admit, because Mr. Holland looks like a cross between Jon Hamm and Brad Pitt.

When Amanda casually mentions her dad, I spot an opportunity to delve deeper.

"Tell me about your relationship with your dad. What's that like?" *Cliché, cliché, cliché.* "Was it hard for you when he was dealing with that big border dispute case? You'd just gotten to Virginia, right? You must've been lonely."

"It totally sucked." There's an innocence in Amanda's eyes when she replies. For the first time, I'm interacting with the little girl in her. Suddenly, no matter how much I want to hate her, that little girl is the only person I see.

In my preoccupation, I've overlooked the needs of a child in distress.

This is one of the low points in my career, and I'm crushed by impostor syndrome. I find myself doubting the grad program that gave me the stamp of approval, and the mentors who encouraged me, and the very system that vested in me the right to sit across from Amanda and others like her.

Impostor syndrome, noun
A persistent feeling of self-doubt and inadequacy, despite evidence of competence or success. Often experienced by professionals who have no business doubting themselves but do so anyway. Side effects may include questioning your entire career and contemplating life choices in the middle of therapy sessions. See also, Lizette's current state of existential crisis.

When I was in Amanda's situation, no one other than Mr. Blessed knew I was pregnant. I'll never forget the pain of that isolation, especially after I lost the baby. But things can be different for Amanda. I can be her support system. Even if my husband is her groomer, I can help her through this. She deserves that, and I'm all she has.

As the conversation continues, Amanda goes into detail about her life in Texas and how hard it was to move across the country in the middle of the school year. She's got resentment toward her parents for the move and seems to wish her dad worked less in general. But overall, her perspective on the whole thing is surprisingly mature.

After some time, Amanda turns the conversation back to her baby and its mysterious father. I'm glad she trusts me enough to go there, though I suspect this particular young woman enjoys the spotlight so much, she'd open up to most therapists in the same way.

Nonetheless, I sit up straight as her tone turns conspiratorial.

"He suggested an abortion initially, you know." Amanda fidgets in her seat. "It was so weird. But I said no, and he dropped it right away. From then on, he was all about being a dad. Never mentioned Clear River again."

My heart catches in my throat at the mention of Clear River. It's the same clinic Arthur wants to use for IVF. Trying to steady my voice, I ask Amanda to repeat herself. She does, her impatience palpable.

I cover up the question with a quick nod, doing my best to keep my hands from shaking. "Thanks. Just…always good to keep a list of places like that. Your situation is much more common than you might think."

I have a strong urge to leave, to run to Arthur and confront him with what I've discovered. Instead, I rely on my cognitive behavioral therapy training to stay composed.

My emotional side argues, *This is proof that Arthur is the father of Amanda's child.*

My rational, CBT side counters, *Clear River is the largest reproductive health clinic for a hundred miles. It's logical that Amanda's boyfriend would recommend it.*

My CBT side wins out, so I keep my ass in the chair and continue the conversation with gentle curiosity. "I don't think you ever mentioned where you met the baby's father. Was it Texas or Virginia?"

"Uh, do the math." Amanda points at her belly. "This fetus has been in me for like, six months. I met the guy right when I moved to Virginia. He was working with my dad on something, and we kept ending up alone together."

My CBT brain shuts down as I think back to Arthur's

trips to work with Amanda's father. This coincidence is too much, too hard to reason away.

Amanda leans forward, talking to me like we're schoolgirls gossiping at the back of the bus. "The first time we had sex was in a construction trailer at my dad's work." She sits back with a satisfied smile. "He went down on me right there in the trailer. Boys my age just don't do that." She flips her hair back. "Best I've ever had."

My mouth goes dry, and I no longer have any comments to offer, clichéd or otherwise. As the session continues, I nod and listen with well-placed facial expressions. But inside, I'm reeling.

Then, just like that, it's over. Amanda leaves, and I'm alone in my office. I think about waking up the other morning to Arthur going down on me, and my stomach churns.

While watering my plants, I mentally review Amanda's session. Doubts about my abilities as a therapist and as a wife creep in. And the idea of my husband giving that young girl "the best she's ever had" fills me with shameful rage. But it also makes sense. He's older. I mean, how much sex is she actually weighing her comment against?

Sitting back in front of my laptop, I pull up the page for Clear River Reproductive Health. The site glistens with images of happy mothers and their newborns, and there's a phone number nested beside the clinic address at the bottom.

Someone at the clinic must have the answers I'm looking for. Has Arthur visited with Amanda? Is he paying for her appointments there?

I need to know the truth.

CHAPTER

TWENTY

A cold knot tightens in my chest as I dial the number from the Clear River website.

I'm afraid the person on the other end of the line will confirm that Arthur and Amanda have been planning their pregnancy there, and I'm not sure what I'll do if that's the case.

The phone rings, and rings. Finally, someone picks up.

"Welcome to Clear River Reproductive Health. For our IVF office, press one. For family planning, press..."

I don't have the patience for that shit, so I jam the number zero to shut the recording up and get connected.

The phone rings again. A sweet-voiced woman picks up. "Clear River Reproductive Health, how can I help you today?"

"Yes, hi." I'm using my "fancy lady" voice, two pitches higher than my natural voice and three levels more articulate.

It's meant to serve as a barrier between myself and my anxiety. Ideally, the voice will give me a sense of control over this situation.

In reality, it does little more than hide a fraction of my

vulnerability. "I'm so sorry to bother you, but I have an appointment there sometime in the next month, and I can't find the details."

The woman takes my information, and I jump back in nervously just as she asks to place me on hold.

"Actually," I say with a laugh, "I think my husband might've made the appointment under his name, so you might not even have me on your books."

It only takes a few seconds for me to rattle off Arthur's full name and birthday, and then I'm on hold.

The hold music, a jaunty tune from a familiar musical, fills the silence. I consider how many women have endured this song during some of their most vulnerable moments, the cheerful melody at odds with the gravity of their situations.

After about thirty seconds, I'm on my feet, looking out my office window. Yolanda, one of a few counselors on shift today, strolls past with a bright smile and a small wave.

A pang of guilt hits me as I turn away, pretending I don't notice her. I envy Yolanda's lightheartedness, but it's too much to handle in the shadow of the burdens pressing down on me.

The hold music stops, and the receptionist comes back on the phone with a loud click. She informs me that besides my husband's appointment last month, they don't have anything for the Yuen family on record.

My mouth goes dry, and I grip the phone tightly. "Last month. Right."

I can't think of any reason why Arthur should've been at Clear River. The news sends a surge of betrayal and anger through me. More than that, I'm embarrassed that my husband has managed such a secret life away from me.

I picture Arthur, arm in arm with Amanda, leading her into the clinic. They're talking to a prenatal specialist, maybe taking a Lamaze class. He's cooing to her as she cycles through baby names, hand on her stomach like she's carrying the most precious package under the sun.

The images freeze me in place, my feet rooted to the scarred floor. I can't move. I can barely blink.

"Would you like to make an appointment for yourself, Ms. Yuen?"

I want answers.

But I know better than to hope for a breach of HIPAA. The weight of my uncertainty presses harder with every unanswered question.

Telling her I need to check my schedule first, I hang up as a wave of dizziness hits me. I steady myself by grabbing the edge of my desk and taking a deep breath. The news of Arthur's secret appointment at Clear River feels like a physical blow, and I can barely process the implications.

I don't feel my feet as I stumble down the hall to Jonathan's office, my mind spinning with unanswered questions.

Amanda was at Clear River. Arthur was at Clear River. Were they there together, planning their future as a happy family?

I literally trip into Jonathan's office, apparently over my tangled mess of thoughts.

Jonathan stands. "Liz. You okay?"

"Just a little off today. Is it all right if I head home early?"

Jonathan guides me to an overstuffed leather chair, his hand on my elbow in a comforting gesture. This man—and this camp, in many ways—are my safety net. Here, I'm valued and respected. And the people here want the best for me because I want the best for them.

Once I'm seated, Jonathan offers me a glass of water, and I'm suddenly impatient with his coddling. Though Jonathan is there to catch me, the vulnerability of falling angers me.

"I don't want any water, Jonathan." The words come out sharper than intended.

Jonathan sets the glass down on a wooden coaster. He looks at me, dumbfounded, for several long seconds. I don't know what to say, so I instead bring my hands to my throbbing temples.

Seconds later, he sits on the edge of his desk and takes a deep breath through his nose. He prods me gently, asking what's going on, expressing concern, and trying to help.

I don't look up. Don't take my hands from my temples.

"Liz. You can talk to me." He slides back on the desk until he's more soundly seated. "Is something going on at home? Something with Artie?"

My husband's nickname is the magic word that unlocks my tears. It's like all the effort I've put into the lie of our relationship is transposed into grief, and I'm officially overwhelmed.

I want to scream. *He had a secret appointment at Clear River. He's been going there with Amanda. I know it!*

Instead, I sit motionless as tears quietly stream down my face. Jonathan has seen them, and there's no use trying to hold them back.

"Liz, what's going on?" Jonathan leans forward, elbows on his knees. "Is this about the whole phone thing?"

I look up. How does Jonathan know about *the phone thing*? "What are you talking about?" I snap.

Jonathan shrugs. "I talked to Will about that text you supposedly got from Regina. He told me about the witness protection thing and having Artie hide the phone for him."

I'm too stunned to utter anything other than, "Oh."

Jonathan picks up a signed baseball from his desk and turns the ball over in his hands. "Will's an idiot. But that's not Artie's fault."

An angry warmth climbs my throat as I watch Jonathan

move the baseball from hand to hand. His movements are too casual, and I fight to hold back an angry scream. "You pried into my personal life. That's...that's messed up. I mean...what else do you know?"

This is Jonathan's chance to tell me about Arthur and Amanda. And if there's anything there, maybe he will...

"I did not 'pry into your personal life,' Liz." Jonathan places the baseball back in its little holder. "I tried to find out who was sending you inappropriate texts. Will brought up the phone thing. All I did was listen."

I shake my head, tucking my legs under me on the armchair.

"Are you under the impression I want your marital advice?" I ask, my irritation masking my gratitude for his concern.

"No." He looks down. "Sorry."

"It's fine." I exhale deeply. "You already started. What were you going to say?"

Is Arthur having an affair with Amanda? How long has it been going on?

He shrugs. "Artie loves you. That's all I've got."

"Jonathan—"

"I'm serious. The guy's been so loyal to you for so long. Even in high school, when you broke up with him out of nowhere, he held vigil like you were lost at sea. You're the only woman he's ever cared about. None of the others have meant anything, not even for a second."

The others?

In an instant, my mind introduces me to dozens of new suspicions and doubts. I'd never known Arthur as a player, but the ground shifts beneath me with such speed, I no longer know what to think.

"Who are 'the others?'"

"I didn't mean it like that. I'm only saying, even though

Artie started up with Hazel pretty quickly after you ended things…even after he married her…all he cared about was you. That's why they got divorced."

The mention of Hazel's name sends an uncomfortable wave of jealousy through me. The jealousy tells me two things. One, I still love my husband, and two, I still hate his ex.

There is comfort in Jonathan's theory. If Arthur's love for me tanked his first marriage, he's that much more likely to be loyal to me now. But I don't want Jonathan to clock that comfort, and I hate that he'd been compelled to tell me in the first place.

"Arthur and I aren't worried about the past." I hold on to my angry tone as the only wall between Jonathan and my real emotions. "And we don't talk about it. So I don't know why you're bringing it up like you're some kind of authority on the topic."

"I'm bringing it up because you stumbled into my office like you'd seen a ghost. And you've been checked out of work for days." He tilts his head, searching my face. "I can help."

I stand up, pulling my purse on over my shoulder. "Can I go home early or not?"

Jonathan gestures toward the door.

"Thank you. I…I appreciate you. But I think I need to decompress for the afternoon." I exit and close the door behind me with shaking arms.

Moments ago, anger about Arthur's potential future with Amanda had consumed me. Now I'm overwhelmed by the need to uncover the truth about his past.

CHAPTER
TWENTY-ONE

My whole drive home, I fantasize about things I can't possibly say to my husband. Each sentence is more incendiary than the preceding. Each is guaranteed to drive him out of the house, possibly for good.

I know you knocked up a teenage girl.
Tell me about the first time you screwed Amanda Holland.
What exactly are your plans for the future?

The perseverations consume every second of the drive. Pulling into the garage, I realize I don't recall passing my usual landmarks.

Before going into the house, I sit in my car and use the "Pick Three" technique I've taught to dozens of campers to quell anxieties. Identifying one sight, one scent, and one sound, I describe them out loud to ground myself in the present.

I breathe in through my nose. "I see my old bike hanging on the wall. It's red and a little rusty, with black writing."

Another breath, in through the nose. "I hear my engine clicking and clacking as the car cools down."

Another breath, in through the nose. "I smell my hand lotion. Lavender and chamomile."

The exercise works, and as I climb out of the car and enter the house, I'm once again rooted to the world around me.

Arthur's not home, but he's left a note for me on the counter.

Headed to the cabin. Back by dinner. Maybe I'll come up from the basement tonight? I love you, Lizard.

He's drawn a wild happy face next to the message, a trademark from the love notes he used to write me in high school. The face has its tongue out and swirly eyes, and it sends an electric pulse of relief through my arms.

This is just an insane set of coincidences. Arthur is still the man I married. And I miss him and need him back in my life.

Just as a smile creeps onto my face, I remember Amanda's declaration that sex with her baby daddy was the "best she's ever had." In an instant, the love and relief in my body mixes with a shot of adrenaline, and I'm angry and jealous all over again.

I bury my head in my hands and place pressure on my third eye, taking another shot at grounding myself. Without realizing it, I'm laughing.

"You're going crazy, Lizette." The laughter builds as I crumple Arthur's note into a ball and throw it across the room.

A dusty bottle of red catches my eye. I check the microwave. It's 2:57 p.m.

By three o'clock, the bottle is uncorked, and I'm headed out to my garden with a glass in hand.

That same ceramic frog looks up at me. *"Ribbit. Are you sure you should be adding alcohol to the mix? Ribbit."*

"Don't judge me, frog. I've got the afternoon off."

Plunging my hands into dirt and working in my garden has always been an escape for me. It reminds me of how small I am. Reminds me that the whole world is powered by sun and water, and I'm no different than the basil plant that sprouts each spring.

Over the next hour, I sip wine, I plant new seeds, I sip wine, I clip dead leaves, and I sip wine again. It's not until I'm lugging my third window box from the garage that my mind drags me into the past.

Arthur and I first spoke during an Advanced Agriculture course at Wildfire High. Yes, that was a real class at our high school, and it still is to this day. Time in the garden often brings me back to that moment we first connected.

"He was so cute." I add potting soil to the window box and aerate the soil with my trowel. "That smile. Those stupid cargo pants."

As I twist the trowel in the dirt, the motion turns angry. "And I broke up with him to carry on with freaking Mr. Blessed."

I shake my head, but the discomfort lingers. Mr. Blessed was charming, but it's his relentless patience that haunts me.

He reeled me in inch by inch—dislodged me from my boyfriend, turned me against my parents, had me believing that he and I were the only true thing in the universe.

To this day, I've never felt smarter than I did with Mr. Blessed. Never felt more seen than I did during those few months. Never felt more confident in any future than the one I dreamed of as Mrs. Michael Blessed, with our baby, and our house, and our perfect lives together.

The same trap that ensnared me now holds Amanda. And there's nothing scarier than that.

I'm not sure what personal trauma created Mr. Blessed's natural propensity for gaslighting. But gaslighting is not a skill that develops out of healthy relationships, happy childhoods, or functional family systems.

"Stop empathizing with your abuser, Lizette. Seriously?" The trowel scrapes along the window box as I drag it through the dirt. There's no chance the soil needs to be aerated any further, but I've accepted at this point that the exercise is more for me than for the well-being of my plants.

I'd believed Mr. Blessed was my destiny. But that belief was shattered one night, as violently as the illusion of safety in my own home.

I'd been asleep when the two men entered the apartment. A creak of floorboards, a whisper of movement...at first, I'd thought it was my mom home early from the night shift or my sister coming back from her friend's place. Then chaos erupted. Rough hands around my neck, pulling me from my bed. A heavy boot kicking me in the ribs.

A baseball bat to my stomach, and then between my legs.

A moment of calm, at last, as I struggled to breathe. Then the bigger man pulling me to my feet. Pressing a gun to the side of my head.

Neither man spoke during the entire attack. But as the gun barrel pushed against my temple, I could've sworn I heard a whisper. Something about getting what I deserved.

I still remember the sickly sweet smell of the cleaning solution on his handgun, like a mix of grape soda and WD-40. I still remember the sound of the hammer being cocked back, the menacing clicks.

The bigger man wanted to shoot me, but the other one stopped him. They left in a flurry, just like they'd arrived.

After the assault, the first moment I'd been alone in my hospital room, I'd called Mr. Blessed on my Nokia. I needed him to come get me, to hold me. We'd get through the loss of the baby together.

He picked up on the first ring. Before I had a chance to tell him what had happened, he said his house had burned down, and he was leaving town with his family.

This, more than the attack, was the greatest pain I'd ever experienced. I must've sounded so desperate, so pathetic in that moment.

"Why?"
"But I thought you loved me."
"I thought we were going to have a family."

Mr. Blessed patiently explained that he already had a family, using his "teacher voice" on me for the first time in months. And then, he wished me the best. In his "deepest heart," he informed me, he'd always love me. But when you're an adult, with responsibilities, you can't survive on love alone.

Mr. Blessed released himself from blame and described himself as "powerless" in our "situation." It stung the worst when he'd told me this was all for my own good.

I drop the trowel into the window box and sit back. I pull up a blade of grass and tear it to pieces. I'm crying.

The ceramic frog looks sad now too. I've even brought him down.

Maybe I should have told somebody about Mr. Blessed. Maybe I should have told Arthur.

But even now, as the thought crosses my mind, I hear my own voice whispering, the voice I'd buried deep. *Don't tell. Don't let it out. Don't let anyone see the shame you carry.*

Wrapping my arms around my knees, I rock back and forth in rhythm with my sobs. Once again, I think back to Arthur visiting me in the hospital.

He'd been there for me like no one else, even though he had a new girlfriend, and we were no longer together. But I couldn't risk our potential future by telling him the truth back then.

Years later, the lie has spun out of control. Telling him the truth now—that I lost a baby that night along with the ability to ever have another one—would kill him.

And if it didn't kill him...

It would kill his love for me.

He'd hate me as much as I hate myself.

CHAPTER
TWENTY-TWO

I wake up face down on the couch. It's nearly nine. The house is dark, and a text from Arthur says he'll be home in a few hours. I rub my eyes and swing my feet onto the carpet.

In the bathroom, I drink from the faucet and catch my haggard reflection. Dragging a hairbrush through my thick brown hair only leaves it looking worse.

As I leave the bathroom, the stairway to Arthur's basement office catches my eye. The steps creak as I descend into his space. I flip on the overhead light, squinting against its harsh LCD shine.

"Holy shit. How does anyone work in this?" I turn off the overheads and flick on the standing lamp in the corner, settling myself into Arthur's leatherette desk chair.

Assorted papers cover the desk—charts, graphs, maps, pamphlets stuffed with boring information about land surveying. I'm not sure what I'm looking for, but this isn't it.

More of the same fills his bookshelf, although one book stands out. *The Modern Man's Guide to Gentle Parenting.* I pull it down with a small smile.

Once again, the pendulum swings, and I'm convinced there's no way my husband has anything to do with Amanda Holland. This guy is a boring-ass, mapmaking nerd. He wants to gently parent *my* child, not the illegitimate offspring of his secret teenage lover.

Unless my inability to get pregnant led him to her...

I head upstairs, where I dig through Arthur's color-coded closet. Reaching past the gun safe bolted to the wall, I pull forward several shoe boxes stowed away on the top shelf. The first box contains every love note I've sent him, including plenty from our early days, way back in high school.

U R CUTE. MAKE OUT LATER?

I laugh, a bittersweet echo in the silent room. More poetic words have never been scrawled in the margins of an Advanced Agriculture homework assignment.

Soon enough, I'm sitting on our bed with dozens of mementos spread out around me. My favorite is a hard copy of Ayn Rand's *The Fountainhead* with flowers pressed between the pages. That was from my brief flirtation with objectivism at the beginning of grad school.

A surge of Rand's self-motivated reason might come in handy right now, as I fight to cut through the fog of empathy crowding my judgment. But you can't flip-flop from one life philosophy to another, so I fear I'm stuck with the empathy that plagues me.

Later, I find what I might've been looking for all along—Arthur's high school yearbook from the time we were together, when he was a senior and I was a junior.

My copy was lost long ago, after the move to Colorado. But I knew Arthur would have his, perfectly preserved and ready to guide me down memory lane.

I pause on my picture. The flower dress and pearls I wore for photo day were my mother's. The clothes had made me feel like a grown-up—something I'd craved desperately, before

I knew what growing up entailed. But looking back, I seem even younger than I was.

Mr. Blessed looks good—he's definitely handsome—but he appears older than I remember. His smile is too wide, his crow's feet too deep, his hairline receding, just a bit. I flip past his photo so quickly that I nearly get a papercut.

A headshot of Hazel Mendez—Arthur's future ex-wife—is marked with a lipstick stain, a phone number, and the scrawled superlative *Best Girlfriend Ever*.

Seeing Hazel's bubbly hearts and phone number in Arthur's yearbook stirs a jealousy I can't shake. After he and I broke up, I secretly got together with Mr. Blessed. And Arthur very publicly started dating Hazel.

I hadn't been jealous then. I'd felt so superior in my grown-up relationship with Mr. Blessed, while Arthur and Hazel were still caught up in their petty teenage emotions. But these photos are a stark reminder of the rocky start I got with Arthur, and how long it took—including the entirety of Arthur's failed marriage to Hazel—to finally find our way back to each other.

The untold stories from that time apart haunt us, casting shadows over a marriage that might still be unstable.

I remember Jonathan's revelation. Was I the reason Arthur and Hazel's marriage ended? And how much of that drama began way back at Wildfire High?

I grab another of Arthur's yearbooks. Flipping through the pages, I stop when I see him photographed right next to Will. Naturally, the twin brothers are side by side on the page.

Will's photo is boring, bur Arthur's is ridiculous. He's wearing a Hawaiian shirt and smiling like he'd discovered the world's sexiest new fashion.

A laugh escapes me as I run a finger down Arthur's face. "No, Arthur. Not hot. Dorky."

Flipping the pages, I hunt for more photos of Arthur.

Wildfire High was where all the kids from the surrounding towns ended up—Shepstone, Putnam, you name it. And as I scan the pages, I pick out kids from all over the county. But I stop turning the page when I spot the varsity basketball picture.

Will is centered in the frame, and he looks like himself. Muscular, confident, wearing the kind of smile only displayed by people with few brain cells. But my heart catches in my throat as I continue to scan the photo.

Myer Whitley stands beside Will, looking far less like your typical jock. There's a dark emptiness behind his eyes, he's not smiling, and his arms are crossed. But Will's got an arm around Whitley, and he's leaning against the kid like the two are good friends.

This is the first time I've laid eyes on Whitley in well over a decade, and that look in his eyes sends a chill through my body. There he is. The infamous Myer Whitley. The boy who would have been questioned for Regina Smith's disappearance if he wasn't hurting another woman the night Regina went missing.

The next guy down the line from Myer Whitley is my husband. I might have remembered he was on the team sooner, but Arthur rarely talks about his sporty days, probably because he barely got any playing time.

Whitley has a hand on Arthur's shoulder. From the look of his knuckles, it seems he's squeezing Arthur way too hard for a team photo. But Arthur wears a big, broad smile, like he's the proudest benchwarmer the team has ever seen, like there's nothing off about the situation.

As I stare at Myer's hand gripping Arthur's shoulder, my mouth goes dry. Why has my husband never mentioned his connection to the suspected killer in our small town?

My worries are interrupted by Arthur's headlights

crashing through the windows and projecting shadows on the bedroom walls. It's 12:03 a.m. My husband's high school memorabilia covers the bed like blood spatter. And I've got three minutes, at most, to hide the evidence of my prying.

CHAPTER
TWENTY-THREE

"Shit, shit, shit." The yearbook tumbles to the floor as I leap off the bed, pulse pounding. The photo of Arthur with Myer Whitley spiked my adrenaline. Now the growl of the garage door opening sends me into overdrive.

I shove the shoebox of love notes back into the closet, barely catching it as it slides out again. A cold sweat forms at the base of my neck.

Arthur calls my name, singing as he comes up the stairs with a smile in his voice. The yearbook lies on the floor. I kick it under the bed as Arthur enters and sets down his work bag.

"There you are." He furrows his brow. "Still dressed? After midnight? Just...standing here?"

I fake a yawn. "Fell asleep on the couch."

He strides over, tucking a stray hair behind my ear with hands that reek of whiskey and hops. His cheeks are tinged with the warmth of his drinks, eyes heavy, hair a tousled mess.

"There you are, Little Lizard." His kiss is soft, his body more relaxed than it's felt in months.

Despite my doubts, I lean into it. Drunk or not, my husband's reaching for me, and I want to reach back.

He stumbles back a step, holding hazy eye contact. "I'm not drunk."

I can't help but laugh. His denial of drunkenness is a private joke as old as our love. The callback reminds me of the ground we've traveled together...sometimes thorny, sometimes smooth. But have we had a good marriage? I've never questioned our connection before. Maybe I'm spectacularly good at deluding myself.

"You know I love you, Liz." Arthur pulls me close again. "I would do anything for you. Like, we can't let some stupid phone come between us. I was trying to support my brother, you know? But it turned out to be a total mess because he's a big, dumb dummy."

"He sure is." I return his smile and settle into his arms.

Arthur kisses me again. "I'm sorry for everything, and everything else, and all the other stuff."

His words blur in my mind, lost in the fog of doubt and fear. *All the other stuff, like your friendship with Myer Whitley? Or your pregnant teenage girlfriend?* My body aches with conflicting emotions as I lean into his kiss.

After several lovely moments, I end our kiss with a firm peck, then circle the bed and grab my pajamas from under the pillow. "You shouldn't drive after drinking."

"I barely drank anything."

I turn away from him to unbutton my shirt. "Uh-huh."

In the window's reflection, Arthur flops into bed, fully dressed.

When I turn back, my gaze lingers on him. I see the boy I fell for, and I wonder if my desire to hold on to that early love has kept my husband from becoming the man he was meant to be.

"Hey, what happened with you and Hazel? Why did you end up getting divorced?"

Arthur's head lolls over to me, his confusion evident. "What?"

That gentle deflection—meant to buy time and gauge my reaction, I'm sure—is all I need to confirm one important fact. Arthur's first instinct is to lie to me about whatever was going on with him and Hazel back then. But if he ended things with her because he still loved me, why would he hide that?

"Is there a reason you're asking me about Hazel?"

My gaze flicks toward the underside of the bed, where I kicked the yearbook seconds before Arthur entered. I can't admit to digging through his stuff, so I hesitate.

"Jonathan mentioned the two of you today. Dropped your divorce into conversation like it was nothing. But he could tell I was clueless about the 'why' of it all. It was kind of, like, embarrassing."

Arthur sits up on his elbows and squints at me. "So you're bringing this up because of something Jonathan said?"

I shrug, masking my growing suspicion. "Wanted to see how you'd respond."

"Damn, Liz. I came home overflowing with love for you. And why is Jonathan bringing up my past relationships? Is that normal workplace conversation?"

"In small towns, yeah, I guess it is."

Arthur climbs out of bed and pulls his shirt off, crumpling the top and tossing it in the direction of the hamper. "We agreed not to talk about the past."

"We did. But that doesn't mean it never happened." I pick up his shirt and add it to the hamper. "There were five years between us breaking up in high school and getting back together. You were married and divorced in that time. That's real shit."

"I know, but..." He hesitates.

"Honestly, I'd never advise a client to bury the past like this. I don't know why I thought it would work for us."

Because I was young. And stupid. And desperately in love.

Arthur pulls off his pants, crosses the room, and places them in the hamper. "We made that agreement because the future is all that matters. I mean, do you want to relive what happened to you?"

I look down, silent.

"I've only ever loved you, Lizette. That was true in high school, and it's true now."

As Arthur takes my hand and kisses me, confusion presses down on my chest. His eyes are pure, and his touch is gentle and loving. I begin to doubt everything I've learned over the last few days.

I have to accept that my feelings are misleading, though I can take sick comfort in the notion that I can't rely on myself. And I have to stop questioning my reality.

I melt into his kiss. And when he presses his forehead into mine, I'm home.

And then he kills the moment. "I won't be angry, you know."

Pulling back, I look into his nearly black eyes. "About what?"

"If we find out you can't have children because of what happened. I'd never be angry about that. I wouldn't leave you."

I open my mouth and close it again, blinking at twice my normal rate. I can't hide my shock, confusion, and fear fast enough.

Arthur might think he wouldn't be angry if he knew the truth. But there's no way he'd stay with me if he found out how long I've been lying to him, how elaborate the lie has become. Or if he knew I'd been pregnant before.

He squeezes my hands. "I'll always be by your side, Mrs. Yuen. I love you."

The callouses on his palms scrape into my skin, and I fight the urge to pull away from his grasp.

"I love you too."

I love you, but if I found out you'd been the one lying all this time, I'm not sure I still would.

CHAPTER
TWENTY-FOUR

As dawn creeps across Wildfire, unease settles over me. Despite going to bed after midnight, I wake up two hours before my alarm, wide awake. Nervous energy pulls me out of bed and into the silver morning light. Arthur doesn't stir as I carefully retrieve the yearbook from under the bed and stow it at the top of the closet, his body emitting a sweet scent as he detoxes from the alcohol.

In the kitchen, I kill a few minutes making pour-over coffee, mesmerized as one drop after another falls through the crystal-clear glass and ripples in the dark pool below. As my Sumatra finishes brewing, the rich aroma permeates the air. I breathe it in deeply while filling my travel mug and set off for work.

As usual, my car is first in the employee lot. I think back to Amanda's depiction of a work-obsessed wife and feel a low growl rising in my chest. Arthur will wake up to the aroma of coffee, but none will be left in the pot.

What kind of wife does that make me?

My office is a hundred feet in front of me, waiting with piles of paperwork, notes to take, and prep work to grind.

Through the dewy field beyond lies five square miles of the Putnam Forest, an opportunity for contemplation with the distant possibility that I might figure my shit out.

Clutching my mug, I venture through the field, hoping I make it into the shade before the morning sun brings the day's heat over the horizon.

I walk for two hours at least, sticking close to camp, before I decide to head back and get started on work. As I scan the forest looking for the path back, I spot Madeline lying on a rock up ahead, gazing at the treetops.

My first instinct is to walk away. She hasn't seen me yet, and I'm not ready to trade my solitude for conversation with my angriest camper. But when a camper is out in the forest early, there's always a reason.

Madeline pauses her music as I approach but keeps her earbuds in. She sits up and pulls her knees close to her body. "When I wake up early, I can't get back to sleep. I come out here."

"I like thinking out in the forest too." I breathe in the moist, fresh scent of pine. "Clear air is good for the brain."

"I don't come here to think. I come here to face my fears." Madeline locks eyes with me. It's a challenge. An invitation to rehash our Regina argument.

It's early, but I'm not one to back down from a challenge.

"You can't get so caught up in all these rumors, Madeline. They'll take over your brain."

"They're not rumors." Her eyes harden. "Everyone knows what happened to Regina Smith, but nobody's willing to say it."

"Who's 'everybody?'"

"Everyone in Wildfire. Everyone in Shepstone. Everyone."

I sigh. Think for a moment about defending my small town and Jonathan's next door. But the girl before me is in pain. It's my job to help her, even though she doesn't trust me. I need to fix that.

"Madeline. I believe you're concerned about Regina. I'm just trying to understand why. Maybe I can help you."

She repeats the rumors that went around the circle the other day, all the gossip and horror story nonsense each new group of campers manages to dredge up. But Madeline speaks with a certainty when she tells me Regina is dead. "Teenage boys killed her and hid her body in the forest."

"Why are you so sure of that?"

When Madeline opens her mouth, it isn't to answer my question. "I know about what happened to you too."

I meet her gaze with equal resolve. "Okay."

"You were attacked."

"I know. I was there."

She pulls out her earbuds, puts them in their small white case with practiced precision, and closes the lid. "When it happened, people said you were lucky to be alive."

"When it happened, you were coloring with crayons." My blood warms. I start picking at the cuticle on my thumb. It hurts, but I can't stop. "Any reason you're bringing this up? Not my favorite memory, and you haven't answered my question."

Madeline reopens the case to her earbuds and snaps it shut. She does it again and again, fidgeting. Each time it snaps closed, I pick at my cuticle deeper, harder, as if the opening and closing of the case is the twisting of a knife.

"I talked to some people back home," she says. "They say you were right about Myer Whitley. He was committing another crime the night Regina Smith went missing. Attacking a girl, actually. Kylie something-or-other. That girl was a camper, too, though. He sneaked her out. Got her drunk at a bar and—"

"The rest is public record." I swallow, pushing down memories of the reports.

"Too gruesome for the public, though, don't you think?" The case clicks shut again. "Is that why you kept the detail from us that day at the lake?"

A blue jay alights from a tree branch, landing in another tree a few feet away. Madeline watches it for a long moment, like she's more interested in the bird than in the horrible history she's dredged up.

"My cousin went to Wildfire High at the same time Myer was there. Way older than me."

So that's your source. Some cousin indoctrinating you on every scary story she can remember from her childhood.

Madeline tips her chin back, considering me as she squints against a ray of sunlight. "Says the guy was a total creep, but the popular kids hung out with him 'cause he had his own apartment above his parents' garage or something, threw ragers. They had a *don't ask, don't tell* thing going on."

I bite a piece of loose skin off my thumb and press it between my teeth. My conversation with Madeline is like a high-stakes negotiation—like she's accusing me of something—but I don't know what.

"But how could Whitley have killed Regina Smith if he was with that other girl that night?" I ask.

"Who knows when Regina was actually killed? It was only discovered that she was missing when he was with that other girl." She flicks her hair back over her shoulder. "But I'd bet good money he was involved. If he was, he didn't do it alone. Maybe he got it started, then left with the other girl. Came back later to help dig the grave."

A sardonic laugh escapes me. "That's insanely dark."

"I thought therapist types weren't supposed to describe things as insane," Madeline continues before I have a chance to reply. "But it makes you think, doesn't it? Lots of bad stuff happened around here back then." She pins me with a knowing look.

I spit out the tiny piece of skin and stare her down.

Madeline's implying there was some kind of violent crew running around Wildfire during the attacks. Thinking back on the timeline, it wouldn't surprise me if this crew had something to do with my attack too. But there's no way I'm introducing that gremlin to Madeline. Not now, not ever.

I am not alone.

Regina.

I'm about to respond to Madeline—by saying what, I'm not sure —when a scream erupts from camp, followed by two more.

"What in the hell...?" I mutter in confusion, looking back toward the cabins. These screams are sharp. Visceral. Not the sound of kids having fun.

A fourth shriek rings out. I pull Madeline to her feet, and we run back toward camp. My heart pounds as horrifying images of dead teenage girls assault my senses. This place has seen so much sadness over the years. I'm not sure it can take much more.

CHAPTER
TWENTY-FIVE

Jonathan paces my office, reading off his phone screen. "It says even baby copperheads have venom as toxic as adults. I freaked out when I saw it."

"Sure. But you can't fuel the panic like that." I hate to lecture my boss, but really? "If you stay calm, the girls will stay calm. If you scream—"

"They all scream. I get it." He locks his phone and pockets it. "I saw it, and I freaked out. This is why you can't disappear into the woods and leave me to do battle with the serpents on my own."

The light on my desk flickers and goes out. I look over at Jonathan as I cross to my closet to grab a replacement bulb. "You grew up in Shepstone, right?"

He nods. "Still hold the record for the youngest drum major in marching band."

"Super cool." I grab a light bulb and turn back to my desk. "Madeline's from there. That camper who keeps bringing up Regina Smith."

I gauge Jonathan's face as I bring up Regina's name and tell him about Madeline's suspicions. Though my conversation with Madeline freaked me out, Jonathan relaxes into the armchair as I speak, unfazed.

When I finish, he looks at me with wide eyes. "None of that's too surprising, is it? Not the first time a camper has started asking about all that stuff."

"Weirded me out, that's all." I switch the light, but it doesn't turn on. "Madeline's fixated on Regina Smith and Myer Whitley. I suspect she's the one who sent me that text."

"Disturbed teenage girls send creepy texts. Not exactly earth-shattering news." Jonathan stands and pushes the light plug more snugly into the outlet. The light flickers on, casting a soft amber glow that warms the room but does little to ease the chill creeping up my spine. "And then there was light."

Frustrated, I put the new light bulb back in the closet and screw the original back into the lamp. "What do you know about the girl Myer Whitley attacked the night Regina went missing?"

Jonathan shrugs. "Kylie Boyd. She was from Shepstone too."

"What happened to her after Myer went to prison?"

Jonathan closes his eyes, head falling back in resignation. "Do we have to go into all these gruesome details? It's early."

I give him a firm look.

Jonathan sits up, his eyes meeting mine with a blend of fear and resignation. "The girl…she, uh…she ended up taking her own life. The whole town showed up to her service."

"Did you go?"

Jonathan looks away. "Might've been the saddest day of my life to that point."

I switch the light off, then on again, then off. Each time the light comes on, I catch a different emotion on Jonathan's face. First sadness, then confusion, then a hint of anger at the corner of his lips.

"That entire year sucked for the whole town," he says. "You want to maybe stop with that light?"

"Sorry." I leave it on. A couple girls walk past my window. I wave, and they wave back, not breaking stride or conversation. Once they've disappeared down the path, I turn back to Jonathan. "Madeline's convinced Myer Whitley had something to do with Regina's death."

"Everyone thought that. But the rumor is he was in the back of a cop car at the time of Regina's disappearance, from assaulting Kylie."

"Yeah, no, I know. I told the campers, um...a tamer version of that. But it would've been hard to say exactly when Regina disappeared." I search his face. "Isn't it possible Myer Whitley could've done both?"

Jonathan shrugs. "It's possible. Regina's body was never found, which means there's no official time of death, or any official...death, you know? She could still be alive, like you said."

"Or maybe...Whitley could've had help. Is that possible?"

Jonathan turns his hands palms up, looking helpless. "I don't know. But the good news is, the guy's been in prison for years, and he'll be there for a long time still."

"Lucky for us he tried to rob that bank, I guess."

Jonathan nods, and my mind flashes to the photo of Arthur beside Whitley on the basketball team. My husband, side by side with a teenage sociopath.

Did Arthur know how terrible Whitley was?

"Back when you were partying at Whitley's house, did you have any idea what he was capable of?"

"Like I said, I wasn't there very often." Jonathan shifts his focus to the window, a contemplative frown forming. "But when I think back on it now, with all my training...there were signs."

I reply with lightning speed. "Like what?"

"The kid was horrible to his mom, for one thing. Treated her like a bad employee, called her a bitch, all sorts of names. A lot of the guys would laugh but it never sat right with me."

I slide to the edge of my chair. "What else?"

"I mean, the parents were way too permissive. He pretty much lived by himself. They'd buy beer for all his parties. There were no rules, no consequences."

Once more, the chummy image of Arthur and Myer Whitley pops into my mind. "Back then, with everything you saw, did you have any inkling of what he might do?"

"Of course not." Jonathan lets out a deep exhale. "But that's the thing with pure evil. Finds its way through the cracks eventually."

"Kind of dramatic, no?"

A serious expression comes over his face. "You didn't know Myer Whitley."

CHAPTER
TWENTY-SIX

My old friend Maggie Gilford gives me a wistful smile as I enter her little plant shop.

The place is beyond serene. Tracy Chapman plays from a dusty DVD player in the corner. Hundreds of plants hang from the ceiling and line old wooden shelves. A grandfather clock ticks quietly, set against the back wall.

Stepping inside the shop is like entering an alternate dimension, and the lavender incense and calming folk music lower my blood pressure as the door closes behind me.

"Hey, Liz. Here for something specific or window-shopping?" Maggie's warm, knowing voice carries a smile as she emerges from behind the counter.

"Not sure yet."

She chuckles. "You never are. That's what I like about you. Just let me know if you need any help."

I give Maggie a polite nod and drift through the store. A three-foot tall ficus pulls me across the room, and I stop inches away. When I reach out to touch it, my hand shakes, and I pull back.

Note to self—acute stress doesn't magically dissolve after two minutes in your favorite shop.

Next, I visit Maggie's "living wall," a rich, natural tapestry of plants hooked up to an automatic watering system that looks like it was stolen from a steampunk sketchbook. The water drips through a series of glass tubes, finding its way to each plant one droplet at a time.

Maggie adjusts the self-watering system, calibrating it with meticulous precision. I step aside and watch her work, enjoying the soft scent of patchouli floating off her skin.

Ultimately, I buy a single orchid and an accompanying pouch of flower food. As she rings me up, Maggie makes small talk, but I linger before I leave, hoping to take the conversation in a more serious direction.

"Hey, Maggie...you've lived here forever."

She pushes a curly gray lock behind her ear. "You calling me old?"

"No, no. Just...I had a question about something that happened here. Long time ago."

"Lemme have it."

I pull the orchid into a ray of sunlight cutting a diagonal across the glass countertop and twist it so the flower faces me. "I want to know about Regina Smith. Do you remember, um, when she went missing?"

"I...well, I-I..." Maggie trips over her words, her eyelids fluttering in an uncommonly awkward moment for a woman usually poised and in control.

"I'm sorry. We don't have to—"

"No, no. It's fine." She gives me an apologetic smile. "Just been a long time. Wasn't easy living here when all that stuff was happening."

I nod, explaining that I was finishing high school in Colorado at the time. And I further explain about the new curiosity among the girls at camp. "Do you think Regina ran away, or was it more, uh…final than that?"

Maggie bites her lip but says nothing, instead returning to the self-watering system and adjusting the knobs for the second time. A long moment of silence passes. I consider apologizing again or repeating the question. She turns back to me.

"Sorry. Can't focus if my systems aren't all in order."

"Of course. Take your time."

Maggie's mouth twists, and she looks toward the street-facing window at the front of the store. "I'm not sure this town has ever been the same since that poor girl went missing." She turns back to me. "There's a darkness here now. I don't know. Maybe you don't feel it."

"I do."

She crosses to the door and turns the *Open* sign to *Closed* before turning back to me. "I was there when they found her locket out in the forest. Little bronze heart. Inside, a picture of the family golden retriever."

The sweet innocence of the image sends a sad warmth through my body. "Oh, man…"

"Regina Smith didn't run away, Lizette. Something happened to her. Something bad. I know it." Maggie fixes her soulful caramel-colored eyes on mine. "Why are you asking these questions now? It's been over ten years."

I'm not sure I knew the answer until I said it out loud. But as soon as I speak the words, I know they're my truth. "I need to find out what happened to her."

"Okay." Maggie hits me with a shaky glare. "Then let me tell you exactly where they found that locket."

CHAPTER
TWENTY-SEVEN

I place my petite white orchid on the floor of the car like a prized possession, getting it situated in its box so it won't tip over on the drive home. Its stem is thin, and its petals are softer than a baby's skin, carrying a fragrance just as sweet.

The delicate flower derives such strength from its fragility, its mere existence a defiant statement against a harsh world.

Can I find that same strength as I bridge the gap between my dark past and the present?

My conversation with Maggie hangs around me like fog as I click my seat belt and start the car. Virginia dusk settles in, casting a tranquil glow over the world. In my rearview mirror, the sunset sneaks through a break in the gray clouds like light from under a closet door. The beauty offers a brief respite, but I can't shake the heaviness of our conversation.

As I turn toward the highway, the dwindling light invites quiet reflection. I pull off the side of the road, shut off the engine, and let silence cover me.

Soon, my mind drifts back to Maggie, each word we'd shared lingering. I'd told her I needed to find out what happened to Regina Smith, and it felt true when I said the words. But now, as the sky darkens above the trees, I'm not sure I want to face that horror. Not sure I can handle what I might find.

Doubt crawls over my scalp and down my neck.

My gaze falls on the dashboard where my phone rests.

The screen lights up with an incoming email—a spam message from a big box store—and I'm plunged back into the twenty-first century.

Grabbing the device, I look up Myer Whitley and scan article after article. Each headline paints a clearer picture of the man who tore this quaint little area apart. My jaw tightens as I read, the reality of his actions bringing a rush of memories and unresolved fears to the surface.

Wildfire Teenager Arrested for Assault of Local Girl.
Myer Whitley Released Early Amid Controversy.
Whitley Arrested in Connection with Bank Robbery.

The articles, mostly from the *Putnam County Gazette*, depict a tortured young man evolving into a troubled adult. Each piece reads like a rap sheet, painting a progressively grimmer future for Whitley.

I grip the phone tighter. The air in the car is hot and humid. I could fix it by rolling down the windows, but I can't pull my focus from the screen for even a second.

"This kid was a monster."

I'm on a sleazy-looking website now, signing up and making a payment so I can get a background check on Myer Whitley. I bang through the purchase pages in ten seconds flat, entering my information, paying, and clicking as fast as I can.

Next. Next. Next. Agree to terms of service. Review Information. Confirm Purchase. Download PDF.

Whitley's juvenile records are sealed. At seventeen, he was convicted of a DUI. Less than six months later, he was charged with the crimes against Kylie Boyd.

I run a new search. *Kylie Boyd, Myer Whitley, Camp Wildfire.*

An article comes up. Kylie had been fifteen at the time, attending Camp Wildfire over the summer, most likely for an eating disorder or a burgeoning substance abuse problem, like most of our campers. Like Whitley, she'd been a resident of nearby Shepstone.

I'd worked with so many girls from the area over the years. In my mind, I knew her so well, even though we'd never met. Oversize Shenandoah sweatshirt. Pink short shorts. That classic teenage tan that whitens teeth and lightens hair.

Kylie Boyd, Shepstone, Obituary.

I can't bring myself to read the obit, so instead I click back to Myer Whitley's background check. I'm searching a long list of breaking-and-entering charges, looking for a crime that might match what happened to me. I want to finally have a name and a face to match with one of my attackers.

There are several cases of Whitley attacking women in the forest or stalking them through wooded trails. And Whitley was questioned in two Putnam County kidnappings. And there's plenty of paperwork surrounding Kylie Boyd.

But there's no record of him attacking a woman in her home with a bat or any other object.

I set the phone on my lap. I'm in my memories now. The bigger man grips the baseball bat and holds it high above his head. Both men are masked.

Back to my phone. Scanning police records, background information, articles on his crimes. Whitley never used a weapon, not until the bank robbery. Never bothered to hide his identity. No matter how much I want to make the connection, it's not likely he had anything to do with what I suffered. But the date of my attack is so close to the date of Kylie's death and Regina's disappearance. By this point, I'm nearly convinced we all suffered at the hands of the same men.

I toggle between pictures of Kylie Boyd and Regina Smith. The mischievous sparkle in Regina's eyes belies a bold confidence, like she's a precocious kid about to belt a stunner on *American Idol*. But Kylie's energy is gentle and demurring. She doesn't know how beautiful she is. And that's probably what made her Whitley's tragic target.

Jonathan's words play on repeat in my mind. *"That's the thing with pure evil. Finds its way through the cracks eventually."*

My gaze lands on a photo of Kylie posing with her school soccer team. She's got her arm draped on the girl beside her, like how Arthur had his arm hung across Myer Whitley in the basketball picture.

I fixate on that photo for what feels like five minutes. Maybe more. A call from Arthur pulls me from my trance. The sun has fully set now, and I wonder if the bright colors were ever there at all.

Suddenly aware of sweat dripping down the small of my back, I start the car and answer the phone. "Hello?"

Arthur's voice is tense and concerned. "Lizette. It's almost eight o'clock. Where are you?"

He's right. It's 7:53 p.m. and I'd told him I was heading home almost two hours ago. "Sorry. Got caught up at work."

With promises to be home soon, I hang up, then pause before closing out Myer Whitley's background search. All of Wildfire concluded Whitley couldn't have hurt Regina because he'd already been arrested for the attack on Kylie that night.

But Whitley's background report makes it clear...the guy had violence coursing through his blood. And what if he was capable of greater evil than people knew?

CHAPTER
TWENTY-EIGHT

Arthur had told me he loves me last night, and I'd responded in kind. Then we'd gone through the motions for the rest of the night, polite but distant. But I'd forgotten to leave him coffee when I left this morning, then I'd stayed late at work, living out Amanda's stereotype of a wife who deserves to be cheated on.

When I get home after my marathon research session on Myer Whitley, it's almost eight thirty—way later than I'd promised—but the theater of our polite marriage continues into its second act. Arthur greets me with a kiss and sits at the table while I eat cold pizza left over from his meal.

We're nice to each other, without daring to be kind.

After two hours of premium cable, he's asleep beside me in bed. I lay awake a few minutes before grabbing my laptop and navigating to the website for the Virginia Department of Corrections.

If I'm going to find out what happened to Regina and see if it connects to my unsolved case, I'll have to talk to the man rumored to have hurt her.

As I navigate the website in incognito mode, the LCD light casts ghostly shadows in our dark bedroom.

I click over to Linden River State Prison and hit the *Visiting an Inmate* button. Several options pop up—*Sending money, Sending mail, Phone correspondence.*

It takes nearly thirty minutes to complete my application, starting with a series of yes-or-no questions.

Are you a current or former VADOC employee, contractor, or volunteer?

Are you currently under active parole or probation supervision?

Have you ever been convicted of a felony as a juvenile or adult?

The more questions I answer, the more suspense builds in my stomach. Every creak in the house sends a jolt of adrenaline through my veins. Several times, I look over at Arthur, convinced I'll find him watching me. Every time, he's still sound asleep.

What is your relationship to this inmate?

Friend is a lie, but it's the only option that fits, so I select it, the word leaving a bitter taste in my mouth.

Next comes a battery of questions that are far more personal than I'd expected.

First name, middle name, last name, social security number, date of birth, place of birth, driver's license number.

Each question is a tiny invasion, and I'm grateful I never legally changed my last name from Silva when Arthur and I got married, even though I use Yuen personally and Silva professionally.

Next, I'm asked to detail every aspect of my physical appearance.

I pause on the drop-down for eye color.

The options include multicolored, gray, maroon, and even pink. For a moment, I imagine a pink or maroon-eyed visitor at Linden River, their gaze as unnerving as the bars and concrete. The image sends a shiver down my spine.

Though the process to apply is interminable, the approval email from VADOC arrives less than five minutes after I submit.

Confirming Your Scheduled Visit to Linden River State Prison—Myer Whitley.

Linden River is a level-five state prison in central Virginia. Housing over a thousand inmates and nearly as many employees, it's situated in a river valley with nothing but fields for miles around.

As my car descends a winding hill, the facility looms ahead, a sprawling compound etched against the enormous gray sky. Razor wire fences glint in the morning light, casting long shadows that claw at the prison yard.

Minutes later, I step into a concrete holding area, the air thick with chemical cleaner and stale sweat. After passing through one security checkpoint and then another, I relinquish my personal effects and follow a guard down a long hall to the noncontact visitation area.

I expect this room to look more like the movies. But in real life, everything's much dirtier than it is on TV.

Plastic partitions bear the grime of countless visits. The wooden desk in front of me is scarred with the initials of past visitors. And the fluorescent lights above cast a sickly pallor across my hands.

Each booth is equipped with a heavy black telephone, the only means of communication between the visitor and the inmate. The cords, short and reinforced to prevent any potential weaponization, coil on the metal desktops. Each side of the plastic barrier offers a small, steel chair, forcing occupants into a rigid, uncomfortable posture.

For a moment, I'm alone, and I'm considering getting up and telling the guard I want to leave. But before I have the chance, Myer Whitley takes a seat across from me.

His depthless gaze locks onto mine, and the cacophony of the prison fades from my consciousness.

"Not sure I know you." His voice holds even less dimension than his eyes.

Stumbling through my words, I explain that we were students at Wildfire High together, and that I work at the girls' camp in Wildfire now. At my mention of the high school, he laughs nostalgically.

The laughter brings a moment of levity that breaks the tension enough for me to breathe.

"Wildfire Wildcats bleed blue for life!" He claws the air and roars, exposing a mouth of rotten teeth and a cotton-white tongue. An image that won't leave me anytime soon.

I force a grin. "Yep."

"Still don't know what you want to talk to me about, though." Whitley's accent is twice as thick as Arthur's, and he's got that "good ole boy" southern thing not even Will can pull off. He repeats his question with a sharper twang and an angrier edge. "What you want from me, lady?"

It hits me that I have no satisfactory answer for this question, and all at once, I'm floating above my body, questioning my sanity. I see every action I've taken to land opposite Myer Whitley through the fish-eye lens of an unreliable mind.

Clicking through the VADOC website, driving two hours to a prison on my day off, listing Myer Whitley as my friend on the prison website...

It all led me to this moment, sitting across from a felon

convicted of assault, bank robbery, and God knows what else, with no idea how to get the information I want.

In an ideal world, I could ask Whitley three simple questions and get three honest answers.

What do you know about the disappearance or murder of Regina Smith?

Were you involved in said disappearance or murder?

What was your relationship with Arthur and Will Yuen?

The sharp scent of chemical cleaner reminds me I'm not in an ideal world. Instead, I'm at Linden River State Prison, facing down one of the most infamous men my county has ever produced.

Quickly, I recall my grad school courses on the criminal mind. Murderers and sexual offenders are often narcissists. They love talking about themselves. And if you can get them going, they're far more open than you might expect.

With nothing else to guide me, I fall back on these old lessons, appealing to Whitley's ego as much as I can.

"You've always been known for being…a bit of a mystery. How do you think people see you now?"

I can tell my question both surprises and pleases him. "If people see me as a mystery, it's only because they don't have the capacity to understand me or how my mind works. Most people are too shallow to see what's beneath the surface."

"Interesting. Um…that makes sense." I shift in my chair, searching for another way in. "And is it true you had quite a few admirers back in high school? What was it like to be in the spotlight so much?"

His blue eyes brighten with a spark of vanity. "Oh, yeah, there're plenty who wanted my attention…especially women." He flashes his black teeth, and my stomach turns. "But it's not about the spotlight. It's about having a presence, you know? People are drawn to power, to someone who isn't afraid to be themselves, to lead. I guess they recognized that in me."

This man is delusional. But the more I can bring that out, the better.

"I think people still recognize that in you," I say, pushing the compliment.

He leans forward. "That so?"

I shrug, deliberately avoiding his gaze. "A lot of the girls at camp have been talking about you, actually. And they're, like, really young. Why do you think you fascinate them so much?"

He chuckles, a smug sound that disgusts me. "I did things my way. And I've got knack for connecting with people. It's a gift."

Whitley's smile is enough to shrivel my whole entire soul, but I think I've set him just off-balance enough to turn the conversation.

"I've, um, I've actually been working on putting together a history of Camp Wildfire, and your name comes up a lot with former campers too."

He raises his eyebrows. "Oh, yeah?"

I hate what I'm about to imply, but I have no choice. "Oh, yeah. They, uh…lots of them can't forget you. A couple of them even mentioned writing to you in prison?"

"Never got those letters."

"Is the federal correctional system known for its precise mail-delivery system?"

"About as good at delivering mail as they are cooking." Whitley sucks spit through his incisors and chuckles to himself. "These girls tell you what they had to say in these letters?"

"They remembered your blue eyes, from a mug shot, I guess? Said they could never forget them. I mean, they clearly have a thing for bad boys."

"Do you?"

I smile but can't bring myself to show teeth. "I like 'em more boring than that."

Whitley gives me a lascivious look through the plastic barrier. I can't take much more of this, so I finally make my way to my point.

"A couple of the campers seemed kind of hung up on your connection to one girl, in particular. Uh, Regina Smith? Did you know her?"

A disgusted scowl replaces Whitley's hungry-wolf smile. "I didn't have anything to do with that girl."

"No, I know. But I was wondering if you might know who might have."

"Told you, I don't know anything. She wasn't my type anyway. Wasn't built like you."

Whitley gives me an obscene up-and-down—lingering on my chest—as a smile spreads across his face. It takes all my strength not to spit at the plastic barrier between us, and I toss out my flattery for a more direct approach.

"Kylie Boyd was your type though, right? Why don't you tell me about what you did to her."

Whitley shifts his gaze toward the door, raising his hand in a subtle, practiced motion, signaling a nearby guard. "We're done here."

As the guard collects him, I give all my energy over to my anger and indulge it with a razored tone of voice. "I was attacked back then, too, come to think of it. Were you there for that?"

"Now hold on one second…" Whitley turns back. "I finally figured out who you are."

"And who's that?"

"You're married to Artie Yuen. That guy's a legend!" He laughs to himself. "Do me a favor. Tell him Myer 'Swish' Whitley still bleeds blue."

His use of Arthur's high school nickname gives me chills.

How close was "Artie" to this monster? And what secrets might the two share?

CHAPTER
TWENTY-NINE

"Don't tell me Artie never mentioned how close we were." Whitley's eyes gleam with sadistic playfulness, a sneer tugging at his lips. "Your hubby was like a little brother to me."

I grip the edge of the steel desktop, trying to hide my discomfort. If Myer Whitley's telling the truth, that basketball photo takes on a far more disturbing tone. But there's no way Arthur would've been friends with this guy.

The guard places a hand on Whitley's elbow. "Ready?"

"Actually, give me a few more minutes with Mrs. Yuen here. Conversation got interesting." Whitley settles back into his seat, looking satisfied, like a man who's just eaten a heavy meal. "You look like you've seen a ghost."

I take a minute to gather myself, breathing deep into my diaphragm. My instinct is to get up and run. But Whitley's hateful glare soon turns my fear to anger.

How dare this guy try to undermine my marriage with his manipulative bullshit.

"I'm not interested in old high school friendships. I believe there's a connection between Kylie Boyd, Regina Smith, and quite likely myself. And that connection is you."

This time Whitley weathers my mention of Regina and Kylie with a calm demeanor. He looks wistful as he rubs a smudge off the partition with his thumb. "Absolutely devastating what happened to that Regina girl. Makes sense your little campers are scared. They never caught the guy, right?"

"Right."

He licks his finger and continues rubbing at the smudge, which clouds the plastic further. "How long have you been Mrs. Yuen, by the way?"

"Four years." I answer honestly, curious where this is going.

"So sorry I missed that wedding of yours. Putnam Country Club is a gorgeous venue. It's no Linden River, but still."

Arthur had handled his friend and family invites for the wedding. But there's no way he would've invited Myer Whitley.

Right?

Refusing to be baited, I stay on topic and resist the temptation Whitley is dangling before me. "If you know something more about what happened to Regina Smith—"

"I was cuffed across town when whatever happened to that girl happened to that girl." Myer leans back. "Do your research next time, and you won't waste your whole day coming up here for nothing."

Narrowing my eyes, I refuse to back down. "Way I heard it, the timeline on this whole thing's sketchy. Seems to me you could've hurt Regina and still had plenty of time to torment Kylie on the same night."

Whitley glances off to the side. There's a caginess there that suggests I've struck a chord.

I press more firmly. "Even more likely, you know something about what happened to Regina that you're not sharing. If you have information that could help Regina's case get solved, I bet you could use that to broker a deal on your current charges."

"So you think I know what happened to her, and I'm keeping it a secret and choosing more time in prison...?" He throws his hands up, scoffing. "Why? Out of the goodness of my happy little heart?"

"Out of brotherhood, maybe. Someone like you would've known about every bad plan for miles. But what has that brotherhood earned you, other than a spot behind bars?"

"You sound like a detective on a shitty crime show." Whitley presses all ten fingertips against the plastic, leaning in. "I didn't know shit. Didn't wanna know shit. Didn't care about shit. Was having way too much fun hanging out with Artie and the boys." He pins me with a cheesy, sadistic wink.

He's determined to engage me on the topic of "Artie," and I'm about to resist, when I remember an acting class I took in college.

Improv 101. My instructor—a wiry older guy with a childlike smile—taught us to say "yes, and" to everything our scene partner suggested and to never push back. The class was a requirement for psych undergrads for a reason I didn't understand until now.

Sometimes, you need to buy into delusion to access what's beneath it.

Leaning forward, I give him a conspiratorial smile, like we're two old friends sharing secrets. "Why's it so important for you to tell me you were close with my husband? What happened between you two?"

Whitley shrugs. "Artie and I were tight back then. But he grew up, got himself a wife, sexy little thing, and forgot all about me." His gaze drops from my face to my chest and stays there, the tip of his tongue poking out between his lips.

I groan in disgust—can't hide it—and turn the sides of my mouth down like I've stepped in something nasty on the street.

"Don't make a face like that, pretty girl. It'll get stuck that way."

I roll my eyes. "Now you're the crime-show stereotype."

"Stereotype of what?"

"The sleazy, manipulative predator who gets under people's skin."

Whitley laughs and lets the grin linger. "Maybe. But stereotypes exist because there's truth behind them."

For the first time, I register a middle-aged woman sitting beside me. There's no inmate waiting for her across the plastic, but she's peering hopefully through to the other side, crying.

I doubt Myer Whitley has ever disappointed someone by not showing up. It's more likely he's disappointed people by being there.

"So you blame me for your falling out with Arthur?" I ask.

"How do you know I wasn't talking about his other pretty little wife? The first one."

A flush of shame burns my cheeks as the truth hits me.

"Don't worry. You're both hot." Whitley tosses his head back and laughs. "But if you want to find out who your husband was then, she's the one you need to talk to."

"I'm not here to learn about my husband. I'm here to learn about you."

"You're the one who just asked what happened between us." Whitley runs a hand through his greasy dark hair. "Or have you forgotten that already?"

My head spins. I haven't done a good job keeping my facts straight with Whitley. I know that, and I hate the idea that this depraved convict has been toying with me.

"Whitley." The guard steps forward. "Time's up."

I stand. My steel chair scrapes against the cement, and I wince.

Whitley stands a second later, but his chair hardly scrapes at all. "Quick question before you go, Mrs. Yuen," he says, tone dripping in arrogance.

"What's that?"

The black teeth flash again. "Do you have any idea why sweet, young Hazel left your husband?"

I fight to keep my face from showing my surprise. Ever since getting back together with Arthur, I've assumed his relationship with Hazel just...ended. Then Jonathan told me Arthur and Hazel ended because Arthur was still in love with me.

Now Whitley's suggesting Hazel left him. Someone's lying. Jonathan or Arthur?

Before I have a chance to get more information out of Whitley, he's led away by the guard, and I'm all alone in the noncontact visitation room. As I head back toward the prison lobby, the idea that Arthur hurt Hazel and lost her trust—because that's why people leave—fortifies my insecurities and chips away at the version of my husband I thought I knew.

When Arthur and I made our pact not to delve into each other's pasts, our vow of silence had felt romantic, like we were safeguarding our love from old ghosts. Every day now, that pact feels more like a mutual agreement to live in ignorance, and I regret cosigning that decision.

The lies I've told my husband could ruin us. But what if he harbors secrets even more destructive, secrets that could shatter us completely?

I exit the prison into the blinding afternoon sun. As I walk toward the parking area, rolling farmland stretches ahead. The pastoral landscape collides jarringly with the prison's stark walls and razor wire fences.

My conversation with Whitley has left me with more questions than answers. I need to talk to Arthur, but before I face him, I have to find his ex-wife.

I get in my car, determined. Something tells me Hazel Mendez holds the key to understanding the man I married.

CHAPTER
THIRTY

Until now, I've honored the agreement Arthur and I made when I moved back to Wildfire after college. No talking about exes, no dwelling on the past. It seemed romantic at the time—a fresh start unburdened by history—and a convenient way to keep my own history a secret.

I hadn't intended for things to start up between us again, but he showed up at Camp Wildfire with Jonathan one day, and I found myself remembering the boy I'd fallen in love with all those years ago.

It felt like a second chance at the future we'd lost. A future that had been violently derailed by Mr. Blessed and the brutal attack that marked the end of our affair. The beating that nearly took my life and ruined my ability to bear children.

I'm parked at a Walmart near the prison, in an isolated corner near the back of the lot. The next closest car is at least twenty spaces away.

Pulling out my phone, I type Hazel's name in the internet search bar.

Every woman whose husband has a mysterious ex has been in my position. You want to see the sparkle that attracted your husband in the first place. But you also want to see the dysfunction that tore them apart.

This time is different though. This time, Myer Whitley dangled Hazel in front of me like a winning lottery ticket. *"Do you have any idea why sweet, young Hazel left your husband?"*

Taking a deep breath, I refocus on my phone. A full page of links appears, all related to Hazel Mendez.

The first link takes me to her Facebook page. I anticipated the same sweet-faced brunette I remember from the halls of Wildfire High. Instead, I find a woman I barely recognize.

In her profile photo, Hazel is leaning up against an ATV. She's wearing short shorts and has a tattoo of a vine climbing from her ankle all the way up her thigh.

A cigarette dangles from her lips, and the caption below reads—*Back country last week*! The photo was posted three days ago.

I click into her photo albums and quickly learn that Hazel's been posting consistently ever since high school, with public posts every day or so.

"Who keeps this stuff open for everyone to see?"

This reckless digital footprint must reflect who she was or who she's become. And the fact that she didn't shut down her public sharing with the rest of society unsettles me.

There's an album of Hazel in Cancún with a muscular, tattooed guy. Three albums later, the guy's gone, and she's on a Jet Ski by herself. Two albums after that, she's pictured with another man, this time on a fishing boat down at the lake.

In some of the pictures, Hazel holds a can of beer. In most of the pictures, a cigarette hangs from her lips. In all the pictures, she stares at me through the computer screen with such disdain, I almost believe she can see me parked and lurking.

I'm a disciplined woman, so I force myself to go through

the albums chronologically before I get to one emphatic label. *Honeymoon with Artie!!*

As I scroll through the photos, I'm struck by the contrast between their lives and mine during that time.

While Arthur and Hazel were enjoying what appears to be the vacation of a lifetime— sunburned at a luau, umbrella drinks—I was halfway across the country, finishing high school and preparing for college.

Clicking through the honeymoon album, I cringe as I read one horrifying caption after another.

Me & my baby.
Look at my hubby. Hot, hot, hot!!
I wuv my Artie. Luckiest bride in the world!!!

It's revolting. But the public portrait of Hazel's relationship with Arthur as lovey-dovey makes me question Whitley's assertion that Hazel left him.

I click to the last photo—Arthur and Hazel rubbing noses under the Hawaii stars—and I scoff. "Whitley was just trying to get a rise out of me. What an asshole."

As I close the browser tab, my eyes catch the clock in the corner of my screen. It's 1:54 p.m. I blink in surprise. That means I've been doomscrolling Hazel's Facebook photos for over an hour, and all I have to show for it is a lousy tension headache.

I head back to the search results and scroll through the first page of links. Hazel has a profile on LinkedIn listing her job as a 'retail specialist,' but sometimes that site notifies users when their profiles are visited, so I stay away.

Instead, I explore another of her social media profiles, which shows more boring pictures of a tattooed country girl doing tattooed country-girl things. This account is newer, and it lacks honeymoon and wedding photos for me to scrutinize.

Back on the search results, I see a listing claiming to have access to Hazel's home address and phone number. It's from the same website I used to look up Myer Whitley, so I only have to pay two extra dollars to download the report on Mendez.

I have her number in less than a minute.

A woman answers the phone. She's got a chain smoker's gravelly vibrato, and I can taste the stale cigarettes on her breath.

I'm suddenly hot. I direct the air vent to blow on me, and the recycled air dries the sweat on my forehead.

"Um, hi. Is this Hazel Mendez?"

"Who's this?"

Should I be honest? Shit. Shit. Shit.

"My name is Lizette. Um, Lizette Yuen. I'm married to—"

"You married my ex. I know who you are." A long cough rattles her body for several seconds. "Are you calling me about Artie?"

There's an inevitability in her voice. I can't pin it down, but it's like Hazel has been waiting for this call for a long time. A wave of empathy hits me, leaving me heavy and sad.

All these years, I've worked hard to make this woman a villain, someone who hurt my husband. But what if he was the one who hurt her?

"I know it must be strange hearing from me out of the blue. You're probably wondering why I'm calling and maybe even considering hanging up."

Pausing, I wait for a response. Birdsong filters through the phone. I picture Hazel standing outside, near running water. I glance at my screen, ensuring the call hasn't dropped.

When Hazel's voice returns, it's softer and devoid of the earlier growl. "I considered calling you before. When you reconnected with Artie. When your wedding happened. A few times."

"Why didn't you?"

"None of my business."

"But now?" Our two voices combined barely amount to one whisper. A red car pulls into a spot a few spaces away. Instinctively, I slide down in my seat a few inches.

"Now you called me," Hazel says.

I wait again, but she remains silent, still on the line.

There's something she wants to tell me. Something important.

Honesty is my only course of action, so I swallow hard and let the words spill out. I tell her that I'm having trouble with Arthur. That my trust in him is weakening every day. People have told me he wronged her. "I know I have no right to ask, but I was wondering if you wouldn't mind talking about what happened?"

Now I hear a door close on her end of the line, and the birdsong is gone.

"Artie was a good boyfriend." Hazel's voice resonates with a soft echo, like she's in a bathroom or a long hallway.

My fists clench as I await whatever's coming next. "But…?"

"I don't know."

A gray cloud passes over the superstore. I wonder if another storm's coming. "Hazel…Myer Whitley is the person who told me to track you down. He was at Wildfire High the same time we were."

"What'd you do, go see him in prison?"

My nervous laughter is all the answer Hazel needs.

She replies with a soft laugh of her own. "You really are second-guessing your husband."

"Right now, I'm trying to figure out who he was then, and if there's any chance he's still that person. Was he really friends with Whitley, or was Whitley trying to freak me out?"

"*Friends* isn't the right word." She sucks spit through her teeth like a cowboy chewing on grass. "Will, Artie, all those guys…they used Myer. Even after we all graduated, they still hung out at his place. Just like they did in school, and Myer let 'em because, well, that was the only way anyone was willing to include him."

"Boys can be—"

"There were girls there too. Girls from Camp Wildfire." She's so quick to correct me, I'm not sure I hear her right.

I ask her to repeat herself. She does.

"Imagine how I felt back then. My boyfriend, who claims he loves me, is hanging out drinking with a bunch of wild girls from Camp Wildfire, and I'm not even allowed to be there for it."

The dark cloud has doubled in size, stretching across the parking lot and hanging above my car. Thunder rumbles in the distance.

"Was one of those girls Regina Smith?"

My body relaxes as Hazel says, "No." *Thank god.* But her next words wash the relief away. "Kylie Boyd used to hang there all the time, though. She was from Shepstone, so I knew her."

"Do you know what…what really happened to her?"

Hazel yells at someone to wash up for dinner, then returns to cursing under her breath. "Sorry, what was that?"

"I asked if you know what really happened to Kylie Boyd."

Hazel takes a deep breath and lets it out. "I know Myer Whitley wasn't alone that night. The night Kylie was attacked."

"Who was with him?"

"Some freak in a ski mask. Kylie told me all about it. Stood back and watched the whole attack like he was at the movies."

I flatten my palm against my face as the memory of my masked attacker drains the blood from my cheeks. A smattering of raindrops hits my windshield, and thunder clashes. My mom always used to say thunder was God hanging out at the bowling alley. This was more like God dropping bombs.

I ask for more information, but Hazel insists that was all she had. It quickly becomes hard to hear her over the kids fighting in the background. She starts to make excuses, trying to get off the phone, but I interrupt.

"Before you go, um...can you maybe tell me...what did Arthur, um, Artie... What did he do to lose your trust?" My skin warms with anxiety as Whitley's words fall from my mouth. "I know this might seem random or, like, out of nowhere. But I've been trying to understand some things about his past, and I think you might be the only one who can help me."

A teenager pushing a caravan of shopping carts rattles past my car, tiny white earbuds shoved inside his ears.

Finally, she speaks. "Why should I help you?"

There's a vulnerability behind Hazel's question that softens my perception of her. If there's any truth to what Whitley suggested, her life with Arthur might've been just as confusing as mine is becoming. And if I can't empathize with that, I might as well be dead.

"I think...as a woman...you might be able to help me understand what's going on with my husband. With my marriage."

She grunts in apparent camaraderie.

"My time with Arthur's been great," I continue. "Really. So much of it. But there's more to him that I don't understand. You've been through this. Maybe you can help me make sense of it all?"

"No one's been through the bullshit I dealt with in that marriage." There's a new anger in her voice now, like she's back in the trenches with Arthur, reliving something hard.

Silly me, thinking social media told even a fraction of the real story.

"You guys were young..."

She snorts. I turn up my air-conditioning, but her voice

has dropped, and I can't hear her over its hum. I turn it down again.

"People say that, like, it's some kind of excuse for what he did. Or like I was too stupid to realize what was going on. I realized it. But I forgave him. Over and over and over again."

"Forgave him for what?"

She spits out her reply like it's rotten milk. "Don't tell me you don't know..."

"I don't know what...?"

"I mean, he's done it to you, too, right? That's why you're calling me?"

"What did he do to you?"

"Artie was perfect whenever we were hanging out together. Couldn't ask for a better boyfriend, better husband. I mean, it was like he went to college for that shit."

Sounds familiar.

"But when we were apart, he was cheating. And not just with one girl."

My mouth dries up.

"I confronted him about it, right there at the farmer's market on Highway 9. He denied it. I unleashed on him, told him we were over, told him I'd never trust him again."

"Arthur...he...he's never seemed like a cheater."

"Well, he must seem like somethin', 'cause you're talking to me." Hazel laughs to herself. "We were divorced within six months. It was amicable, but only 'cause we were so broke, we had nothing to fight over."

"And have you seen him since then?"

"For a while, after the divorce, I was convinced he was stalking me. I could never prove it, but I always felt, like, his presence."

"D-did you...did you ever tell..." Shit. I can't even get the words out.

Hazel laughs. This time there's an apologetic tone to it. "I'm sorry, you're still married to the guy."

"No, this...this is why I called you."

"You want my advice on Arthur Yuen?"

I nod, as if she can see me. But the question is rhetorical, because she continues without missing a beat.

"If I were you, I'd run far, far away."

CHAPTER
THIRTY-ONE

I'm going to confront my husband. About Myer Whitley. About Hazel Mendez. And about Amanda Holland.

These are the words I repeat to myself like a mantra as I pull up to the Mountain Grill and park.

The log cabin is as charming as ever, nestled off Highway 9 in Wildfire. We've made plenty of happy memories there, including some from several of our early dates as teenagers.

I'd asked Arthur to meet me here on my way home from the prison. At first, he'd demurred, saying he had a work thing. The words of a man having an affair. But I'd pushed, and he'd agreed to meet me for a late dinner. It's fitting that the Grill is where I'll get my answers about what happened back then, who Arthur was, and who he was secretly becoming.

I enter to find him seated at a raw-wood table pushed up against the far wall. Two sodas bubble before him in plastic Coca-Cola cups. I know mine by the lemon slice perched on the rim, and I grab it as I sit, taking a big sip.

We order—both going with the fried chicken, as always—and Arthur leads the conversation. He starts by telling me how sorry he is about disappearing to the cabin yesterday before explaining how vulnerable he's felt talking about our fertility struggles and building our family.

Paying attention to each word, I occasionally lean in to spot a micro-expression that might reveal the truth. Then I chastise myself for not trusting the man I married and reconsider questioning him about his past.

But I want to know the truth, and the fear of losing Arthur grips me. His past can't be as dark as I suspect. *Can it?* There are two sides...

My paranoia and love for my man are at war. Suspicion opens my mouth to speak, and love closes it. I go through two cups of Diet Coke as Arthur says all the right things.

Finally, he gets up to use the restroom. I take the chance to gather my resolve. I want to regain trust in my husband, and that can only happen if I ask the hard questions.

When he gets back, I jump into the conversation before he has a chance to speak.

First, I need to figure out his relationship with Amanda.

"Hey, someone at work mentioned that big Virginia land use case today. You worked on that, right?"

Arthur scrunches up his face. "Who at Camp Wildfire randomly brought up a land use case?"

"Weirdly, uh...it was someone on the maintenance staff. I guess it impacted their mom's property? I overheard him talking on the phone about it." It's disturbing how natural the lies roll off my tongue. "Didn't you become kind of friends with the attorney after working on that case?"

"Peter Holland. I don't know if we were *friends*, but he came out golfing with me and Will once. Dude has like, three-thousand-dollar clubs, but his short game's terrible." Arthur laughs. "He took seven mulligans. Will hated it. But he stayed in touch with Peter way more than I did."

I smile, spearing a green bean with my fork. "You were never the more social of the Yuen brothers."

Arthur laughs again.

I'm tempted to bring up Amanda—and that can't happen—so I adjust course and seize the opportunity to pursue Arthur's relationship with Myer. "That was true in high school, too, right? I mean...you dated me, so you couldn't have been very popular. Unless, I don't know, were most of your friends from basketball?"

"Eh. I wasn't very popular on the team either."

I reply too quickly. "But you went to parties and stuff, right? I remember Jonathan talking about some kid whose parents let him have the whole team over to drink and hang out. He had his own apartment or something?"

Arthur pushes mashed potatoes around his plate but doesn't eat any. "Uh. Yeah. One of the kids had, like, a free house situation."

"I think Jonathan was saying...wasn't it that kid Myer Whitley? The one who ended up in prison?"

Arthur flags down a passing server, gesturing to the table. "Could we get a box for this? Thank you." When he turns back to me, he's got an impatient glint in his eyes. "Yeah. I think it was Whitley."

I nod, but inside I'm frustrated. I'm having a hard time figuring out the best way to get necessary information out of him. "The girls at camp have been discussing him a lot. They're all fascinated with Regina Smith, the girl who disappeared? Some of them have even tried conjuring her ghost, like, with Ouija boards or whatever."

Arthur rolls his eyes. "Teenage girls love a nice séance."

"Some of them are scared, though. I figured I'd investigate whatever happened with Whitley so I could report back, let them know there's nothing to fear, you know?"

It's getting easier to lie to Arthur, and I'm not sure that's a good thing.

"Were you or Will friends with him at all? Or did you just go to the parties?"

The server drops a to-go box on our table with a polite word or two. Arthur makes a dad joke about eating his leftovers on the car ride home. He's so relaxed.

My frustration comes out. "Arthur, my campers are frightened. Is this not a serious conversation for you?"

"Of course it is." He scoops his potatoes into the tray, taking great care to scrape in every morsel. He flicks his fork and knits his eyebrows. "I don't know why you're bringing this crap up. Myer Whitley was a piece of shit. Everyone on the team used him for his parties but stayed as far away as possible beyond that."

"Sounds kind of mean."

Arthur shrugs, the gesture dripping with disdain. "You didn't know Whitley."

Whitley. That's the second time Arthur has said the name with disturbing familiarity.

"It was fun to have a place to go without parents looking over our shoulders. Plus, he had some hookup, so there was always beer."

"You said you didn't go often."

"Yeah. Because I didn't. I'm just saying—"

"There was always beer. The few times you went."

Arthur tosses a chicken leg into his box and gets to work scraping his green beans inside. "I'm sorry, what's with your tone?"

I shovel a forkful of mashed potatoes into my mouth for lack of a better answer.

"Look, I respect that you're trying to find out what happened with that Regina girl. But Myer Whitley's in prison, as far as I know. Nobody around here's going to want you digging up a bunch of painful bullshit for no reason."

"Okay. But it's weird to me you never mentioned you used to hang out with Myer Whitley, like, at his house."

Arthur reaches toward my plate. "You want me to take this home?"

I pull the plate closer to me. "I want you to focus on this conversation."

He raises his voice enough to let me know he's angry without drawing any stares. "Yeah, well, I don't want to talk about this. I'm not proud that I hung out with Myer Whitley, Liz. The guy was a weirdo. We all saw something was wrong with him, and we didn't do anything about it because we were using him for his house. This was a dozen years ago. Are you serious with this line of questioning?"

"Whoa, okay." I sit back, sliding my leftovers toward Arthur. "Pack up whatever you want."

He shoves the food into the container, sending crumbs spilling across the table.

I blurt out a nagging question before I can stop myself. "But what do you mean you saw something was wrong with him? Did you see him hurting people?"

"No." This time his voice draws the curious look of our server from across the room. Leaning forward, Arthur speaks more quietly. "Whitley's a sore spot for everyone around here. You didn't move here 'til the beginning of high school, and then you left for senior year and went away to college before things got really bad."

"Things were terrible for me, Arthur. Remember? That's why I left town for my last year of high school."

"I know that…I just think maybe you don't get it." He sighs. "You're not, like…from here. You know?"

Arthur calling me an outsider hurts. My trauma-bond with this place is stronger than that of any born and bred resident I've met. "You're making a mess with the food."

"I don't care." He tosses a slice of toast into the box and

shuts it, sweeping the crumbs from the table with the back of his hand.

"I have to ask one more question."

"No. I'm done with this conversation. You're accusing me of something, and I don't even know what."

"I'm not accusing you of anything. But I want to know…" I take a deep breath through my nose, then let it out. "Did you take Hazel to Myer Whitley's house? Did anything ever happen to her there?"

Arthur stammers and then laughs in my face, looking hurt but also hateful. Finally, he pushes back his chair with a loud screech and stands to go. "Do you want me to sleep in the basement tonight?"

"No. I—"

"Okay, cool." He shakes his head like he can't believe my nerve. "Then I guess I'll see you later in bed."

CHAPTER

THIRTY-TWO

I catch up to Arthur as he grabs the door handle of his truck. "I'm not accusing you of anything."

"You obviously are. That's what this whole dinner was about."

"No, it wasn't." He pulls the door open. I step forward and close it again. "I'm sorry for bringing it up."

"It's just...it's embarrassing." He turns to face me, his beautiful black-brown eyes cast downward. "Yeah, I associated with a creepy guy...a hundred years ago. But that has nothing to do with us. I love you, Lizette. I've been trying to make that clear, but you're not getting it."

My secrets beat in my chest. This could be another chance to expose the lies I've been telling since high school, protected by the guarantee of my husband's love.

But to tell him, I'd have to trust him, and I'm not sure I do. I blink away a tear.

The sincere look in Arthur's gaze catches me off guard. Despite my doubts, I feel a familiar warmth spreading through me. His words remind me of the boy I fell in love with, the one who always knew how to make me feel safe. For a moment, my suspicions fade, replaced by a longing for the simplicity we once had.

Arthur must sense my vulnerability, because he takes me by the waist and pulls me so close, I can detect the nutmeg and lemon in his Old Spice. The scent steals my breath. I move closer to him, relaxing into the warmth radiating from his chest.

"I'm never going to stop telling you how much I love you, Liz."

His hand grazes mine. I interlock my fingers with his.

I remember discovering our hands were the perfect size for interlocking. Back then, before Mr. Blessed, I'd had the courage to share my feelings with Arthur every day. Of course, back then, my feelings for him were never complicated.

Before I screwed everything up.

He leads me to the darkened picnic area beside the restaurant, lifts me by the waist, and leans me against the edge of a picnic table. As I shift to find my balance, my foot slips into a patch of mud, which splatters up my leg. But the sensation is fleeting, forgotten as soon as we're alone under the moonlight, and he presses his lips to mine.

This very bench is where we had our first kiss. Arthur, a senior at the top of the class. And me, a plain-Jane junior. There's no way that memory's lost on Arthur.

I want to surrender myself to the nostalgia, but I also want to turn away, to withhold my affection until I get closer to the truth.

But what truth am I after, exactly?

And would I recognize the truth even if it smacked me in the face?

CHAPTER
THIRTY-THREE

The longer we kiss, the more my emotions surge. Arthur still hasn't told me if he'd taken Hazel to Meyer Whitley's apartment. I still feel guilty for...so many reasons. The disconnect between my body's response and my churning thoughts grows until it's unbearable. I can't just sit here, in such a meaningful place, and act like a single kiss can make all that better.

My hands, which have been pulling him closer, now press against his chest. Pushing Arthur away, I climb off the picnic table and step into the darkness. The air is heavy with sticky humidity, and I nearly slip as I cross the muddy parking lot.

Arthur follows, his footsteps squelching behind me. "Lizette. What happened? What's wrong?"

I shake my head.

"Lizette!" He catches my arm and spins me toward him.

I try to pull away, but his grip is tight. We freeze for a moment.

When he speaks again, his voice trembles slightly. "You don't want a baby with me, do you?" He speaks as if the possibility is occurring to him for the first time, and his words hit me like a sucker punch.

I try to speak but manage only a few choked sobs. My face is warm with tears. And we must be near the dumpster, because the sour odor of trash invades my nose.

"You won't get checked out." His fingers dig into my arm. "And I know for a fact my sperm are fine. I got checked at Clear River last month."

My eyes widen. He hadn't been there with Amanda, taking a Lamaze class or picking baby names. Instead, he'd been there checking on his own reproductive health.

For us.

It's not easy for any man to face the possibility of impotence. I know it must've taken a lot of courage on Arthur's part. He must've been driven there by frustration and confusion after months of our failed attempts to conceive.

"You didn't have to..."

"One of us had to do something." His voice carries a grave tone that gets amplified with his next statement. "And I knew there was no point in trying to convince you to go and get tested. I took care of my side of the street."

The night holds its breath, the distant chirps of crickets and rustling leaves fading into a tense silence.

I'm fully sobbing now. The tears come from a deep sense of overwhelm, anxiety and guilt, and from the fear that Arthur has finally seen me for who, or what, I am.

This is yet another opportunity for me to unburden myself of the lies that plague me. "I...I..." Honesty will not rise from my stomach, no matter how much I want it to spill out.

"What, Liz? Come on. Just...whatever it is, tell me."

I wipe my tears away with the back of my arm and scrub my hand across my face. My cheeks are warm and wet. I already know how bloated I'll be in the morning. And how little I'll care.

"You're treating me like a criminal in my own home. It's like...you're sabotaging our relationship to avoid building a family with me." His voice breaks as he continues. "What's so bad about me that you don't think I can be a dad?"

The words slice through me. I'm not sure I've ever felt worse in my life as I place my hand on Arthur's, twisting his wedding ring as I grab on.

I search for the strength to uproot my long-buried secret, but all I manage is bland reassurance. "Of course you can be a dad. You'd be a great dad."

Arthur pulls his hand away. "If you believe that, then I'm so confused. It's like...you've got something going on in your head that I can't fix, and you need to figure it out."

"Arthur—"

"You've been hiding something from me, Lizette, and it's way worse than a stupid phone in a truck. I mean, yeah, that was dumb. But I'm not the one putting off the future we've always talked about. You are. Only you can figure out why, and only you can fix it."

"Arthur..."

"I'm sorry. I gotta go home." With that, he turns and walks toward his truck, his footsteps heavy. The parking lot lights cast long shadows that expand as he walks away.

I follow him, choking out words like "I'm sorry" and "wait."

Arthur doesn't reply or look back until he stops walking and screams into the night, "Just fucking stop!"

I freeze. He turns to face me, pulling his keys from his pocket. "I'm going to the cabin tonight."

"Arthur...we can talk about this."

"If you want to talk, why don't you run to camp and process it with your little boyfriend, Jonathan?"

I stumble back like I've been shoved. Arthur's gone in a

cloud of dusty gravel before I regain my composure or find the words to reply.

CHAPTER
THIRTY-FOUR

I'd waited half an hour to come home from the restaurant, hoping that would give Arthur time to grab a few things before escaping to the cabin. But it looks like I didn't stall long enough.

His truck is in the driveway.

Shit.

Panic rises in my chest. I need time alone to process everything that's happened and decide what to do next. And I don't have the energy to continue our fight right now.

I idle next to Arthur's truck for a while before killing the engine. The parking receipt from Linden River sits on my dashboard like the proverbial smoking gun. I shove it in my pocket as I get out.

The storm never materialized up near the prison, but it must've hit Wildfire hard. Branches are strewn all over our front yard, and the chimes that hang from our porch are tangled on the lawn, limp and lifeless.

I step over them and head toward the porch. But I freeze mid-step as the back door bangs closed and Arthur's voice floats toward me.

Heart racing, I hurry to the side yard and peer through a crack in the fence.

Arthur paces under the motion-sensor light, chewing at his thumbnail in a pose I'm far more accustomed to from my angsty campers than my self-assured husband. He's still in his button-down and chinos from dinner—but he's traded his muddy boots for clean ones—and he's speaking quietly.

Struggling to hear, I pry my face away from the fence and press my ear against the wood. My eyes squeeze shut as I focus, desperate to pick up any small shred of conversation. The fence is warm against my body. It smells faintly of the stain Arthur applied last weekend, bitter but also clean and fresh.

I turn my head and look back through the fence. Arthur steps a few feet closer. My body wants to run, but this is my chance to see the real man, unadorned with whatever mask he might wear for his naive wife.

He turns toward me. Time slows, and his lips fill my field of vision as I try to read them.

My husband's voice is tense and urgent. "Promise me you won't try to find it. You'll only make things worse." He turns away, and I lose track of his words.

He angles back toward me, and I catch another strained sentence. "If you touch her, you're dead."

Arthur's voice is angry now, and my body tenses, bracing for him to throw the phone against the fence I'm hiding behind. But after ending the call with a calm, careful movement, he runs a hand through his hair and heads back inside.

I drift away from the fence, my mind reeling. Arthur's words echo in my head.

"If you touch her, you're dead."

My legs are weak as I make my way to the front of the house, each step an effort to appear normal.

As I reach the porch, the front door opens. Arthur stands

there in his socks, his expression a mix of surprise and... something else. Wariness? Guilt? I can't place it.

"Lizette? What are you doing out here?" His voice is carefully neutral.

I fumble for my phone in my purse, grasping for the lie I'd prepared. "Um. Emails. I had work emails. Just wanted to get them figured out before I came inside."

Arthur narrows his eyes, studying me. "You're checking your work email at eleven o'clock at night?"

I nod. "Just something I had to handle. It's all good now."

He turns and heads inside, and I follow, my heart pounding with each step.

As we enter the house, I pause to hang my purse and place my shoes beside Arthur's in the foyer. The sound of his footsteps recedes as he continues into the kitchen, and I force myself to follow, stepping from the entry hall into the heart of our home.

In a practiced routine I've seen hundreds of times, he shoves a decaf pod into the Keurig and snaps the lid closed.

"So," he says, his back to me as he watches the coffee brew, "what were you really doing out there?"

I look Arthur up and down. Who has he been talking to? Who has he threatened to kill? *And who does he want to protect? Me or Amanda?*

She's *my* camper. It's *my* duty to protect her.

"I told you. I had to take care of something for work. These kids need me. I can't just let things slide."

Arthur pulls the coffee cup from the machine and places the mug before me. I wrap my hands around the warm ceramic, but as the heat seeps into my palms, something inside me snaps. The normalcy of this moment—Arthur making me a cup of decaf, like this is any other night—is unbearable. And the gulf between this simple act and the weight of our secrets is too wide.

I need to confront him with the truth—any version of it—and before I know it, I'm talking. The words come out faster than I can stop to consider what they are.

"You know I have a duty, right?" I push the coffee away. "It's, like, my job to protect these kids, so I take that very seriously. It's stressful. It's a lot."

"Yeah, sure..."

"You don't understand. Every single kid is like one of my own. I would do anything to protect them."

Arthur turns back to the Keurig and starts a second cup. Water drains through wet coffee with an irritating squelch.

"Seriously? You're making more coffee right now?" I'm losing control, and I know it. My voice raises three decibels. "I'm trying to tell you something!"

Arthur turns back, scrubbing a finger in his ear like he'd failed to hear me. "I want a cup of coffee. I don't get why you're so mad."

"You don't even know what happened to me, Arthur. These kids might look like adults, but they're just young girls in grown-up bodies. What happens to them now can and will mess them up for life."

The truth is an avalanche. I don't know if I'm standing at the top of the mountain, looking down, or if I'm about to be crushed.

"Lizette. Calm down. We can—"

"Shut up! Stop talking! Now!" I've never screamed like this at anyone other than myself. My arms are shaking. I shove the coffee mug farther away, and it spills across the slick, suburban granite.

Arthur rips off a paper towel and cleans the spill. "You're making a mess."

I tear the paper towels from Arthur's hand and pin him with the wild-eyed look not of a woman scorned but of a woman who's suffered permanent damage at the hands of so many careless, selfish men.

Accept the avalanche. Give the truth to get the truth. It's the only strategy I've never tried.

"I was raped, Arthur."

My raised voice roots me in the present. It's like I'm on drugs and every word is another painful, satisfying hit.

Arthur blinks in confusion.

"When we broke up in high school, I had a relationship with a teacher. Mr. Blessed. He...he took advantage of me. It was statutory rape."

The color drains from Arthur's face. "What? What, what, what..." He stammers as he tears off another sheet of paper towel and dabs at the spill.

"The counter's clean!" I tear the paper towel away from him again.

His eyes are wide, his breathing shallow. "What...what teacher?"

"I just told you. Mr. Blessed."

Arthur's expression twists in confusion. "The AP Psych guy?"

"It was after we'd broken up."

"But Mr. Blessed was like...wasn't he married?"

"Yes. It was an inappropriate affair." There's a mean edge to my voice I can't control. "And I thought I was in love."

"Fuck, Lizette. No. No way!" His voice falls to a shaking whisper as he repeats himself. "No."

I tell him everything. The way Blessed groomed me with special attention. The way he controlled me with his eyes, his text messages, his power. The way my trusted teacher convinced me our love was real.

The way I'd believed every word he'd ever whispered.

When I'm all done, Arthur shakes his head. He's still muttering, "No, no..." Then he slams his fist down on the counter and looks me in the eyes. "No fucking way, Lizette! No way you kept this from me!" His voice waivers. "We were young. I mean, maybe he was inappropriate, but you've gotta be misremembering. People do that. They...they create false narratives. It happens all the time."

I should've expected this reaction. On some level, I can hardly blame him, and I'm tempted to backpedal. But I'm going to have to dig up the painful past if I want a better future.

"It started with an email." I press my fingers to my throbbing temples. "He told me I looked cute in my little red skirt in class that day. I remember when I read it, I felt, like... electric. The hottest teacher in school thought I looked cute."

Arthur makes a guttural noise, like he's both disgusted and devastated.

"The next email came later that night. He wanted to tell me I'd gotten a perfect score on the assignment he'd just graded. And he wanted to clarify that he particularly loved the way the skirt brought out the curves of my body. And my ass."

I remind myself that my shame is valuable. It's a reminder that I've grown. And that I'll never make the same mistakes again.

"Lizette—"

I push forward. "As soon as I opened that second email, I possessed the most powerful secret in the world. It was...it was seductive. You know? Sometimes, I think that's what drew me to him. I mean...what teenage girl doesn't love centering herself in a story of forbidden love?"

"That's...that's...that's stupid! Why would you let him—"

"Arthur," I push forward again with stern solemnity. "You need to tell me you love me. Okay? You need to tell me you believe me. Right now."

"Of course I believe you." His shoulders nearly drop below his chest. He's crying now. "You...you were a victim. I believe you."

Is he convincing me or himself?

I'm conflicted. But watching Arthur cry over my lies and my mistakes is harder than I imagined it would be.

My instincts tell me to comfort him. It's backward, but I can't help wrapping him in a hug. "Hey. I'm all right, aren't I? I'm here."

He collapses into a deeper sob. "It...it shouldn't have happened."

I haven't even gotten to the worst of it. Telling him the rest feels impossible.

"That's not all that happened, Arthur."

He recoils, widening his eyes like a trapped animal. "What do you mean?"

Arthur's still crying. I pause to give him a moment. There's no gentle way to approach the rest of this, so I put it baldly, like an objective third party.

"You already know about the guys who attacked me in high school."

Arthur narrows his eyes. "Did...did Mr. Blessed do that to you? That monster—"

"No. Arthur. No."

"So what, then?"

My throat constricts as I force out the hardest truth. "The attack did permanent damage to my body."

Arthur's focus drills into me with a terrifying intensity. "What are you talking about?"

Deep breath, Lizette. You can do this.

"After that night, I had to have surgery. A hysterectomy."

I was hoping Arthur would show understanding after I named the procedure, but his brow remains furrowed.

"That means I can't get pregnant."

Arthur shakes his head. "You mean like, you're going to need IVF or something?"

It hurts worse repeating it for a second time. "I mean I can never carry a child. They removed my womb, Arthur."

"No. No fucking way." Arthur clenches and unclenches his fists like he has no idea what to do with his fury.

I take a step back. But he's suddenly and oddly unaware of me. Like…the news has turned him deeply inward.

"That cannot be true! Lizette. You…you…you get periods!" He waves his arm wildly, in the general direction of the bathroom. "The…the stuff you have…the bad cramps you get…for fuck's sake, Lizette, I put that heating pillow in the microwave for you every month!"

I look down at my hands, twisting my wedding ring.

Arthur slams his palm on the counter. "Is that all a lie?"

My voice is heavy and dry. "Yes and no." I glance up at him. "I have severe mittelschmerz each month."

"Mittel fucking what?"

I nearly smile at that. "I no longer have a uterus, but they left my ovaries. Each month, I release an egg like any normal woman would. But for me, there's tremendous pain during the process. I also have all the hormonal and mood shifts, bloating, stuff like that."

He's shaking his head as if to keep the lie from settling into his brain. "There's gotta be something they can do. You just need to go to more doctors."

Does he really not understand what a hysterectomy is?

"My uterus is gone, Arthur."

"Why'd you let them do that? I'm sure they could've saved you. Modern medicine—"

"I was bleeding internally." I remember the pain so clearly. "There were no other options at the time. The surgery was necessary to save my life." I take a deep breath. "The good news is that I do still have eggs. Like you said before, we could try surrogacy or adoption—"

"No!" He grabs the coffee cup and throws it into the sink.

The handle breaks off the mug and coffee explodes, splashing out all over the sink and his shirt.

"Fuck!" When Arthur spins back to me, his eyes are hollow and desperate. He's seeing me for the first time in the context of my lies. "Lizette…"

I wait for the punch, whether by fists or by words—does it really matter?

But I don't move. Don't turn away from whatever is going to happen next. Revealing my truth has brought an eerie tranquility over me. Nonetheless, somewhere in the back of my mind, a voice whispers…

"If you touch her, you're dead."

CHAPTER
THIRTY-FIVE

Arthur looks at me like I'm a stranger who's inhabited the body of his wife.

Can I blame him?

In that unfamiliar look—betrayal, abandonment, who knows what else—I see a man who's gone through the looking glass. A man who might never feel love for me again.

Very slowly—and with no words passing between us—he wipes the spilled coffee from the counter and rinses the cup. With that simple chore done, he dumps it, along with the broken handle, into the trash bin.

Pulling his clean boots back on, Arthur goes outside and crosses the deck, peering over the railing. The motion-sensor light flicks on, bringing his form into stark relief.

I walk to the sliding glass door but don't follow him outside. Worry creeps under my skin as I wonder what he'll do next.

When he turns back, his voice is distant and cold, almost judgmental. "Projecting. That's the word for what you've been doing, right?"

I don't understand. "What?"

With the light behind him, darkness silhouettes Arthur's face. "You've been trying to connect me to Myer Whitley. Accusing me of lying and deceiving you…trying to make me the bad guy, when you're the one who's been lying."

I can't blame him for thinking this way, but the hurt cuts deep.

"Don't you have an ounce of sympathy for what I went through? Your first reaction is to…turn it around on me?"

"I guess, yeah!" Arthur pounds the railing. "What happened to you sucks. But you've been lying to me this whole time. And for what?"

"Because I was afraid. And we had a pact. No talking about our past relationships, remember? But more than that, you were adamant that you didn't want children in the beginning. Then, three years later, you changed your mind. Honestly, I thought you'd change it back, so I didn't want to go through the horror of talking about what happened to me if it wasn't necessary."

"And the tampons?"

I roll my shoulders to release some of the stress. "You bought them for me, remember?"

He squints at me. "When?"

"I was in terrible pain one month early in our marriage, and you went out and bought me chocolate and other things to help me with my 'period.' You also bought me some pads."

He blinks rapidly. "And those are the same boxes?"

"Yes. You never asked me about it again, and I just let you believe what you wanted to believe."

Not hard to do with a man who doesn't know what a hysterectomy is.

"This is unreal." He mutters something in a derisive tone as he turns away. I can't make it out, but I know it's hurtful.

I don't know what to say next. I don't know what to do.

"Arthur…please say something."

When he turns back to me, his face is caught between vulnerability, anger, and fear. "Are you cheating on me?"

How is this my marriage?

"What? No." My shame twists into disbelief, then anger. I can't believe he'd accuse me of this.

"Is it Jonathan?" His almond-dark eyes narrow. "I deserve to know."

"I'm not cheating on you." My voice is my mother's at her angriest. Terrifyingly calm. "And if that's your response to what I've shared, then I don't know what we're doing here."

He turns away from me. Several tense seconds pass, and I hit him with a few more pointed questions.

"How can you think I'd do that?"

Nothing.

"Don't you know me at all?"

Silence.

"You need to remember who I really am and stop being so closed-off and—"

Arthur cuts me off with a primal scream. As the sound echoes through my soul, he grabs a deck chair and throws it against the railing. The chair bounces back against his shin, and he kicks it away, sending it tumbling across the deck.

He rubs his shin, cursing loudly.

I've never witnessed such an outburst from him. It should terrify me. Instead, it makes him seem weak. But as he glares at me, I see he still has some fight left. "You've lied about everything! Baby names, nursery wallpaper, washable diapers, toys...all lies."

Arthur's not wrong, and I should feel terrible. But I'm witnessing this scene with a cold detachment that surprises even me.

Cold detachment, noun

A state of emotional numbness in which resentment builds until a person simply checks out, observing their partner's emotions with the same level of concern as one might have for a stranger's grocery list. Often triggered by intense stress or an overwhelming urge to not give a damn. See also, why Arthur's tantrum is having zero effect on my guilt levels.

He matches my detachment with a half-cocked grin. Contempt is the first of psychologist John Gottman's famous "four horsemen of divorce"—criticism, defensiveness, and stonewalling are the others—and we're riding them all.

The realization shakes me, and the moment of cold detachment soon drops me into a sea of insecurity.

I know my lies are unforgivable. But second chances aren't built on paranoia. They require honesty, vulnerability, and genuine support.

"Arthur. I'm the victim of something terrible. I should've told you these things a long time ago, but I was weak and afraid." I press my hand to my churning stomach. "I know we had a pact, but that was misguided. So if you have anything you've been keeping from me, I want to hear it, and I'll do everything I can to support you, no matter what."

This is your chance to come clean, Arthur. Tell me about Whitley. Tell me about Hazel. Tell me who you were talking to on the phone.

Turning away from me, Arthur picks up the chair he threw and returns it to its place at the table. He then straightens the other chairs.

I can't take the silence anymore. And I need to make a bold play for the truth. "Why doesn't Hazel Mendez trust you?"

He blanches. "What are you talking about? Who?"

Seriously?

"I'm talking about your ex-wife, Arthur. Not some summer fling." I advance, he retreats. "What ended your marriage?"

He answers through a small laugh. "That was forever ago. I...I don't know."

"Did your marriage end because of something that happened at Whitley's?"

"Barely went there." He takes another step back. "You're confused."

No, I'm not. Not this time.

"Arthur. We're telling each other the truth now. Okay?"

"Don't talk down to me, *Lizette*." Arthur's smile stops just short of cruel as he mimics me. "I'm your husband, not some creepy teacher who tricked you into thinking he cared about you. And you lied out of...out of..."

"Out of fear. Out of love!" I shout over him before dropping to a deadly calm. "Explain your own bullshit. Then we'll talk."

"I'm not going to let you make this about me. You're the liar here." He jabs his finger at me. "We're talking about you right now."

"No. We're talking about *us*. Our relationship."

Arthur shrugs. "Not how I see it."

I stare at him for a long time.

"Okay, whatever. I'm going to bed. And you need to go to the cabin." Without waiting for a reply, I go back into the house and stride toward the staircase.

Arthur follows me inside, his footsteps heavy. "Lizette, wait."

I ignore him, my legs trembling as I climb the stairs.

"You can't just go to bed." Arthur's voice is a mix of anger and desperation. "We need to talk about this."

I keep climbing to the top of the steps. "Talk about what?

How you've turned my trauma into an accusation against me? Or how you refuse to be honest about your own past?"

"Lizette."

I spin to face him. "Go to the cabin."

I enter the bedroom and remove my pajamas from the dresser, my movements automatic. As I get ready for bed, I hear Arthur storming out and starting his truck. For a moment, I almost waver.

But then I remember his accusations and his refusal to be honest after I laid all my lies at his feet. I go to the bathroom and wash my face.

Seconds later, I'm looking at myself in the mirror, and my determination disintegrates into the sinking pit of my stomach.

By the time I make it into bed, tears are streaming down my cheeks.

Unloading my secret opened me up. At least there's that.

As the night stretches on, my tears subside, replaced by a growing resolve. Arthur's evasiveness has only fueled my need for the truth, and if he won't give me answers, I'll find them myself, just like I've been doing.

Wiping away the last of my tears, I roll over and sip my water. Amanda Holland is only twenty minutes away at Camp Wildfire. And I won't rest until I learn everything about her relationship with my husband.

CHAPTER
THIRTY-SIX

Sunday morning, I wake up and drive straight to camp. I'd hoped sleep would settle me. But as I park, my mind spins.

Jonathon and I rotate weekends, so this should have been my day off. But I can't stay at the house another second. I'd rather work.

One moment, I indulge in conspiracy theories about Arthur and Myer Whitley. The next, I berate myself as an unhinged wife, struggling to handle my husband's past.

Then I remind myself that I'm as much of a liar as Arthur, and my lies touched the past, present, and future.

Why hadn't Arthur questioned me more when I told him about Mr. Blessed and the hysterectomy? Why had he directed his anger at me instead of at Mr. Blessed, the school, or even my mom—anyone who should have known what was happening? I couldn't understand why he was more focused on my mistakes than on the people who'd failed me.

But then it hit me—there's one possible reason Arthur would've been more concerned about my lies than what Mr. Blessed did to me.

Amanda.

"If Arthur's the father of Amanda's baby, he's no different than Mr. Blessed. His lies are worse than mine," I mutter to myself, shouldering open the door to the building. "That's unforgivable."

As I charge toward the counselor's lounge, I'm convinced either Arthur impregnated Amanda or I've completely lost control of my mental faculties.

I burst into the lounge, where a curly-headed junior counselor is eating his breakfast. "Where's Yolanda?"

The counselor nearly drops his biscuit. "Overnight camping with some girls. They should be back soon."

"Is Amanda Holland with them?"

"Uh, yeah, think so."

"Get her. Bring her here. Tell Yolanda I sent you."

The counselor blinks, then scrambles up. "On it."

He leaves, and I head to my office. It's perfectly clean in there, but I tidy up anyway, turning my anxious eye on anything slightly out of place.

I'm repositioning a spider plant when Jonathan finds me. He knocks softly before entering. The scent of his spiced aftershave—subtle hints of chicory and vanilla—precedes him.

"What are you doing here?" He soft-closes the door and turns to me. "It's your day off."

I manage a weak smile, trying to dismiss his concern. "Just came to sort out a few things."

He doesn't seem convinced. His gaze, full of worry, sweeps over me. "You look like you've had a rough night."

Catching my reflection in a window, I do my best to straighten several fly-aways and run my hands over my wrinkled blouse.

Jonathan, in stark contrast, is impeccably dressed, his white sneakers spotless. I can't help but comment, a light jab to ease the tension. "Not all of us can look like we're fresh out of a catalog every morning. Your shoes are so pristine, it's creepy."

A gentle smile breaks through his concern, but his eyes remain serious. He knows me well enough to see through the facade.

If I don't tell Jonathan some version of the truth, I'm going to live under the shadow of this unraveled moment for months. I don't want to lose his respect, and I need someone to talk to. "Arthur and I had a huge fight."

He steps closer, his voice softening. "I'm sorry. Do you want to talk about it?"

I pick up an old magazine, rolling and unrolling it in my hands. "I might seem paranoid, and maybe I'm losing it, but—"

"You're not 'losing it,' Lizette. You're going through a hard time."

Grateful for his support, I nod, taking a deep breath. "Thank you." I pause, gathering myself. "It's just that...I have these suspicions."

As I confide in Jonathan, his touch is light on my arm, grounding. "What suspicions?"

I meet his gaze. "I think...Arthur might be cheating on me."

As I lay out the details—Arthur's past actions, the secret phone—Jonathan steps away from me and paces.

"Are you sure?" His voice is low, tinged with disbelief.

I nod. "I know how it sounds, but the evidence..."

Jonathan runs his hand through his hair. He seems overwhelmed—like the happiest couple he knows is having serious problems.

For a second, I consider telling him everything, including my suspicions about Arthur and Amanda. But all that's unfounded, and I don't want Jonathan removing me from future contact with Amanda.

He might sense my animosity toward her, which I genuinely feel, and that would be reason enough to keep us separated while she's here. I can't afford to be cut off from the one person who can confirm my suspicions, selfish as that sounds.

I end with a meek smile and turn up my palms like a half-hearted stand-up comedian. "That's all I've got. So, uh, thanks for coming. I'll be here all week."

"That's...that's a lot to carry." Jonathan steps toward me, his green eyes wide. "Can I hug you?"

Throat tight, I nod.

As he embraces me, the care and protection in his hold seems to swallow up my heartbreak.

When I step back, Jonathan is there, steady and reassuring. "How can I help you through this? What do you need from me right now?"

His question is not a mere pleasantry. It's an offer of genuine support, reflecting the core values we teach here at Camp Wildfire. Empathy, respect, and understanding.

Jonathan sets both his hands on my shoulders, clasping down like he's setting the top on a manhole cover.

He's so close, I can see the flecks in his eyes.

"You're doing the right thing, Lizette."

He's so close, I can see the light pink undertones in his lips.

"But you need to be careful. I would die if anything happened to you."

He's so close, his breath warms my face. It smells sweet.

I murmur my next sentence with a soft jaw and softer eyes. "Arthur accused me of having an affair with you, you know."

He doesn't miss a beat. "That's 'cause he knows you deserve better."

As Jonathan's fingers graze the nape of my neck, the world stills, and the air between us crackles with possibility.

Leaning closer, his gaze turns intense, hungry. Like he's

glimpsed something in me he desperately wants to explore. "I've always admired you, Liz."

Am I about to make Arthur's accusations come true? I don't want that.

But the current has caught me, and I'm not sure I have the strength to swim out from under it.

I lean forward, and so does Jonathan. A sharp knock shatters the moment.

CHAPTER
THIRTY-SEVEN

I step away from Jonathan, take a cleansing breath, and open the door. Amanda waits for me across the threshold, and I greet her with a practiced smile.

"Amanda, glad you could make it. Come in."

"Glad I could make it?" Amanda edges into the office. Her skin radiates an ethereal glow, exaggerated by her pregnancy, and she carries her pronounced belly like a treasured possession. "You pulled me from the camping trip by the lake. What's up?"

I mutter an excuse about urgent paperwork.

Jonathan, now a few steps away, shoots me a cautionary glance, asking if I'm good in here. I give him a reassuring nod.

He responds in kind. "Ms. Silva, you interrupted the camping excursion for paperwork?" He offers Amanda a sympathetic smile. "Apologies. Seems you got the less fun therapist today. I wouldn't have done that."

His attempt at humor fades under Amanda's piercing stare. Chuckling awkwardly, Jonathan makes his escape under the guise of needing to handle his own paperwork, his laughter trailing off as he retreats down the hall.

In the silence that follows, I take a moment to gather my thoughts, my gaze drifting to the cast-iron plant perched on the windowsill. I run my fingertips along its leaves, the familiar texture grounding me as I contemplate how to approach the delicate conversation ahead.

"This one's been troublesome lately," I say. "It's supposed to like bright light, but since I moved it onto the ledge here, the edges have crisped up."

Amanda's response is swift and direct. "Cast irons thrive in bright, *indirect* light. That spot'll kill it in less than two weeks."

I flash her a grateful smile, my mind racing. If I'd fully thought this through, perhaps I wouldn't have summoned her here. But no manual exists for this kind of confrontation, so I allow myself a sliver of grace as I sink into my desk chair.

"Do you need me to sign something?" she asks, her tone edged with impatience.

"Actually, please, sit. It's something personal. It couldn't wait." My voice falters as I start the digital recorder on my desk.

Amanda clocks the recorder and sighs. "Ugh. So this is a therapy thing." She guides her pregnant body into the armchair across from my desk with a dramatic sigh.

As Amanda sits, the scent of her honeysuckle perfume drifts toward me. I hate that she doesn't have the typical pregnant person's aversion to strong scents—not just because honeysuckle isn't my favorite, but because the fragrance reaches deep into me, pulling a nostalgic lever I wish would stay buried.

I smelled like that once. And I wonder if that girlishness might have been what attracted Arthur to her.

Taking a deep breath, I prepare to reveal my most closely guarded secret for the second time in less than twenty-four hours. I remind myself I'm the adult in this scenario. As such,

I move forward with a measured approach that disguises my puddled insides as confidence, self-awareness, and growth.

"Thanks for coming in, Amanda."

"Uh-huh, what's going on?"

I give her a tight smile. "When I was your age, I fell in love with a man named Michael Blessed."

Amanda shifts in her chair and throws me a skeptical look. "Okay. So...this is about you."

I give her a tight smile. "Kind of."

Amanda keeps her suspicious eyes on me.

My chest heaves, and I launch into my story.

First, I tell her how Mr. Blessed—a much older man—seduced me. I tell her we fell in love in the halls of my high school and over email. And I tell her that his love made me feel invincible.

She leans forward a few inches when I tell her about my first night with him, making love in the basement of the school, some classroom-turned-storage room, beside shelves of dusty old trophies.

"Then I found out I was pregnant." I watch Amanda's eyes widen. "I was terrified, but also...excited? It felt like proof of our love."

Amanda nods, her hand moving to her pregnant belly.

"But the baby...it didn't work out." I clear my throat, looking for the strength to relive those horrible moments. "There was a break-in at my mom's house while she was at work. I was attacked. I...I lost the child. Now I can never have one."

Once I'm finally through, Amanda sits back and blinks her big blue eyes at me. "Is it possible Mr. Blessed is the one who attacked you?"

The comment, innocent enough, taps into the molten-lava core of my psyche. Any other day, I might've broken down crying right there in front of my camper.

Of course I'd considered the possibility. I'd almost told the police about my relationship with Mr. Blessed. But the idea that he would've orchestrated or participated in my attack hurts too much to take seriously, even now that I've pegged him as a sociopath.

Yep, that's me. The ostrich, blindfolded, with its head deep in the sand.

I loved him. Maybe…part of me still does.

And a break-in gone wrong makes more sense anyway. The men who attacked me made off with my mom's jewelry, and there was no way Mr. Blessed would've stooped that low.

He had principle. He was distinguished. He was—

"Ms. Silva?" Amanda turns up her palms. "Have you considered it?"

I shake my head, casting my eyes downward. "It wasn't him."

She shrugs, like *whatever*, and sits back in her chair. "Can I go now?"

"Soon." I let out a deep sigh. "I'm not done with my story yet."

Amanda rolls her eyes. I grit my teeth at her ability to perfectly portray teenage entitlement, even when faced with the deepest, darkest secrets of the adults she's supposed to respect.

From here, I'm headed toward an emotional retelling of how the drama of my teenage life has impacted my marriage in the present day.

My hope is to turn the conversation toward Arthur, to open to a picture of him on my phone, and to gauge Amanda's reaction when she sees it—us. Together, happy, with so much of our lives before us. But Amanda beats me to it.

She cocks her head and poses her final question like Lesley

Stahl on *60 Minutes*. "How come you call your ex 'Mr. Blessed' instead of using his first name?"

"That's easy. Because he was my teacher. And that's what he wanted to be called."

Amanda nods. "Makes sense." A dreamy smile softens her expression, though her eyes tell a different story. They're watching me closely. "I call my man Mr. Yuen."

CHAPTER
THIRTY-EIGHT

Everything makes sense now, even if it's painful. At least I no longer need to pretend. The realization that Arthur is just like all the other men I've known brings an unexpected calm. As I breathe in deeply and exhale, my anxiety begins to dissolve.

I meet Amanda's gaze and prepare myself for a difficult conversation. She knows me only by my maiden name, so she might not be aware of my connection to her lover. There's no choice but to be direct.

"Arthur Yuen?" I have to confirm.

She lifts her chin. "Yes."

"Do you know Mr. Yuen's my husband?"

She glances down and blinks away tears. Several escape, gliding down her marble skin. "I figured it out a few days ago."

Amanda's tears confirm the vulnerability I'd suspected lurked beneath her guardedness. To say I see myself in her would be an understatement.

She and I are not only connected by the shared trauma of teenage pregnancy and inappropriate relationships with older men. We've both been manipulated and lied to by Arthur Yuen.

"What Mr. Yuen did to you is wrong, and if we don't stop him now, he's going to do it to someone else."

Amanda picks at a worn spot on the arm of her chair, pulling at a loose thread and then scratching at the torn fabric beneath. She's gathered her legs under her body, so her pregnant belly protrudes more than normal.

I hear commotion out my window. Yolanda's leading the girls from cabin twelve out of the forest and back toward camp. She's wearing a beige safari hat, and the girls are taking turns trying to grab it off her head. They're so young, playing like puppies out in the field.

Resting her hand on her belly, Amanda squeezes her eyes shut. The juxtaposition weighs heavy on me. I offer her a sip of water or seltzer from my mini fridge, and she declines both.

"Amanda?" At the sound of her name, she lifts her chin an inch in my direction. "Out of all the camps in the country, how did your parents decide to send you to Wildfire? So close to my…to Mr. Yuen."

"He's the one who told me about it. We…we've been able to get together a few times since I've been here."

My mind conjures images of Arthur leaving the house after fights with me to "go to the cabin." He pulls up to the edge of camp and kills the lights on his truck, waiting for Amanda to slink out of her cabin in short shorts and a hoodie.

They spend the night exploring each other's bodies in the back seat before he deposits her back at *my camp* with a dumb smile on her face.

My cortisol spikes. I want to grab Arthur by the neck and strangle him in broad daylight.

I'm grateful Amanda doesn't clock the rage as my nostrils flare, and I cover it up with a tiny cough.

"I don't want you to be mad." The look in Amanda's bloodshot eyes screams of sincerity, however deluded she might be.

"I'm not mad. I'm furious, but not with you. You can tell me anything, Amanda. I'm here for you."

"It's just…" She once again picks at the armchair. "He says he wants to have this baby with me. He wants a family. With me."

Her words sting, an unexpected blow that sends ripples of pain through my chest. I pause, needing a moment to collect myself as the reality of their plans hits home. It's a harsh reminder of the life I almost had with Arthur.

A life now being offered to someone else. A child.

Amanda breaks the silence with a soft, mouselike apology. She tells me she had to tell me the truth, and that I deserve her honesty, "woman to woman."

I fight back a loud, insulted guffaw when she hits me with the "woman to woman" line, nearly losing my grip on my empathy. But this child is not my enemy. She's a victim, just like I once was, and it's my duty to help her.

Looking into her eyes, seeing her raw honesty, anchors me.

I have a duty, so I step back from the edge to remain the responsible adult in the conversation.

"As a mandated reporter, I'm required to inform authorities of inappropriate conduct involving a minor, in any form, to the authorities. This conversation, like all the others we've had, is being recorded for everyone's protection and in case situations like this arise."

I remind Amanda that both she and her parents consented to these recordings on her intake form.

Her mouth gapes, and her face turns red. "You can't do that!"

Though tempted, I refrain from informing the young woman that Mr. Yuen should've considered these implications before sending her to therapy with his wife.

"I don't have a choice."

Resisting the urge to give Amanda any openings to protest, I grab a cold bottled water and set it on the coffee table in front of her with a comforting smile. Then I excuse myself and slip into the hallway to call the police, instructing Amanda to remain in the office as I shut the door.

CHAPTER
THIRTY-NINE

I step into an empty activity room, leaving the door slightly ajar, and lean against the rough, exposed-brick wall near the entrance. From this position, I have a clear view of my office, allowing me to keep watch for any signs of Amanda trying to escape.

Chief of Police Roland Prentice already sounds annoyed, though we've been on the phone for less than a minute. "Explain why I can't bring Will in on this. That's all I need."

I look back at the office where Amanda's waiting and reply with a lowered voice, "Because this crime is directly related to a member of his family. I can't say this more clearly, Chief Prentice."

"You're lucky he wasn't the one who picked up your call."

"That's why I called your direct line. Do I have your word or not?"

Chief Prentice sighs, and I can almost hear his eyes rolling back in his head. "Okay, fine. What is it, Lizette?" He then clears his throat, his voice dropping. "This about Artie?"

Closing my eyes, I see Myer Whitley using the same pet

name for my husband. *Artie.* Like the predator I'd married is an innocent kid playing stickball out in the tall grasses.

"His name is Arthur."

"Just come out with it. What's goin' on?"

I look around. The walls are lined with bad teenage art. A day-old box of doughnuts. Dirty coffee cups with dried drips down the sides. A stack of empty coke cans. This activity room is exactly the kind of place where horrible secrets are revealed.

Over the next several minutes, I recount everything Amanda told me. "I have an audio recording of Amanda confessing her relationship with Arthur, but you'll need to get a warrant before I can release it."

The chief groans like he's in agony. "This is your husband, Lizette."

"Was. Or will have been."

"Lizette—"

"No. Nuh-uh. He's a danger to a minor who's currently living in your jurisdiction." I press my lips together, afraid my emotions might peek through.

"Liz—"

"I'm going to contact CPS as soon as I'm off with you. They're going to notify the parents. But the Hollands are in Asia for work, so I'm going to request that Camp Wildfire act as Miss Holland's guardians until they can get here. Should be fine. We have the paperwork to support it."

"Hold on a second." Prentice barks orders at someone.

"Are you going to take this seriously or not?" I look down the hall. My office door remains closed.

"Lizette, are you sure you want to do this?"

"Of course I don't want to do this, but he committed statutory rape. He needs to be arrested or brought in for questioning or something. Today."

"That...that's your husband."

"You already pointed that out." I take a deep breath and let it out. "But I refuse to let you bend the law because of that unfortunate reality. And Arthur's brother being on the force shouldn't change things either."

Prentice grumbles in reluctant agreement, and we end the call.

I pocket my phone as I head for the door. Just as I step into the hallway, Yolanda hurries toward me.

"Good, you're still here." She pants and doubles over. "What were you doing in the activity room? You look pale."

A knot forms in my stomach as I take in her distressed state. Something else has gone wrong. "You don't look so great yourself. What's going on?"

She straightens and runs a shaky hand through her hair, struggling to collect herself. "Madeline...she's been acting weird lately, all paranoid and secretive."

My jaw tightens. "And...?"

"She's missing." Yolanda tosses her hands up. "I started noticing her strange behavior for, well, since she got here. But now...now she's just gone."

The knot in my stomach constricts as images of Madeline abducted in the forest flash through my mind.

"Okay. She probably hitched a ride into town and tried to find some idiot to buy her beer. It's not the first time this has happened, and it won't be the last."

Yolanda slightly relaxes her shoulders, nodding aggressively. "Okay. That's what I think too. That's what I've been telling myself."

"What do you mean, that's what you've been telling yourself? How long was she out of your sight?" I take a breath and bring my tone back to even. "Tell me what happened. Please. Madeline was under your care on my day off."

Yolanda wrings her hands, and her head swivels around

the hall, as if she's looking for someone in an imaginary audience to offer her a lifeline.

"Yolanda." I step into her field of vision and take her hands in mine. "Talk."

Once she gets over her nerves, she spills everything that happened over the past twenty-four hours. She bloats the story with irrelevant details—what she ate for lunch, which girls paired off for activities the day before—before getting to the important facts.

Madeline didn't join Yolanda and the others on the camping trip out to the lake the prior night. She'd stayed back at cabin twelve instead, complaining of a migraine and insisting she needed the comfort of a bed to recover.

Yolanda claims Jonathan said it was okay and asks several times if she's going to lose her job over this.

Taking one problem at a time, I call in Jonathan from his office and fill him in on the situation. He confirms that he gave Madeline permission to hang back and is careful to take responsibility, which sets Yolanda at ease.

He and I take turns asking Yolanda a series of important questions. Though I agree that Jonathan ultimately bears responsibility, each of Yolanda's answers adds to my anger.

Yolanda didn't learn Madeline was missing from cabin twelve until she arrived back at camp from the lake. She has no clear picture of how long Madeline has been gone. And her preoccupation with her job security leaves a bitter taste in my mouth.

As we talk, Jonathan tries to lead us into his office, but I keep the conversation in the hallway so I can keep an eye on Amanda. "Yolanda, you need to circulate around camp, find out what the other girls know. Start in cabin twelve and widen it out from there. Can you do that?"

She nods and hurries out, apologizing.

"You want me to call the police?" I ask, clenching and unclenching my fist.

Jonathan shakes his head. "Let's start by searching camp ourselves and see what we can turn up. If we don't find her soon, we get the police involved."

A small wave of relief washes over me, just enough to steady my breath. "Are you sure?"

"I mean, how many Madelines have pulled this stunt before?" he says. "They always turn up, and we've never brought the cops into the mix in the past. If we do, they create a report, and it's a whole thing…"

This is the perfect moment for me to bring him up to speed on the Amanda situation. The camp's reputation is so delicate. "Incidents" like these can ruin us. But as I open my mouth to get it over with, Yolanda hurries back and calls Jonathan away.

"Jonathan, wait," I say as he hurries out.

He turns back.

"Um…" *I can't stay and search for the missing camper because I need to go home and watch as my husband is dragged away by police.* "I, um, I…have to take care of something at home. I want to help, but—"

"Madeline's going to turn up any minute. You do what you need to do."

"Are you sure?"

He gives a little salute. "Everything's going to be fine. I promise."

Once Jonathan is out of sight, I make a quick call to Child Protective Services about the Amanda situation. They need documentation to coordinate a plan with the police department. But they say Camp Wildfire will be permitted to continue care of Amanda in her parents' absence as soon as we forward over the necessary paperwork, which is all part of our intake process.

CPS also makes it clear a paternity test will be a necessary part of the process, either now or down the line. I make a mental note to talk to Amanda about it, and, if she agrees, to get her in for the test as soon as possible.

If she doesn't agree? That's a different story.

The faster we get that paternity test, the sooner Arthur will be conclusively proven guilty, and I'm glad Amanda will be under our care at Camp Wildfire until then.

I enter my office to find Amanda lounging in the armchair, flipping through a magazine. She looks up, and I close the door quietly behind me.

"You can go back to your cabin now."

"For real?" Her eyebrows lift slightly as she leans in. "What happened?"

"I informed the police and CPS, and I'll keep you updated, okay?" I don't mention the paternity test, but I mentally schedule it for sometime in the next twenty-four hours. Hopeful thinking? Probably. But it's all I've got.

Amanda gets to her feet with a groan. She pauses before she leaves my office. I'm shocked she's not crying or screaming or hitting me.

We both know her days with Mr. Yuen are over.

CHAPTER
FORTY

Imagining Arthur cuffed and behind bars fills me with dread. I drive home with the windows down, hoping the gusts of hot afternoon air will distract me.

My tires rumble against the asphalt, the vibration settling deep in my bones. As I speed past, a family of deer turns away from a patch of berries, startled by my sudden intrusion. I envy them—their ability to escape danger so effortlessly. My own life feels like it's hurtling down a one-way road with no exits in sight.

A huge, anvil-shaped cloud hangs high in the sky, foreboding, like something straight out of a cartoon, waiting to drop. I almost laugh—how perfect. An anvil, of all things. Irony personified. I'm living in a twisted joke, where the punchline is my own husband's betrayal.

That cloud looks like it's ready to crush everything beneath it, and I wonder if it's the universe trying to warn me—or mock me. Is this what Wile E. Coyote felt right before the anvil dropped? Knowing something heavy and inevitable was coming but powerless to stop it? And here I am, speeding toward the truth, about to be flattened.

Thoughts ricochet around my mind, bouncing between Arthur, Amanda, Madeline, and the looming police investigation. Anxiety pulses through every cell in my body as I tap the steering wheel.

Halfway home, I realize I opted to keep Jonathan out of the loop, but that others might clue him in on Arthur before I get the chance. "Chief Prentice wouldn't call Jonathan before me, would he? It's Jonathan's camp, but…no. He'd give me the chance to tell my own boss."

My knuckles whiten on the wheel.

"I should've seen Arthur for the creep he is the day we got married. Smug smile. Stupid-ass tuxedo."

My spinning mind passes the minutes at three times the normal speed, and I'm soon shocked to find myself pulling into my driveway. Several clouds darken the sun, and Arthur sits on the front steps, blanketed in the summer gray sky.

He's clutching that light-blue teddy bear that has gone to bed with us every night for the last six months. For Arthur it's a symbol of hope, for me a reminder of my lies.

The way Arthur squeezes the teddy bear thickens my hatred for him. No shit he chose a teenager over me. He's still a baby himself.

I slam the car door harder than intended and cross toward him, stopping in the front yard. The grass is cold and wet from the sprinklers. I step onto the front path and stare at him and his little teddy for a minute straight.

When I speak, my voice drips with hatred. "Your mom gave you that teddy bear the night you told her we were trying."

His fingers stroke the plush fur, but he says nothing.

I ignore the muted plea for sympathy. "I was so mad at you for telling your whole family our private life. It was… manipulative."

He finally looks at me. "You never said that."

"I was too caught up in my own shit to worry about yours." I step closer to him. "You never asked what was wrong anyway. Never wanted to know how that stupid bear ended up on the floor every morning. I threw it there after you fell asleep. Every night."

Arthur pulls the teddy bear closer to his chest and smooths the hair on its forehead. The way he takes care of the thing—like it's a real child—repulses me. "You're starting another fight because you don't want to talk about your lies."

I let out a short, loud cackle before reining in my feelings. I'll never get through to him if I shout or act in a way that he'll define as crazy. I must be calm. I must keep my shit together.

"How many girls did you hurt at Whitley's apartment, Arthur?" I'm proud of how soft my voice is. "You want to talk about lies, let's start there."

"Okay."

His voice is firm, even honest. *This is all part of his con.* I decide to give him enough rope to finish himself with and gesture for him to talk.

"I've always known you had, like, a bad relationship with your past," he says. "That's one thing neither of us lied to ourselves or each other about."

That's true, and I acknowledge it with a nod.

He sits up a little straighter. "The mistake, for me, was that I used your tragedies as, like, a shield. I decided I didn't have to be honest about my past because yours was so sensitive. That wasn't right."

Fury flares, and I tamp it down, forcing myself to breathe.

Arthur's voice grows tender as he continues. "You're right about Whitley's apartment. I mean...we did some messed-up shit up there. 'Boys will be boys' doesn't even start to cover it. I was...we were...we were like an unofficial fraternity, but we weren't even eighteen."

I believe him. But Arthur's seemingly genuine revelations

about the past have nothing to do with his present-day transgressions or his abuse of Amanda Holland. I wait, expecting him to keep deflecting, avoiding the ultimate truth until he sees it in my face.

I already know what you did, but please, keep talking.

"Looking back, I don't recognize who I was then. I've read a lot about it, about how teenage boys are thrill-seekers or whatever. It's a trait of the developing brain. But that hasn't helped me feel any better about who I was then."

I scoff. *Every teenage boy and girl has an undeveloped brain.*

"We had girls over and…I mean…sometimes they were so out of it and consent, like, wasn't a thing then. I don't know. I didn't understand how messed up it was for years, until after you and I were together."

I don't believe him.

He sets the teddy bear down on the top step and stands. "Once you and I got together, after you moved back from college, I knew I was done with all the shit I used to do. Cut Whitley out of my life completely. Changed into a man that somebody as incredible as you could love."

Sounds great. But how about you fast-forward to the part where you impregnated a teenager? My heart wants me to scream the question, but I keep my mouth shut.

He takes a step toward me, looking at me the way he did when I walked down the aisle. "I love you, Lizette. And I get it, I understand why you didn't tell me what had happened to you. I mean…I can't imagine how hard all this fertility stuff must've been for you." He licks his lips. "We can adopt if you want, or we can get a surrogate. It doesn't matter, as long as I have you."

Arthur's gaze drifts past me and narrows at something in the distance.

I hear it too—the low rumble of engines growing louder.

Not the wail of sirens, just the muted pulse of urgency, like a heartbeat closing in. The police cruisers turn onto our street, red-and-blue lights flashing across our front yard.

Arthur's face tightens, his jaw clenching, and he takes a half step back, his body rigid. His eyes dart from the cruisers to me, panic creeping into his features. For a moment, he looks like a trapped animal, and I almost feel a sting of pity.

Almost.

Moving in slow motion, Arthur turns toward me, blinking.

I'm afraid I might cry, but I fight tears back with tight lips and squeezed fists. "I know about you and Amanda Holland."

The flash of recognition on my husband's face is all I need just before Chief Prentice parks the cruiser, steps out, and walks toward us.

Arthur's mouth hangs agape. For a moment, a flash of self-preservation dilutes the shame and sorrow on his face.

As Chief Prentice leads him away for the interrogation, Arthur's gaze stays locked on mine. A pathetic plea flickers behind the sullen resolve in his eyes. Some part of him must've known this reckoning was inevitable, yet he still balks at facing its harsh reality.

I hold his stare, refusing to let guilt and sorrow break my stoic exterior. All I allow is the faintest quiver of my lip as they pull him into the back seat.

His eyes are glossy and half open, focused yet disoriented. While it hurts me to see him like that, it also brings me indescribable satisfaction.

Mr. Blessed didn't suffer for a second because of what he did to me, but Arthur will never hurt another teenage girl.

Soon, the police cars are pulling away, I'm sure watched through many windows by nosy neighbors. This means my broken marriage—and all the horrible facts I've been blind to—will soon be the talk of the town.

A small tax on a new life, more than worth paying.

My phone rings as the squad cars turn the corner and disappear. It's Jonathan. Turning away from the building crowd and walking toward the house, I answer and press the phone to my ear.

"Liz, we...we can't find Madeline." His voice is tight with worry. "We're going to have to involve the police."

CHAPTER
FORTY-ONE

"Only three cop cars? For a missing fourteen-year-old girl?" I park and head toward the main building. I'd spent the rest of the drive going ten miles above the speed limit, desperate to get to camp and help.

Not much help here.

My feet crunch over the gravel lot as I charge forward, a plume of dust rising behind me. I spoke with Jonathan in more detail on the drive over, and he informed me he was keeping the campers in the cafeteria until the police let everyone know it was safe to return to the cabins.

I'd given him a quick headline on what happened with Arthur, freaked out he'd learn about the affair from the cops before getting it from me, but it seemed like his brain was too full to truly comprehend what I'd said.

Stepping into the cafeteria, I find all ninety-nine remaining campers sitting, bored, at the dining tables. Madeline is a notable absence.

The cafeteria reeks of old lunches and damp wood, and a low murmur of hushed voices punctuates the occasional scrape of chair legs on linoleum.

The campers' faces are pale and drawn. And their eyes dart toward the door every time it creaks open, as if they're expecting Madeline to enter at any moment. Or maybe their parents. They'd all been encouraged to call home while I was away.

I move through the rows of tables, my footsteps echoing. Amanda makes eye contact, but I look away. Right now, I need to put the Arthur situation aside. There's a sea of anxious faces before me. They're all vulnerable, and they all need my help.

Each time I pass a table, I stop and let the girls know I'm here if they need to talk. We discuss coping mechanisms in times of stress, and I do what I can to let the campers know they're safe here with police supervision.

In the corner, I spot Jonathan, his expression grim as he surveys the room. He catches my eye, and an unspoken understanding passes between us—something is very wrong, and we are the only ones who can set it right.

The weight of this responsibility presses down on me, intensifying the suffocating atmosphere.

I meet Jonathan under the American flag in the far corner of the room. "Have you checked the security cameras?"

He shakes his head. "You're the only one who knows how to operate the system. They wanted to get out into the forest as soon as possible, but they'll want to review the footage later, for sure."

Jonathan's eyes flicker with desperation before he restores a facade of strength and perseverance. But that flicker is all I need to grasp just how hard he's taking this.

I hug him, and we share a deep breath together before stepping apart.

"This thing with Arthur...I'm so sorry. You doing okay?"

I give him a small nod but don't want to discuss it further.

"Are you fine in here right now? If you can hold it down, I can—"

"Check the cameras?" Jonathan manages a minuscule smile. "I promise...after all this...I'm going to get over my fear of technology. Maybe I'll even get a smartphone."

"Then I won't be able to make fun of you." I give him a reassuring touch on the elbow. "Call me if you need anything?"

He nods, and I hurry out of the cafeteria and toward my office, wringing my hands as I get closer to the truth.

Four tries, and I can't access the camp's CCTV system. This is the first time I've had to log on for months, but there's no way I've forgotten the log-on info, and no one else at camp is tech-savvy enough to change it.

I try once more. The system flashes and threatens to lock me out if I attempt to log on one more time and fail.

"Has the whole system been rebooted or something?" When I glance around my office, it's like I'm seeking someone to validate my experience. But no one's in here but me, my plants, and a growing sense of foreboding.

A search dog barks in the distance, and the hairs on my arms stand on end.

Finally, I give up and create a new username and password to access the camera system. After triple-confirming via codes sent to my phone and email, I'm in.

In a few clicks, I access the file folder for the past twenty-four hours, but when the folder opens, there are no individual files stored inside.

"What the hell? Not a single camera has recorded anything for an entire day?"

A police officer walks past my window. I avert my gaze and keep clicking through the folder. A tense fear grips the back of my neck. *Is this a horrible coincidence, or have our cameras been compromised?*

In three more clicks, I navigate out to the main folder where the files for the entire year are stored. There are plenty of files, but none for the previous forty-eight hours.

"That can't be..." I click out and then open the folder again, hoping for a miraculous change, scared that I did something to cause the files to disappear. Despite my prayers, the files are just...not there.

Seconds later, I dig through the virtual trash, but they're not there, either, and they're not hidden anywhere else on the laptop. For all intents and purposes, our CCTV footage is useless, and it will not be any help finding Madeline.

I sit back and think about what else I might be able to do to help. Jonathan hasn't called, so he's got things locked down in the cafeteria. And the police are handling the search out in Putnam Forest.

That means cabin twelve is empty.

I bite at my thumbnail, considering sneaking in there to search for evidence. Highly unlikely either Jonathan or Chief Prentice would sign off on the idea, but right now I'm rogue, and it's my duty to make the most of that.

The door to my office locks with a satisfying click, and I head down the hallway. This is my chance to make a difference for Madeline.

I hurry toward cabin twelve, breaking into a light jog after my first few steps outside. The overgrown grass swishes beneath my feet, sending a sweet, rotting scent into the air.

In the distance, search teams scan the forest, but I stay low and out of view as I run, moving like I have something to hide.

Wooden floorboards creak as I step past a strip of crime scene tape and enter cabin twelve. An unsettling stillness hangs in the air, and the cabin's usual chatter and laughter is now replaced by eerie quiet.

I pull out my phone, my fingers trembling as I check for a message that tells me Madeline has been found.

Staring at the screen, I will it to light up with good news, but there's nothing. No messages, no updates. Just an empty inbox and the increasing weight of dread settling in my chest.

I scan the empty cabin. The bunks are neatly made, each bed belonging to a terrified girl sitting with bated breath in the cafeteria. I scrutinize the room, hoping to find an overlooked detail that might lead us to Madeline.

The cabin offers no answers. It only echoes my fears. Outside, a gray cloud passes in front of the sun, and a shadow covers the camp. It's a reminder that seconds tick away, that we might be running out of time.

Madeline's name is written on construction paper above her bunk. I open the trunk at the foot of her bed and find a neat stack of clothing folded inside.

Sitting on the edge of the bed, I run my hands over the crisp white sheets. With a deep exhale, I lay back and close my eyes. My trip to Linden River feels like forever ago, and it's only gotten more chaotic from there.

My eyes burn so badly, I have no choice but to close them. Heavy bones pin me to the bed, and the desire for sleep seeps into my psyche like I've been hypnotized.

I sit up, blinking the sharp pain of fatigue away. "No sleep. Can't do that."

As I force my exhausted body out of Madeline's bed, something hard under a bottom corner presses against my palm.

Without thinking, I pull up the covers. There's nothing under the comforter, but something hard remains beneath the fitted sheet.

I pull up the sheet and, once again, nothing out of the ordinary meets my naked eye. But when I crouch, I spot a slit in the mattress, and when I reach into the slit, my fingers close around a small metal box buried between two springs.

I open the small box.

Inside is a vape pen, a smartphone with a black cover, and a small notebook. The vape pen is strawberry-banana flavored, and the phone won't power on.

As I grab the notebook, I'm brought back to the many journals I'd filled with private writing when I was Madeline's age. I lay the notebook on the bed and flip it open to the first page. There, in large, angry block letters is one simple message.

I am not alone.

CHAPTER
FORTY-TWO

I'm lost in Madeline's haunting message as voices approach the cabin. I stare at her secret phone, tempted to take it with me. I know I can find a charging cord, but being able to access the device is another matter. Tossing it back in the box, I leave it for the authorities to find. They'll have better luck hacking the password than I would.

In a few seconds, I've righted the bed, grabbed the notebook, and hurried toward the back door. It seals behind me with a quiet click as Yolanda leads a young cop through the front entrance, discussing what needs to be done to clear the bunk for the girls to return.

Suddenly I'm a fugitive at my own camp. I hadn't needed to leave the cabin, and the police would've accepted any one of dozens of reasons why I was in there. But I felt a need to escape, and now I'm hurrying across camp, looking for someplace to hide.

I'm uncharacteristically coordinated as I jog through the grass before breaking into a full-speed run, clutching Madeline's notebook tightly.

When I step into the forest, the smell of grass is replaced

by the sweet scent of decaying wood, and breaking branches crackle under my feet as I stumble deeper into seclusion.

I haven't been this alone in days, or perhaps in my entire life. But Madeline is with me, in the pages of this notebook and possibly somewhere in this forest.

Sitting on a fallen tree, I ignore a chorus of coyotes in the distance and open Madeline's notebook. The first page gives me pause, just as it did back in the cabin.

I am not alone.

Madeline must've used her secret phone to send that exact message to me.

But what had she wanted to accomplish with her cryptic note? And why had she sent it only to me?

I turn to the second page of the notebook to an Emily Dickenson poem written in angry, angular letters. Though it's only midafternoon, it's shady enough in the forest to make reading a chore.

Turning on my phone flashlight, I place the device close to the page. I recognize the poem's first line from an undergrad poetry class, "The Loneliness One dare not sound—" but the rest of the piece has been scratched out so completely that the page beneath it is torn.

My heart beats in my throat as I turn from one page to the next, hunting for some clue as to where Madeline might've gone...or been taken. Voices call out to each other back toward camp—cops searching around the bunks—and sweat dots my forehead.

I don't know why I'm embarking on this mission in secret. And if I were watching my actions in a movie theater, I'd be screaming at the girl on the screen to go someplace safe.

But all the worst things that have ever happened to me have taken place in my own home or with people I've loved, so I trust the unfamiliar now.

The notebook is a whirlwind of teenage angst. There are a

dozen half-finished stories, mostly about woodland creatures, guardian angels, and nymphs.

Then there are exercises I'd prescribed in therapy, including ten pages covered with the words *I love myself*, which hits different in this macabre light.

An old photograph has been taped onto a page in the middle. It shows two girls hugging one another. One is clearly recognizable as a young Madeline, no more than five or six years old.

The other girl is fifteen or sixteen, with gorgeous strawberry-blond hair. She's wearing a Camp Wildfire sweatshirt and smiling wide, squeezing young Madeline close under her arm. The girls are backlit, so there's a soft glow behind their heads.

Underneath the photo Madeline has scrawled a short letter.

Dear Kylie,

I know you never would've killed yourself. Someone hurt you. I'm going to find him, and I'm going to hurt him worse.

First you were my cousin. Then you were my angel. Now you're my guardian angel. Please look out for me. I miss you every day.

Love,

Madeline.

"No wonder Madeline was so obsessed with what happened back then," I mutter. "Kylie Boyd was her cousin."

From the notebook, it's clear Madeline believed Kylie's death was murder mislabeled as suicide, and she got herself sent to Camp Wildfire so she could finally solve that mystery.

It takes willpower, but eventually I pull myself away from Madeline's letter and continue through the rest of the notebook.

Much of the handwriting has been traced over so many times, it's illegible, but the words on the last page are perfectly clear. My throat tightens as I scan the letters, reading several times to make sure it's correct.

On the top of the page is a headline. "Murderers and Rapists," I say out loud. Below that are the names *Myer Whitley* and *Arthur Yuen*.

My hands tremble as I turn the notebook into the phone's light, hoping my eyes are deceiving me. But the names remain clear. I try to swallow, but my mouth is too dry.

Arthur had confessed to engaging in questionable activities at Whitley's place in high school. He'd painted his sexual exploits as less than consensual, but in that confusing, drunken, high school way.

It was all unforgivable. But it had fallen far short of murder, far short of true evil.

As I lower the notebook to my lap, I see that the other side of the page bears the names of three women written in all caps.

REGINA SMITH.
KYLIE BOYD.
LIZETTE SILVA.

My phone light shakes in my hand as I read my name plainly written in the notebook.

Did Madeline know something about my childhood trauma that I don't? And what does it all have to do with Arthur, if anything?

I'd suspected my attack could have been committed by the same men who hurt Regina and Kylie. Now I'm almost sure of it.

Back at camp, another dog barks as a police ATV speeds past the cabins. I stand, unsure if my plan is to walk back to camp or farther into the forest, but my legs wobble and threaten to give out beneath me.

My heart aches with a sharp, twisting pain that leaves me breathless. I squeeze my eyes shut, willing the nightmare to end, but when I open them again, the words are still there. My name is still there.

The air in the forest is thick and suffocating. My breath comes in short, panicked gasps as the enormity of the situation settles over me.

As I return to my seat on the fallen tree, I flip through the notebook to the last page. There, I find a series of hand-drawn maps leading from cabin twelve out into Putnam, alongside scribbled labels like *Sleeping Man Rock*, *Smoking Willow*, and *Chair Mountain*.

Scanning the maps, I cross-reference Madeline's scribbled maps with what Maggie Gilford at the plant shop told me about where the police found Regina's locket a decade prior.

I stand with new strength in my legs, peering into the treetops with a cold resolve settling on my shoulders.

"Madeline was hunting for Regina Smith's body."

CHAPTER
FORTY-THREE

Recent rainfall has left Putnam with its insides showing, and it's impossible for me to walk more than a few steps without landing in several inches of space-black mud or standing water.

I call out for Madeline every minute or so. Other than that, I only hear the sucking sound of my sneakers in the mud. I should've worn my duck boots. But when I woke up this morning, I had no idea that by early evening I'd be following a missing camper's map deep into the forest.

Few people know the trails beyond Camp Wildfire better than me. The familiarity of the paths brings a small comfort, but today, even the familiar is threatening.

The air is thick with damp earth and rotting leaves.

Madeline's first set of directions start at camp and lead to Sleeping Man Rock. I know the rock because I'm the one who gave it that name, based on its unique structure that forms the outline of a sleeping man.

Despite the mud, I make it out to the rock in no more than ten minutes and follow Madeline's directions to go left.

I walk confidently for a few minutes, following the new,

less muddy trail with solid footsteps. At the next landmark, I pause and look around the dense underbrush.

Sunlight catches on the glistening leaves of ivy that twist and climb up the trunk of an old tree. I curse at the sight of the invasive species, choking the life out of everything good.

A distant rustling makes me freeze.

I spin toward the sound. Sunlight filters through the canopy, casting shifting shadows that play tricks on my eyes. What looked like a person melts into the dappled green darkness. My pulse pounds in my ears as I lean forward, the deceptive interplay of light and shadow unsettling.

The police are out here searching too. But the forest is huge, and I can't hear or see another soul around me.

When I step forward again, my foot sinks deep into a patch of mud, the cold, wet grip pulling at my sneaker as if trying to bring me to my knees. I yank my foot free with a grunt, and the mud seeps into my sock and onto my skin.

I grit my teeth against the discomfort and continue.

My mind races with fear, anger, and a hope that I'm not too late. When my phone buzzes, my heart leaps, but it's just a notification. Less than five percent battery life remains.

Dread settles in my stomach. My phone is my lifeline to the world outside this forest, and I need it to stay safe.

I'm on the verge of a total meltdown—convinced I've lost Madeline's trail—when I break through a dense thicket and stumble into a clearing.

The soft, melancholic coo of a mourning dove echoes. Its haunting call, usually background noise, seems amplified in the silence.

I hold my breath and scan the area. There, at the edge of the clearing, is a small, weathered marker. I hurry over and crouch to examine it.

It's a wooden cross. I assume I'm not lost after all and that the cross was made by Madeline. But I can't be sure, and I'm struck by the sensation that someone is with me out in the woods.

I turn in all directions. The afternoon sun creates deep shadows beneath the trees, transforming familiar shapes into menacing silhouettes. My eyes dart around, catching the shimmer of water trickling toward me from the nearby hills.

Regina went missing during the wet season, and although police dogs had led search teams to high ground, it's possible one of these mountain streams carried her locket to this very spot.

By this point, Madeline's maps are wet and stained with mud from my hands. I flip through the pages, frantically moving from one map to another and trying to compare them in my mind.

That's when I spot an important discrepancy.

"These maps are tracing two different paths to this spot. Coming from two different starting points."

Did Madeline suspect Whitley had an accomplice the night Regina Smith died? *And could that second killer have been my husband?*

"Maybe the killer dragged the body through here, and the locket got lost along the way."

But where would he have been going?

Thinking back to my explorations through the wilds of Putnam Forest, I recall an overgrown footpath not far from here that connects all the way to my house in Wildfire proper.

My feet are headed there before my brain makes the decision to go.

Less than five minutes down the old path, a snarling animal catches my attention. I pivot, seeking the source of the sound. It's so loud, as if it's coming from all around me.

The snarl is interrupted by the sound of tearing flesh and the crunch of bones.

My heart races. It's still a couple hours before a coyote's

usual feeding time, but they're opportunistic feeders and will eat whatever they find, no matter the hour. I take solace in the sound of its eating—content as long as it hasn't noticed me.

Yet.

I nearly turn away until a horrible thought occurs to me. As much as I don't want to see what the animal is eating...I have to. A girl is missing.

Please, God, no.

Continuing in a slow, careful circle, I hunt for the coyote. Where is it?

I nearly complete a full turn before I spot it. Almost camouflaged among the shadows, a coyote stands, thin and wiry, its fur matted and patchy. Its pointy ears twitch, its attention fixed on something just beyond my line of sight.

I press a hand to my stomach. The fur around its mouth is wet and dark, glistening in the dappled sunlight—blood. Fresh blood.

Pushing through the fear—hesitation could be deadly—I take a step toward the animal, raise my arms above my head, and scream as loud as I can.

The coyote jerks its head, startled, and for a second, its gaze meets mine—hungry, defiant, unafraid. Every heartbeat seems to stretch forever before the animal bolts into the thick brush and vanishes into the trees. Silence rushes back, heavier than before, pressing down on me from all sides.

As I catch my breath, my gaze falls on the coyote's meal. A flash of pale skin and the red stain of blood—so much blood.

I move closer, my feet moving as if through water, heavier with each step. My eyes focus, and a wave of cold weight crashes over me. A young woman lies on the ground, her body twisted at an unnatural angle. Her throat is a jagged red line, her stomach torn open, entrails spilling onto the forest floor.

It's Madeline Miller.

I stagger back, a scream clawing its way up my throat. My

legs give way, and I fall to my knees, the impact jarring, but I barely feel it. The air is thick with the cloying scent of blood and decay. It's a foul mix that makes my stomach turn. Bile rises in my throat, and I fight the urge to retch.

My vision blurs, and I blink hard, forcing myself to look at her. Madeline. Dead. Mutilated. Her lifeless eyes stare blankly at the forest canopy as flies feast on what little moisture remains.

As horrible as what's in front of me is, a sickening realization twists inside me, leaving me breathless. A girl is dead at Camp Wildfire, and somehow, some way, I know—I just know—I'm connected to this.

The coyote's bloody muzzle flashes in my mind, and I shudder, dread settling deep in my bones. I should have been here sooner. I should have found her. But now it's too late.

Far too late.

CHAPTER
FORTY-FOUR

Nearly three hours have passed since I discovered Madeline Miller's body.

Now, as evening falls closer to night, I find myself at the police station, a headache growing under harsh fluorescent lights. My husband sits in a cell somewhere close by.

The air-conditioning chills my skin, but the shiver running down my spine has little to do with the temperature.

As I await my interview, the weight of Madeline's death presses down on me. The image of her lifeless body, ravaged by the coyote, is seared into my mind. I don't know how I'll ever shake the gruesome memory.

Heavy footsteps jolt me from my thoughts, and I glance up as Will approaches. He moves with the weariness of a man burdened by the weight of his own secrets, his once-vibrant eyes dull and insincere.

Though he's only four minutes older than Arthur, at the moment, Will looks beyond his age. His formerly athletic frame has been softened by years of neglect. His jawline has disappeared beneath a layer of stubble and exhaustion, and the dark circles under his eyes have circles of their own.

DON'T TELL

He sits beside me and wraps me in an enormous hug, his arms warm and firm. It's our first embrace in years—maybe since he was best man at my wedding—and while it's strange, the hug offers an unexpected comfort.

There's a softness in his gaze I've never seen before.

Is this moment real? Or is it another Yuen brother manipulation?

"Sorry for the wait. It's been crazy here." Will releases me, his hand lingering on my shoulder. "Come on back. I'll try to make this quick."

Quick? I've been waiting here for hours.

I swallow my snark but can't help my disbelieving tone. "You're interviewing me? Isn't that a conflict of interest?"

"Yeah…I mean, this isn't an interview. Not officially. I figured you'd prefer a familiar face, before the chief sits down with you and takes a statement. Everyone else is tied up. But if you want—"

"No, it's fine. Let's get it over with."

He nods. "But, hey, uh, everything's recorded in the interview room. So, uh, you and me, we're gonna talk out in the hall."

Will heads down a long corridor, with me a few feet behind him. Once we're alone at the far end of the hall, the mask falls.

"Some bullshit, you accusing Arthur of this."

I laugh in his face. "The girl told me he did it, Will. You're going to have to accept that, because it's gonna be a long road for him."

Will leans forward, speaking under his breath. "My brother was not *grooming* some teenage girl, Lizette."

He says the word *grooming* like it's preposterous.

I repeat myself, talking slow and loud, like Will's the idiot he is. "She. Told. Me. He. Did. It."

"Whatever, but—"

"'Believe women,' ever heard of that? She straight-up told me 'I call my man Mr. Yuen.'" I shake my head, a realization hitting me. "I guess that means you were lying about that phone, then. Covering for him."

Will's face flushes red, hopefully from deep-seated familial shame. "I haven't told you any lies."

"Whatever you say, man." I stand a little straighter, pulling my purse close to my body. "Was there something else you wanted to ask me about, or can I wait for the chief inside?"

I move toward the interview room.

He steps in front of me. "Wait."

I pause, and we make eye contact. "What?"

"You gotta just...tell me what happened at the camp today. Why'd you run into the forest? And what's up with that notebook?"

"The police confiscated it. Why don't you take a look?"

Will looks down sheepishly.

I laugh. Of course they don't let him access important pieces of evidence like that. I should've known.

"Just tell me, Lizette. And be honest."

His condescending tone pisses me off. "You want honesty?"

He shrugs.

"Let's talk about you, then." I fix a steady gaze on him. "You and Myer Whitley were tight in high school, right?"

"We're not talking about me." He shakes his head like there's water in his ear. "I'm not the one who was found next to a dead girl's body in the woods."

I ignore him and continue my train of thought. "Honestly, I'm probably the only person in Wildfire who didn't know you and Arthur were close with Whitley. Guy's kind of a monster, though, isn't that correct?"

"Lizette, I'm going to ask you to please stay on topic."

"Oh, but this is on topic. The notebook your little officer

confiscated from me had Myer Whitley's name in it. Madeline was pretty convinced your little pal was a killer and a rapist on top of being a terrible thief."

Will laughs. It's a jock-like chuckle that would make sense in a high school locker room setting, but not here. "Lots of people hung out at Whitley's place in high school. You'd get that if you were a true local."

"The longer I live here, the happier I am I left for the time that I did. This place is kinda fucked. Don't you think?"

He hits me with another all-American laugh. The smile makes his face fifteen years younger, but there's no helping that beer belly or the fear behind his eyes.

"Does Vicky know about the girls you and Arthur used to bring back to Whitley's place? Does she know Regina Smith was one of them? I bet she'd like the details."

I make a small leap by including Regina among the campers who hung at Whitley's place, but the timelines make sense together, and my instincts tell me to push forward with the theory.

Will trips over his own tongue before getting a full syllable out. "I-I...um. I don't—"

I bulldoze over him. "But why did Regina have to die? That's what I'm trying to figure out."

"No clue what you're talkin' about. For all I know, that girl is still alive." He clears his throat. "Mind if maybe you answer my question now? A camper was killed under y'all's supervision."

I raise an eyebrow. "I bet you have no clue what happened with Kylie Boyd either. Were you and Arthur involved with her 'suicide?' Or just with the cover-up?"

Will's Adam's apple pulses as he swallows a big breath. Though neither Whitley nor Hazel implicated him, the realization of his involvement overwhelms me.

Arthur had deeply admired his twin brother back in high

school, and there was no way Will hadn't pulled him into the depravity.

My brother-in-law hits me with a forceful look, every muscle in his body tense like a snake ready to strike. I'm beginning to worry he might throttle me.

Fear and adrenaline set my nerves on fire. I meet Will's gaze, steeling myself for the possibility of a physical confrontation. Though I'm confident in my ability to defend myself, the thought of testing that belief against Will's rage, strength, and training is far from appealing.

He breaks the silence with a thick, derisive laugh, heavy with every cigarette he's smoked behind his wife's back. "You're aware you don't know what you're talkin' about, right?"

I wrinkle my nose and give him a small nod. "Pretty sure I do."

"But you don't, Liz." He sucks spit through his teeth like he's a cowboy. "Only evidence against your husband is the accusation of a disturbed young woman who was being coerced and secretly recorded by her hysterical therapist."

"The recordings were not a secret. And I'm not—"

He holds up a finger. I hate that it silences me immediately. "Artie's already been released. And he's going to stay that way until we secure warrants for your patient files and run a paternity test on your lying little camper."

"Amanda Holland is not—"

"Unless a paternity test confirms my brother knocked up that girl," he shouts in my face, "he's never going to see the inside of a jail cell."

I lean in, my voice low and steely. "The truth always surfaces, Will. And when it does, no one, not even you, will escape its reach."

CHAPTER
FORTY-FIVE

Chief Roland Prentice approaches, coffee cup in hand, as Will and I wait outside the interview room. He's wearing jeans and a rumpled button-down. His once deep-black hair is now peppered with silver, and his expanded waistline strains against the confines of his wrinkled shirt.

Both Will and I straighten our postures. Will opens the interview room door and gestures me inside. Avoiding Will's glower, I step into the room.

Chief Prentice follows me in, and we each take a seat at a metal table in the center of the room. He gets comfortable, straightening his coffee cup and clearing his throat with authority. Will hovers at the open door, watching.

The chief turns to him with tired eyes, squinting against the overheads. "Officer Yuen, you're dismissed."

Will hesitates before exiting without a word.

The door clicks shut, and Prentice turns back to me with arched eyebrows. "Okay, then."

Prentice starts the recording and recites the standard police preamble. The formal procedure is at odds with my memories of him. Back in high school, he was always waiting for his daughter after dismissal with a soda and huge, goofy smile. Now he's a different man entirely.

He lifts a hand, palm up, and invites me to tell my story. But I need to know that Will isn't standing outside listening through the door, so I stand up and open it, peering into the corridor.

The hallway's empty.

I close the door and resume my seat. "Sorry. Just...nervous, I guess. Will said some things I didn't want to hear."

"He's concerned about his brother."

I lift my chin. "And that's a massive conflict of interest."

"Spare me the soapbox." His lips press into a thin line. "Officer Yuen is gone now, right?"

I glance around, searching for a two-way mirror, just to be sure he isn't watching me from the other side. Seeing none, my shoulders drop—if only a little.

Chief Prentice winks, a brief spark of camaraderie. "Bet he didn't even thank you, did he?"

Huh?

"Thank me for what?"

"You found the missing girl. Got ahold of her secret notebook. Accomplished more in an hour or two than my officers managed all afternoon."

Chief Prentice leans back in his chair, studying me with a calculated gaze. His fingers drum a steady beat on the table, filling the silence between us. I find myself at a crossroads, wondering if I can place my trust in this man, a familiar face from my past, as he undoubtedly reassesses his perception of me.

"Why don't you start by telling me what's in that journal you found?" he says.

"Your officer has it. Look for yourself."

"What's your professional opinion?"

I narrow my eyes at Chief Prentice. Unless I'm going to

take control of this entire investigation on my own, I need to trust someone within the police department. Based on Prentice's attitude toward Will and his seniority in the department, he's both my best and only option.

He leans back, his chair creaking under the strain. "We don't have to go into all this right now if you don't want," he says, his voice softer now. "With Arthur, the camp...I'd understand if you need a break."

After my attack, I'd spoken to so few people about the actual details of the beating. Even after Mom had found me a special therapist in Colorado, I'd only talked about what happened in broad generalities. And I'd always remained silent about Mr. Blessed.

My psyche had paid the price for that silence. Worse yet, the price was paid by Mr. Blessed's potential future victims, some of whom he might still be hurting.

As of today—right now—I'm done living in silence. My heart races as I take a deep breath, steeling myself for what I'm about to say. I sit tall as I look Prentice in the eye, ready to unleash the torrent of thoughts I've been suppressing.

Suppression, noun

The act of consciously pushing away thoughts, emotions, or memories that are too painful or uncomfortable to deal with. Often mistaken for "strength," but typically results in heart palpitations, restless nights, and the eventual explosion of repressed feelings. See also, why I'm about to spill my guts to Prentice.

After a moment of internal struggle, I reach my decision. "I think Myer Whitley, Will, and Arthur did a lot of bad stuff toward the end of high school."

Chief Prentice runs a hand over his stubble. "Okay."

"They're behind whatever happened to Regina Smith. And I'm pretty sure they were wrapped up in Kylie Boyd's 'suicide' too."

The chief looks away. "Never made sense to me, that girl taking her own life like that. Just didn't line up."

My chest heaves as I take a deep breath and let it out. "Right. And uh…I guess…I have a pretty strong suspicion those guys were responsible for my attack too. Do…do you know about my attack?"

A muscle pulses in his jaw. "I've read the cold case. Nasty business. You think Artie was involved with that?"

My eyes water, but I draw on all my remaining strength, and the tears recede. "I'm not saying I know who did anything. But it seems to me Whitley's at the heart of it. And Will or Arthur or someone else was involved. Think about it. It can't be a coincidence that Madeline showed up dead in the exact spot she suspected Regina had been buried."

Roland nods. "It's like someone knew she was getting close, and they killed her to send a message."

"Or to keep the truth from coming to light."

"So the person who hurt Madeline tonight…"

I anticipate Chief Prentice's question. "Seems to me it's the exact same person who killed Kylie Boyd and probably killed Regina Smith."

"But Whitley's locked up at Linden River."

"I know. I visited him there."

Roland chuckles. "With your determination, we should get you working on the force. You're brave too." His eyes harden. "Couldn't have been easy calling us in on Artie like that."

The stabbing pain of heartbreak surfaces in my chest and radiates throughout my body.

My marriage feels like a dream from the distant past. But

Arthur exists as surely as his victims do, and my cheeks warm at the thought.

"Will says Arthur's already out on bail," I manage, my voice barely above a whisper.

Roland's voice is solemn. "The system has its flaws."

I force a tight smile. "What happened to me back in high school, Chief Prentice…it's the key to all this. I can feel it."

Chief Prentice looks away again and lets out a world-weary sigh. "Yeah, I been thinkin' that too."

A lump forms in my throat as I consider the path that lies ahead. The truth could break me. But if I want peace, I'm going to have to confront the chaos.

CHAPTER
FORTY-SIX

After leaving the police station, I'd headed straight back to camp, where chaos had taken root. Parents were calling nonstop, demanding answers or arranging early pickups, while state authorities combed through every detail of their investigation.

The camp buzzed with a mix of fear, grief, and tension as counselors did their best to console the campers, many of whom were scared and confused. I spent the rest of that Sunday evening fielding questions, speaking with the police, and preparing statements for the media. By the time I finally collapsed into bed, it was well past midnight, and the relentless day had drained both my body and mind.

I arrive back at camp the next morning just in time for an all-hands meeting with the campers.

Jonathan meets me at the cafeteria entrance, his face ghost-white. "This is one of the worst days of my life."

If this is the worst day of your life, you should consider yourself lucky. Madeline will never have one of those again.

"I know it's hard." I place my hand on his, and he squeezes it.

Jonathan's face shows a day's worth of stubble, which is a look I've never seen on him before. "Hopefully, the medical examiner will provide answers. Until then, these girls need to hear from us." He sighs. "It's like I'm about to face a panel of judges who have the power to execute."

"I'll be right next to you for backup if you need it."

He nods and pushes through the double doors into the auditorium. Quiet chatter gets louder as we enter, every eye turning to face us.

On typical days, Jonathan walks with a casual, confident ease. Today, he moves with stiff rigidity, like he's walking the plank toward certain death. I mirror his posture, standing tall with my chin up.

Over the past eighteen hours, time has lost all meaning, but the clock on the far wall tells me it's just a couple of minutes before ten. The kids should be out on activity right now, kayaking, jogging, or—God forbid—exploring Putnam Forest.

By the time Jonathan and I climb the short staircase to the stage at the far end of the room, the conversation has reached a considerable din. Jonathan holds up a hand to silence the kids, but it accomplishes little.

After everything that's happened, I don't blame them for needing to talk. I scan the room for Amanda. She sits with her usual group of girls, elbow to elbow as always. I wonder if she'll ever tell them about me and her and "Mr. Yuen." But none of the other girls are looking at me, so the answer is almost definitely no.

Jonathan calls for quiet three times before the girls fall silent.

He confirms that Madeline is dead and the police are investigating. But he refuses to speculate or go into any further detail.

Jonathan informs the students he's spoken with their

parents. More than twenty are coming today to pick up their girls. The rest are comfortable with the additional precautions in place at camp—new cameras, new locks, added security—and have elected to keep their kids at Wildfire for now.

These wealthy parents, with their busy social calendars, view this tragedy differently than I would.

After Jonathan works through the logistical concerns for the departing campers, he turns to a discussion geared toward helping the girls process their emotions.

He begins by assuring them that he and I will be there to talk as needed. But he soon wavers off course and launches into an impromptu eulogy for Madeline Miller.

Jonathan describes Madeline as the "main character" of her life, a young woman who touched the lives of so many. He dives into her natural curiosity, her determination, and her unshakable sense of right and wrong.

Soon he apologizes to the campers, his voice growing shakier with each word. "This is my camp. That incredible young woman I just described was my responsibility. And I failed her."

Jonathan steps away from the mic and turns to me, implicitly asking me to take over. Tears stream down his cheeks, and his eyes are bloodred.

Sniffles and sobs echo from the gathered campers, many of whom broke down in lockstep with Jonathan.

I step to the microphone and fend off tears of my own. "It's okay to grieve."

Anyone who wasn't already crying now is.

I close my eyes and allow the gravity of the moment to sink in.

The energy crescendos and holds for a few beats before dying down to a whisper. This moment of shared humanity is powerful, and I wait two full minutes—until the room is silent again—before I say a word.

Later, as the campers stream toward the exit in a stupefied haze, I catch up to Amanda as she fills her water bottle at the fountain.

Her gaze hardens when she sees me approach. "Leave me alone."

The conclusion of our last tense conversation replays in my head. After reminding her about our recorded sessions, I promptly used them to have her lover arrested.

Hard to blame the girl for her hostility.

"I get it. I'm the last person you want to see right now." A group of girls slows as they walk past. Once they're gone, I continue. "Just thought I should let you know…the police are going to come interview you today."

She lets out a frustrated sigh. "Were you able to contact my parents?"

A simple head shake is the only response I can muster.

"Figures." Her tone drips with contempt. "Typical careless bullshit."

I place a hand on Amanda's elbow, but she jerks away, spilling water onto my feet.

I retreat a step. "The police department is securing a warrant that will compel you to get a paternity test. That's—"

"To prove Mr. Yuen's the father." Amanda caps the water bottle and wipes the excess water off on her sweatshirt.

An inappropriate lightness settles over me as I realize I've avoided the fate of carrying a sociopath's child. I quickly squash the uncharitable thought and return my focus to Amanda.

"I'm telling you so you're not taken by surprise. If you want to get ahead of it, I can go with you to the clinic."

Her lips curl into a sneer. "Seems like you might be the one who wants to know who the dad is, and this has nothing to do with CPS."

She's right, but I don't have the time to care.

"I'll take the test, but only because I'm prepared to testify that everything between my baby's father and me was consensual." A pause, her voice softening. "And when he's released, which won't be long, I want my son to know how amazing his father truly is."

My heart tightens. "You're having a boy."

Amanda raises her eyebrows as if to say, *Obviously*.

I manage a faint smile. "Arthur pretended he didn't care. But...he always wanted a boy. I know he did."

Amanda looks down, unscrews the lid to her water bottle, and caps it on again. "I'll take the test tomorrow, first thing." And just like that, the mother of Arthur's son disappears into the sea of campers, almost like she was never there at all.

I run into Jonathan a few minutes later, out in the empty hallway. His eyes are still red from crying, and my steps are weighted by the strange mixture of devastation and relief coursing through me.

We lean on one another, and he wraps an arm around me. He lets out a long breath and pulls my head closer against his shoulder. "I'm sorry."

I look up, seeking his eyes, but I don't find them. "For what?"

"You wanted to call the police about Madeline right away, and I stopped you." He bites his bottom lip. "She'd been gone for hours by the time you found her. If I'd called the police when you'd asked, it could've saved her."

Unsure what to say, I move out of his embrace and find my hand nestled in his.

He pulls me under his arm yet again, and the two of us slouch against a bulletin board together, ruffling the papers pinned to the cork.

A long moment passes until I finally speak. "Jonathan?"

His only reply is an exhausted grunt.

"Why can't I ever tell the good guys from the bad?"

He slouches farther against the bulletin board. A thumb tack presses into my back, but I ignore it. "That's overgeneralization, Liz. Plus, a twist of all-or-nothing thinking."

I groan. "Cognitive behavioral therapy haunts me everywhere I go."

"I'm just saying, life is long, and you've been right far more often than you've been wrong. I trust your instincts more than anyone's."

"Other than your own?"

"Well, yeah, but that goes without saying."

We share a beleaguered laugh as I burrow into the crook beneath his shoulder. I know it shouldn't matter, but his gentle reminders of the good I've done for the campers over the years offer a glimmer of comfort.

Time and again, Jonathan's presence has been a steadying force, his support extending beyond words into genuine acts of kindness.

As I gaze up at him, longing nearly overcomes me. I want to close the distance between us. I want to surrender to the intimacy of a kiss.

But just as I start to lift onto my toes, the echoes of Arthur's accusations reverberate through my thoughts. I refuse to grant him the satisfaction of validating his theories about me and Jonathan.

Not until he's behind bars.

CHAPTER
FORTY-SEVEN

I fall asleep around midnight with my phone in my hand, halfway through one of many articles about Madeline's death. When I wake up, it's almost six thirty in the morning, but I swear, it feels like I've only had my eyes closed for twenty minutes.

My phone is ringing, but it's no longer in my hand. *Must be buried in the sheets somewhere.* It's my habit to nudge Arthur until he finds it for me, and in my exhaustion, I paw at his side of the bed.

But he did not come home last night. I haven't seen him since the police took him away three days ago, and I'm not sure I care if I see him again.

The phone is under my nightstand, ringing with a call from someone with a Wildfire area code.

"Hello?"

Chief Prentice greets me. I sit up on my elbow.

Outside, a mockingbird is perched on the branch of a tree with a worm dangling from its beak. The morning sky is bluer than usual. The day more still.

DON'T TELL

"Had a discovery over by camp I wanted to fill you in on."

I'm sitting all the way up now, blinking the last drops of fatigue away. "You need me to come in? I'm taking Amanda Holland to Clear River for a paternity test this morning."

Chief Prentice clears his throat. "No need to come by. Just, uh...more bad news, I guess."

"It's Regina Smith, isn't it? You found her body."

He lets out a deep sigh, and that's all the confirmation I need.

I let out a sigh of my own and pull the comforter closer to my body. The fresh pine scent from laundry day still lingers, and I breathe it in deep.

"How did they dispose of Regina's body?"

For a moment, the chief doesn't say anything. A loudspeaker crackles somewhere at the police station. He finally comes back to the phone speaking in a grave tone. "It was charred. Burned up bad."

The mockingbird takes off from the branch, fluttering its wings and disappearing until it's a fleck in the far distance.

"Any idea how they killed her?"

Chief Prentice starts to answer, but a loud thud from the first floor pulls me out of the moment, and I get to my feet. There's another thud, then another.

"I gotta go."

Hanging up, I pull on jeans and a t-shirt as I pad out of the bedroom and down the stairs. "Hello?"

No reply.

My heart pounds in my chest as I descend the stairs, each step creaking under my weight. The house feels different—alien, almost—now that I no longer think of it as *our* home.

Pausing at the bottom of the stairs, I strain my ears. Another thud, softer this time, comes from the direction of the kitchen. I spy Arthur near the toaster, biting a piece of toast like he hasn't eaten in months. He looks up when I enter but quickly returns his attention to his food.

I go to the front entrance and grab an umbrella from the stand before going into the kitchen. Better than nothing.

My husband's face is more stubbled than it's been in years, his hair is disheveled, and the scent of the beers he drank the night before pollutes the room.

"You need to leave." My voice is shakier than I'd like.

Arthur fills up a glass of water and drinks it in one gulp, spilling half the water down his front.

"Arthur. Get out."

A second slice of toast erupts from the toaster, and I jump a little.

He grabs it, rips it in half, and takes a bite. In a flash, he reminds me of the coyote I found eating Madeline Miller's entrails.

Might as well be.

"You know, I'm so angry at you right now." He throws the bread on the counter, shaking his head. "I never touched that girl. Tried to tell you that, and you wouldn't listen."

"Stop lying." I laugh in his face. "It's pathetic. You're a creep, and now everyone knows it."

Arthur lets out a guttural yell, then reaches into his hair and pulls hard.

"That's good, tough guy. Rip out your hair. Really cool." I taunt him. And I like it. Nonetheless, I keep my distance across the room.

Arthur grabs the second slice of toast and forces it down the garbage disposal. The sound is harsh and metallic, and I wait until he's turned the disposal off before I continue in a calm and calculated tone.

"Amanda told me what you did to her, Arthur. Or should I say 'Mr. Yuen?'"

Arthur looks at me like he's going to have an aneurysm.

"That's because she was protecting the real father, you idiot! Think about it. You totally stopped asking about that guy once she said it was me, I bet."

My cold, detached energy gives way to a rage that's been boiling for months. "I know you worked with her dad! You met her on-site in D.C. Used your stupid secret phone to talk to her!"

"That's not true!" Arthur's screaming now too. "Fuck, fuck, fuck!"

"Will you stop cursing? You sound like an idiot."

"Just because I met the girl, you think I knocked her up. That's insane, Lizette. I knew you had issues, but you're completely nuts."

Gaslighting, noun

A psychological manipulation tactic in which someone makes you question your reality, often to avoid accountability. Side effects may include self-doubt, frustration, and the overwhelming urge to throw something. See also, why I'm suddenly the "crazy" one in this conversation.

"Right." A ferocious scoff erupts from my throat. "I'm the one who has issues?"

"Yeah, you do!" He flings the bag of bread, and it hits some water glasses on the counter. They fall to the floor and shatter.

I back up a step. "I talked to Hazel, too. She told me you cheated on her. Told me you stalked her after you two divorced."

He opens a cabinet and slams it closed three times, screaming louder each time the cabinet slams. "That's a lie! These are all lies!"

"So you didn't cheat on her?" I'm gripping the umbrella like a club.

"What happened with Hazel has nothing to do with my relationship with you. I...I already told you, I was a piece of shit. But not with you. You're special."

In the past, I'd always liked when Arthur had told me I was special. But this time, the words come off like the obsessed declarations of an unhinged man.

"You had a secret phone," I remind him. "And Amanda told me—"

"Why would you trust a pregnant teenager at a camp for disturbed young women more than you trust your husband of many years?"

"But Myer Whitley—"

"Convicted bank robber. Locally famous creep! He's more trustworthy than I am?"

Licking my lips, I reach for more words, but they feel thin, even as I say them. "Will said the phone was yours."

"My brother? You don't even like him."

I do not.

"And you...you also talked to Hazel? Well, everyone knows she's trustworthy. One of our most reputable citizens. She got caught selling meth a few years ago."

I squeeze my eyes tight, fighting back the confusion as Arthur talks circles around me. "No, no! Stop talking!"

Arthur laughs, picking up the spilled bread from the counter and taking a bite. "Whatever."

The mottled granite countertop fills my field of vision. I cycle through the facts, convinced they point to Arthur. Now I'm talking more to myself than to him, and I'm far too preoccupied to care how crazy I might seem.

"They found Regina Smith's remains exactly where Madeline Miller turned up. Whitley's got to be the one who killed Regina. But he couldn't have been alone. And he was probably there the night they got Kylie Boyd, too, her cousin. And then...that's right when I got attacked. It's got to be connected."

"Lizette." Arthur fixes me with his big nearly black eyes. Suddenly, they're filled with compassion. "I think...all this stress might be getting to you. You know, they say a hysterectomy can mess with a woman's hormones. Push her into early menopause."

My mouth drops open. "What?"

He takes another bite of bread, chewing slowly, his eyes never leaving mine. "Maybe that's what's happening here. Maybe you're...losing it, just a little. You've been so emotional lately, so irrational. It's not your fault, really. It's just your body doing what it does."

"No..." Tears well in my eyes as anger and frustration bubble up. "There's a connection here. You...you..."

"What?" He turns up his palms with a mocking smile. "I killed all those people and got away with it?"

A tear runs hot down my cheek. I haven't considered the possibility that I could be wrong. But Arthur's words burrow into my mind like termites, gnawing at my doubts. What if he's right? What if I *am* losing it?

What if I've cost myself one of the only good men I've ever met?

"All I've ever wanted to do was love you." His mouth turns downward in a disappointed frown. "We were going to put the past behind us, and now you've ruined it."

More tears fall, and I lower the umbrella to my side. I'm too confused to reply, too afraid of saying the wrong thing. My phone rings, and when I glance at the screen, a ripple of worry runs through me.

It's Camp Wildfire. What now?

Sniffling, I turn away from Arthur and answer.

The voice is tiny, like it's coming from a little girl curled up on her bed, holding a blue teddy bear to her chest. "Ms. Silva?"

I recognize her immediately. It's Amanda.

"Yeah?"

"I don't think I can do this."

CHAPTER
FORTY-EIGHT

Amanda's waiting in the parking lot when I pull up to Camp Wildfire. She's wearing black slacks and a button-down top that stretches over her belly, along with several jangly pieces of costume jewelry.

It's as if she's trying to look as adult as she can for the paternity test, which is quite likely one of the most adult moments of her life. I would've done the same thing.

She slides onto the passenger seat without looking me in the eye. I compliment her outfit, and she grunts a hasty, "Thanks."

"How you feeling about everything this morning?"

"I'm feeling coerced. And like I want my phone. And like I don't want to do this."

Too bad. The warrant has already been sent to the clinic.
"Amanda—"

"No." She crosses her arms, then uncrosses them, clearly fidgety without her device. "I want to go back to my bunk."

I turn out onto the highway, my grip tightening on the steering wheel. I can't back down now. "How about I keep driving, and you tell me more? If we get to Clear River and you don't want to go in, that's fine."

I don't feel a bit bad about that lie. Sometimes, a little deception is necessary to protect someone. Even if they don't realize they need it.

"You only want this paternity test so you can get the evidence you need to send my boyfriend to jail." Amanda shifts in her seat, her hand protectively covering her belly. "And I don't want to do that."

She's rehashing our talk from yesterday morning almost verbatim. But I expected this, and I won't waver from my position.

I take a breath and decide to be deeply honest. "I understand. I really do. Arthur's my husband, the man I promised to love in sickness and health." Tears burn my eyes, and I blink them away. "But when I thought about sickness, I thought things like heart attack or cancer. That I could handle."

Glancing over at her, I'm glad to see she's watching me closely.

"But this..." I reach over and hover a hand over her swollen belly, careful not to touch her. "It's not just him having an affair, even. It's that he abused you. I know you don't see it that way now, but one day you will. I promise."

We're silent for several miles before she finally speaks. "I'm sorry."

I grip the wheel tighter. "I know. I've been in your shoes before, so, yeah...I know." Another mile slips by before I speak again. "CPS and the police have already secured a warrant for the paternity test. You don't really have a choice in the matter."

"Like I care. You're the one who said I had to get ahead of it." She crosses her arms, sinking into a typical teenage persona. "And I don't even know if I believe you."

"Amanda, we talked about this yesterday. If I don't take you in for the test, the police will. And every local newspaper will be there to take pictures of it." I glance at her belly. "What about your son? All kids deserve to know for sure who their father is."

Even if their father is a statutory rapist adulterer who should rot behind bars for the rest of his life.

Amanda looks at me. "But I only…did it with Mr. Yuen."

"And Mr. Yuen is saying that's not true, which means a paternity test is the only way for your child to know for sure."

Amanda's leg bounces, and she rolls down the window. Observing her in my periphery, I clock all the signs of a teenage girl on the verge of a breakdown.

I pull over the car, place my hand on hers, and squeeze.

"No matter what happens, your baby's going to lead a good life. You know that, right?"

She shakes her head and scrapes a tear away with a long pink nail. "No. Why? I'm still in high school. I don't know anything about being a mom. And my parents are, like, totally self-involved."

"Yeah, but they're rich," I deadpan, aiming to ease the tension. "That helps a lot."

Shock flashes across Amanda's face before she dissolves into laughter. "I guess that's true."

I squeeze her hand again. "I'm not telling you it won't be tough. I don't know from experience, but I've heard that raising a child is challenging. I've also heard that it's totally worth it."

She rubs her belly. "I've heard that too."

"Your son will have an incredible life, no matter who the dad is."

Amanda dries another tear with her business casual blouse. "Even if the dad is…your husband?"

I squeeze my eyes shut as conflicting emotions race

through my body. The first is compassion. Beyond that, there's pity, sympathy, and rage.

Amanda squeezes my hand tighter before I have a chance to respond. "I'm glad I met you, Ms. Silva. Wish my own mom cared about me how you do."

Words fail me. My face says what my voice can't—how deeply her words have touched me.

"I'm...I'm sorry. About Mr. Yuen." Amanda pulls her hand away, the physical closeness apparently juxtaposed too severely with the "woman-to-woman" betrayal. "I bet you're going to find somebody really great one day."

To be reassured you're lovable by the teenage girl who arguably stole your husband is both surreal and humbling. But I was Amanda once—I know how naive she is—and that's the reason I'm able to keep my head on straight in this conversation.

"Thank you." My smile softens as I pull back onto the road. A few minutes later, I turn into the Clear River parking lot and kill the engine. Amanda's no longer crying, and she's totally pulling off "pregnant teenage business leader."

As we walk into the Clear River waiting room, the conversation turns toward the brighter side of childbirth.

Amanda tells me she's going to give the kid an androgynous name, because that's what's in right now. And while we sit in the waiting room, she cycles through a long list of these names to gauge my reactions.

The list is unorthodox—as any list of names generated by a troubled teenager might be—but several are charming. My favorites are "Cotton" and "Blue," though I don't tell her that for fear that she'll use one of them.

Amanda gets up to use the bathroom. I watch her shuffle away with a wistful smile, feeling oddly nostalgic for my own time as a teenage mother-to-be. There's an angry glory to it, something triumphant in satisfying a biological drive before you're old enough to drink.

I roll my eyes, groaning. *Get a grip. That's nothing to be jealous of.*

As I wait for Amanda to come back, my mind drifts back to my argument with Arthur in the kitchen. I'd never seen him so angry, so vehement. It was as though he'd seen the darkness inside himself for the first time and couldn't handle it.

The nerve, insisting I wasn't listening or being fair to him. And *menopause*? The absolute, unbelievable, despicable—

"Amanda Holland?" A nurse juts her head into the waiting area and glances around.

"Here." I raise my hand and move to stand.

"Are you Amanda?"

"No, uh, she's just in the bathroom." I check my watch. Amanda's been gone for almost five minutes. "She'll be back any second."

I remain calm while I check the restrooms. She isn't there.

CHAPTER
FORTY-NINE

"Amanda!" Bursting through the double doors, I survey the waiting room with a sweeping gaze. "Where is she?"

My fear runs on several parallels. Amanda could have been taken by whoever killed Madeline. Abducted in the bathroom and dragged to a waiting pickup without the assailant breaking a sweat.

I should've brought security with us from camp.

Or she could've decided to back out of the paternity test and escape Wildfire with Arthur behind the wheel.

I should've waited outside the bathroom.

But I thought she'd finally started to believe in me and that she actually planned on going through with it.

I never should've trusted our bond.

No matter the situation, there's a high likelihood Amanda's in danger. And these next few minutes are crucial.

As I charge down the hall, peering into every empty room, I call the police department and get the chief on the line.

"She's gone!"

His slow drawl patronizes me. "Now slow down, Lizette. Who's gone?"

An arrow overhead points to the Nursing Room. An image of Amanda flashes into my mind—wistfully watching a new mother nurse—and I'm suddenly sure that's where she is.

Breaking into a jog, I hurry toward the room while briefing Chief Prentice on the situation. He sticks with the slow drawl and asks one stupid question after another.

"Amanda!" I shout as I burst into the room. A Hispanic woman, sitting on a rocking chair and nursing an infant, jumps at the sound. Air gusts from a cheap oscillating fan in the corner. A TV blares some morning show at top volume.

"Did a girl come in here?" I scan the room. "Pregnant teenager? Long blond hair?"

The woman shakes her head, and I'm out of the room.

As I blast through the exit and charge toward my car, I return to the phone call and recap the situation for Chief Prentice with anxious, hurried words.

His response is equal parts condescending and infuriating. "Calm down, Lizette."

It takes all my strength to keep my voice on this side of steady. "Do you not see the pattern here? Do you not see how urgent this is?"

I kick an empty coffee cup aside and cut behind a parked ambulance, carving a direct path to my Outlander in the corner of the lot.

Light glints off the roof of my car and catches me in the eyes. I blink away the stars and hurry forward.

"She can't have gone far on foot," the chief says. "I'll get a couple guys over there to search the area around the clinic."

"I'm telling you she was taken! You need to get a grasp on...on..." I trail off as I unlock my car and slide behind the wheel.

There's a note resting on the passenger seat where Amanda had been sitting on the ride over.

I end the call and pick up the folded piece of paper. It's

warm, as if still holding Amanda's body heat, and it smells ever so faintly of her honeysuckle perfume. With trembling fingers, I unfold it to reveal a message written in Amanda's loopy handwriting.

I begin reading but can't get past the first line.

Arthur is not the father of my baby.

I reread that line three times before the note falls from my hand.

Leaning over, I retrieve the note from the floor mat, my movements slow and mechanical. I smooth out the creases and force myself to read the entirety of Amanda's message.

Arthur is not the father of my baby.

The father of my baby is a much better man. We love each other, and he's going to take care of me. I don't feel bad for lying to you, because you deserved it for not believing in my love.

Please don't look for me.

Amanda.

The words blur as tears well up in my eyes. I need air. Desperately. I fumble with the door handle and spill out of the car, gasping as the oppressive heat and humidity hit me.

My legs feel weak, barely capable of supporting me. I lean against the car for a moment, trying to steady myself, before sitting down on the asphalt.

The hot blacktop burns the backs of my legs, but it's nothing compared to the scalding shame from Amanda's letter. Her lies don't bother me. She's a teenager, after all. What makes my entire body tremble is the crushing realization that, if what Amanda says is true, Arthur was right about me all along.

"I was Amanda's hysterical therapist."

My words taste bitter in my mouth. The truth settles over me like a lead blanket—I've failed. Failed Amanda, failed as a therapist, failed to stand by my man. The ethics board will have a field day with this. Best case, I'm looking at a formal reprimand, maybe a suspension. Worst case...I shudder at the thought.

Even if I keep my license, my reputation in Wildfire is shot. Who'd trust their child to a therapist who couldn't see through a teenager's lies?

And it's not just Amanda.

Madeline was in my care, as well, and now she's dead. I made accusations against Arthur, which now appear to be wholly false.

How many mistakes can one therapist make before it's too many?

I press my palms against my eyes, trying to stem the flood of tears threatening to spill over. I've worked so hard to help these girls, to make a difference. But I've done more harm than good.

I need to report this, to face whatever consequences come. But first, I need to find Amanda. I owe her that much, at least.

With shaking hands, I reach for my phone. It's time to call Chief Prentice back.

The chief of police arrives on the scene in a cruiser and steps out in a surprisingly crisp uniform.

I'm leaning against my car, staring off into the distance, trying to steady myself. His boots thud against the pavement, each step like the tick of a clock counting down to the moment my life completely blows apart. The sound grows louder, like the earth is rumbling a warning about the shit that's about to go down.

I thank Chief Prentice for coming, explain the whole situation, and hand over Amanda's note. Prentice's brow furrows as he reads her message, then reads it for a second time. Finally, he lets out a heavy sigh, his shoulders sagging.

I scrutinize him. "What are you thinking?"

"This is a mess." He rubs his forehead. "We have a pregnant teenager in the wind, possibly with an older man who took advantage of her. And we've wasted valuable time chasing down your innocent husband. We need to move fast now."

The comment about my "innocent husband" lodges in my throat. "I agree. Wherever Amanda is, she's in danger. Who knows what this guy might do to her, or that baby, now that there's so much attention swirling around the camp?"

The chief twists his mouth in a pained expression. "I'll put out an Amber Alert." He looks over at me. "You got any ideas who the real dad might be? Has she said anything? Given you any clues?"

As he runs a hand through his graying hair, my mind races, piecing together fragments of conversations and odd moments from the past two weeks.

I recall Will's strange behavior when I first mentioned Amanda's pregnancy. His eyes had darted away, and he'd changed the subject abruptly.

Then, the other day, I overheard Arthur arguing on the phone in hushed tones. *"If you touch her, you're dead."*

Could Arthur have been offering his brother advice on what to do in the situation? Had Will's initial impulse to solve his problems been to hurt Amanda?

And then there's the secret cell phone. What if Arthur had been hiding it for Will, and Will had used it to communicate with Amanda?

A chill runs through me as I remember Arthur mentioning that he and Will had gone golfing with Amanda's father when Mr. Holland was in town. Will had stayed in touch with Holland after that, hadn't he?

The pieces start to fit together, forming a disturbing picture.

Sure, any adult male could have impregnated Amanda. But I'm beginning to think Amanda was talking about Will, not Arthur, when she claimed her boyfriend made her call him Mr. Yuen.

She must have regretted sharing the name as soon as it fell from her mouth. Because when I assumed she'd meant my husband, she'd gone along with it, and had even cried to sell the story.

At first, it seems like a stretch. But I've seen plenty of teenage girls pull even quicker one-eighties. When hormones mix with insecurity and fear…all the typical rules of engagement go out the window.

Hell, maybe Amanda had planned on sacrificing Arthur all along. And maybe Will had put her up to it.

My heart races as the suspicion solidifies. Will Yuen, respected police officer, Arthur's fraternal twin brother…could he be the father of Amanda's unborn baby?

The thought terrifies me. I've seen the anger simmering beneath Will's calm exterior, glimpsed the potential for violence in his eyes.

But I've learned my lesson about making accusations without solid proof. And accusing the chief's right-hand man of statutory rape and kidnapping? Not something I can do lightly.

I realize the magnitude of the dangerous game I might be playing. But if Will is behind this, who knows what he's capable of, what he's done in the past, or what he might do next?

My imagination creates a chilling vision of Amanda's name scrawled beneath mine in Madeline's notebook, another tragic entry in the list of young women whose lives were permanently changed or cruelly ended by local men. My jaw clenches so tight, I hear my teeth grind.

The weight of my failure crushes down on me. Amanda is

my camper. My responsibility. And I let her slip into the clutches of a potential killer.

If I don't find her, and soon, she'll be more than just another statistic. She'll be the next chapter in Wildfire's dark history, another whispered tragedy passed down from one woman to the next, for generations.

I can already hear the hushed conversations at the grocery store, see the pitying glances from neighbors, feel the suffocating weight of collective grief that will blanket our town.

"*We're cursed*," they'll say. *"How could this happen again?"*

I refuse to let that be Amanda's story, and I won't let her become another dead girl for the gossip mill.

With renewed determination, I straighten my spine. I might've failed Amanda once, but I won't fail her again.

I'm going to find Amanda Holland. And God help anyone who stands in my way.

CHAPTER
FIFTY

It's afternoon before I'm pulling out of the Clear River parking lot. The shock from finding Amanda's note has given way to a steely resolve, and I roll down my windows to let the summer breeze brush my hair from my face.

American flags dot the road leading toward Wildfire, marking the Fourth of July parade route. The Fourth is a huge party day in Virginia. Every fire truck in town cruises down main street, along with a marching band, show horses, and every old fogy with a classic car.

This year, the pall of Madeline Miller's death will hang over the parade. What if another teenage girl is added to the collective trauma?

Prentice put out an Amber Alert right there in the Clear River parking lot. I told him what Amanda was wearing when she went missing, along with all other personal details, and he contacted Virginia State Police and passed on the relevant information.

Within half an hour, the alert was on the state's department of transportation message boards along all major highways, and Wireless Emergency Alerts had been sent out to every phone in the area, including mine, which was briefly reassuring.

Finally, the chief mobilized all available Wildfire units to search for Amanda and coordinated with nearby jurisdictions for additional support while also pushing the story to local news outlets and community alert systems.

As I watched him work, I developed a new respect for our small-town police chief. So much so that I almost felt bad keeping my insights about Will Yuen to myself.

But I'm done trusting people, and while I'm glad the alert went out, I have a strong suspicion this problem started and will end with me.

The road stretches out before me, a ribbon of asphalt cutting through the Virginia countryside. My fingers drum against the steering wheel as I weigh my options. I need information, and I need it fast.

I pull to the side of the road and reach for my phone. The number I'm looking for is buried deep in my contacts—Vicky Yuen. Will's wife.

My thumb hovers over her name for a moment before I press the number. The call connects to Bluetooth, and I roll up the window to eliminate outside noise.

As wild and unpredictable as Will is, Vicky's always been the boss in that relationship. He transforms into a church mouse around her, only occasionally grumbling about the power imbalance of his domestic life.

Will and Vicky, like Arthur and me, found each other young.

There's a certain blindness that comes with youth, a reductive way of seeing the world—and each other. When we're young, love is two-dimensional, with no gray areas, no shadows. The lack of nuance makes everything easy to understand, like a Saturday morning cartoon.

Those of us who find wisdom with age gain the

perspective that, in fact, all people are three-dimensional. We all cast shadows, and very rarely are those shadows worthy of judgment of any kind.

But most people cling to their two-dimensional universe. They add wrinkles and warts and weight to the cartoon characters they love or hate but still struggle to see the nuance. And by the time they do, it's often far too late.

I have a strong feeling Will Yuen never stopped seeing the world in two dimensions. And as I dial Vicky's number, I wonder if she's stuck there too.

Vicky picks up after two and a half rings. "Liz. Hi."

"Just looking for Will actually. Have you seen him?" I wince. My voice is pitched up too high, and I hope Vicky didn't notice.

She replies with a hard edge. "What do you want with Will?"

"Um…" I start, pausing as a truck rumbles past, its draft rocking my car slightly.

"It's nuts what you did, you know." Vicky's words hit me like a slap. "Accusing Arthur like that. And now I hear he's not even the one who did it. I'm ashamed to go out in public, and the parade's coming up."

"The thing is, this camper told me she was involved with a man named Mr. Yuen, so you could probably understand why—"

"I don't wanna hear it." Vicky cuts me off. "Why trust some messed-up girl over your own husband? I mean, sweetie, you seem mentally unstable."

Vicky's insults hurt, but I refuse to be sidetracked. "There was a secret phone in Arthur's truck. And the girl mentioned one, and—"

"Oh, I know about the phone." Vicky scoffs. "Will came clean about the stupid witness protection thing. Said he won't do it again but, hey, he's a cop. And an asshole. So whatever."

"Vicky, you need to let me talk. I think Will—"

"I don't need to let you do anything, Lizette. You're tearing up this whole family, sending Arthur to jail, making my husband more stressed out than I've seen him in years." Her voice rises another decibel. "I mean, he had to go up to the cabin today just to 'think.' You know how pathetic that is to me? My husband is a doer. He doesn't sit around and mope!"

The cabin. Of course.

As Vicky continues her tirade, my mind races. Isolated in the woods, that cabin is the perfect place to hide a pregnant teenager. Miles of hiking trails loosely connect the cabin to the camp, but it's a pain to reach by car.

"And another thing, you rotten, backstabbing..."

As Vicky's voice fades into white noise, I cut her off mid-sentence. "I'm sorry. I...I've gotta go."

How could I have been so blind? The cabin is where Arthur always goes when he needs space, where Will probably goes to escape Vicky's domineering presence. And now it might be where Amanda's being held.

The path leading up to the cabin is treacherous, winding through dense forest. But I know every twist and turn, and as I pull onto the highway, a grim determination settles over me.

Whatever I find at that cabin, I'm ready. Ready to face the truth, no matter how dark. Ready to save Amanda, if she's there to be saved. And ready to confront Will, even if it means facing the monster lurking beneath the surface.

As I drive, my thoughts spiral further. If Will is capable of this, what else might he have done? A disturbing possibility surfaces. Could his involvement extend beyond Amanda? My mind flashes back to my own attack, to Regina, Kylie, and Madeline.

Could Will have been involved in each of these incidents and gotten away with them?

It might be a long shot, but he could've leveraged his position in the police force to make sure his teenage wrongdoings stayed secret.

The magnitude of what I'm considering—a corrupt cop, a conspiracy reaching back years—turns my stomach, and a cold sweat breaks out on my forehead.

I suspect I was meant to die the night of my attack. If it hadn't been for the second man, I would have. But I survived, and I'm determined Amanda will too.

I let out a deep exhale and press down on the gas. I'm fighting for all of us now, and I will not fail. My tires crunch over dirt and gravel as I climb the steep and winding trail that leads to the Yuens' mountain cabin—the grown-up equivalent to Myer Whitley's high school bachelor pad.

My car rattles over uneven ground, while dappled light casts shifting shadows through the trees, distorting my perception.

I've made plenty of mistakes lately, mistakes born from... emotional thinking. And this could be another. I could be wasting valuable time better spent helping my campers or searching for Amanda Holland someplace else.

My heart plummets as I crest the hill. Will's police cruiser sits parked in front of the cabin, a symbol of safety twisted into a harbinger of dread.

I carefully navigate my car behind a dense thicket of bushes—ensuring it remains out of sight—and turn it to face the main road in case I need a fast escape. As I step out, the scents of charred wood and smoke drift toward me from the direction of the house. The absence of smoke from the brick chimney suggests someone's burning something behind the cabin.

I consider calling 911, but there is no time for that, not if that smoke means what I think it means.

Crouching low, I make my way along the perimeter, using

the natural cover of the landscape to conceal my approach. The path to the rear of the property is paved with slates my father-in-law meticulously laid when he purchased the cabin five decades ago.

Now they're a rainy-day gray, covered in a lush carpet of evergreen moss. I tread cautiously, my feet threatening to slip with each step.

Up close, the log cabin bears more signs of the senior Mr. Yuen's handiwork. The porch sags in the middle where he ran out of money for "good wood." And the whole place has the look of something rushed, held together by patchwork repairs between decades of neglect.

As I near the gate to the backyard, a thick wave of smoke forces me to retreat a couple of steps. A cough builds in my chest, but I suppress it to maintain my cover, causing a painful burn to spread throughout my body.

Regina Smith's remains were found charred in the forest. Am I too late?

I inch closer and peer over the gate into the backyard. A large pit, freshly dug, gapes like a wound in the ground, with mounds of dirt piled high around its edges. Smoke rises in ghostly wisps from the pit, and tendrils of fire lick the air just above the rim.

The scene before me is nightmarish, like some grotesque cross between a burial ground and a funeral pyre. I steel myself for the horrors I might be about to uncover.

The crackling fire is the only sound I hear, its intermittent pops unsettling in the mountain stillness.

Will isn't tending the fire. Is Amanda's body already in the pit? No, I can't think like that. Maybe she's inside the house. Maybe there's still time to save her.

I tighten my grip on the gate latch. The cold metal bites into my palms as dread crawls up my spine. I have to find Amanda before this nightmare spirals out of control.

I take a deep breath, and my lungs once again flood with the thick, acrid smoke. There must be a chemical mixed in with the charcoal, because the smoke stings my throat more than any country bonfire I've ever attended. And my eyes are burning too.

Would a young woman's body create this kind of chemical reaction? I force the thought away.

I edge toward the cabin, my heart pounding as I search for any sign of movement within.

A branch snaps under my foot as I approach a smaller window on the living room side of the home. The window is lopsided, just like the house, and the glass is old and single-paned.

I press my forehead against the pane.

Will is nowhere to be found.

But there's Amanda Holland.

She's sprawled across the living room couch. Her chest barely moves with each shallow breath. An arm dangles limply off the cushions, fingers brushing the floor. Her mouth is open, and a pool of drool has darkened the fabric beside her slackened face.

CHAPTER
FIFTY-ONE

The cabin has three two tiny bedrooms on the second floor and a very simple first floor layout.

Beyond the foyer, the entire level consists of one large, open-plan area divided into a living room on one side and a kitchen on the other. The kitchen boasts a large, square island with pots and pans suspended above. And the living room is sparsely furnished, featuring only the faded plaid couch where Amanda lies unconscious across from an old, boxy TV set.

A glass coffee table takes up the remaining space in the middle of the floor. And Amanda's couch is on the same wall as a screen door, which leads out to a mossy patio area, itself opening out to the forest beyond.

I watch from my hiding place outside as Will comes in from the foyer and stalks past Amanda's body. He's wearing torn jeans and a tattered t-shirt. The kind of clothes you don't mind ruining when you're painting the house or killing a pregnant teenage girl.

He elbows his way through the screen door. I duck and hold my breath, praying he doesn't see me. His footsteps crunch across the backyard. Then comes the sound of scraping metal, and the fire roars louder.

Ten seconds pass, then ten more.

I peer through a crack in the back gate. The fire jumps toward Will's face, but he doesn't flinch as he stokes the flames with an iron rod. A wave of revulsion washes over me as Will sips from a mug.

This man's enjoying a cup of coffee as he prepares to roast the mother of his child.

I peek at Amanda again. She remains motionless on the couch, and no one else has appeared in the living room beside her. This could be my only chance to help her.

With a quick glance back at Will—still savoring his cup of coffee—I fall back a step before turning and hurrying toward the front door.

When I rush across the mossy path, my feet give out, and I slip to the ground. My leg slams into the exposed slate, the rock scraping my skin. I bite my lip to stay quiet as pain arcs through my leg up to the base of my spine. Panting, I rise again quicker than I fell.

My jeans are ripped, there's a throbbing gash in my kneecap, and a drop of blood slides down my shin. But I'm driven by an urgent need to get to Amanda before Will finishes what he's started.

I cross the darkened foyer in three quick steps, entering the main body of the cabin. The ancient wood floors creak beneath me.

Through the window, I watch as Will continues to stand on the far side of the firepit, facing the cabin. His face is intermittently obscured by the smoke from the pit, but I can make out a flat expression as he gazes down at the flames.

I'm at Amanda's side within seconds, kneeling on the shag rug and pressing a hand to her neck. There's a faint pulse, and her body is warm. But when I shake her, she doesn't move.

Prescription pill bottles dot the coffee table beside her, with several pills scattered across the glass top. My hand trembles as I stretch toward the pills—thinking of both Amanda and the risks to her unborn child—but I pull back as Will turns away from the firepit and stalks back toward the cabin.

I scramble from the living room and into the adjacent kitchen on my wounded knee, leaving a smear of blood on the floor behind me. Will steps through the screen door as I drag myself behind the kitchen island, positioning myself on the side farthest from the living room. I pull my knees close to my body, trying to make myself as small as possible.

Will cannot find me here. If he does, I'm going to die. So is Amanda.

And so is her baby.

Will's filthy work boots clomp through the kitchen, where he sets his coffee on the island and disappears into the foyer, soon thumping up the stairs with the slow rhythm of a blacksmith's hammer. Peering around from the other end of the island, I consider running back to Amanda, but Will descends the stairs seconds later.

With the slow and methodical movements of a practiced killer, my brother-in-law moves the coffee table out of the way and spreads a drop cloth on the floor beside Amanda's limp body. Once it's in position, he grabs his coffee and sits on the couch beside Amanda, taking one last slurping sip.

Amanda moans, smacking her lips like she's thirsty, before settling back into her drugged-up stupor. Will moves his head in a way that tells me he's scanning her body. He sets his empty mug on the floor by his boots, wrenches his phone from his pocket, and taps out a text.

His leg shakes as he writes the message, muttering, "Hurry up already."

Overcome by fear, I duck back behind the island...and hit the back of my head on a cabinet with a thud.

I don't have to look to know Will is staring in my direction.

He sputters something inarticulate and then speaks. "Is this blood?"

As I look down at my bleeding knee, my arms and legs shake. Only an idiot gets injured on a mission and then drags her bloody leg across the floor for the killer to see.

There's a quiet clicking from over near Will. Again, I don't need to look to know what's happening. He's holding his gun. It won't be the police-issue Glock he usually has on his hip, but something more sinister, like the sawed-off shotgun he parades about every time there's company at his house.

I hold still and listen as Will stalks toward the kitchen. He stops on the other side of the island, breathing heavily through his mouth.

He's scared too. If only I could use that to hurt him.

My heart pounds so loudly, I'm sure he can hear it, and I hold my breath as his footsteps draw nearer, praying he'll somehow overlook my hiding spot.

Will takes the long way around the island, circling from the living room side, as his slow, deliberate steps draw closer and closer.

Panic surges through me. I can't just sit here—I have to move. I scramble to a crouch, heart hammering in my ears, and try to crawl away, my hands slipping on the smooth floor. Desperately, I glance around for anything to use as a weapon. When I spot a vase on the counter, I lunge for it, gripping it tightly with both hands.

Before I can throw the vase, he's already on me. Tears stream down my cheeks, a mix of fear and heartbreak, but my defiance only seems to amuse him. His mud-covered hand grabs a fistful of my hair, and he yanks me up with force so brutal it sends a shock of pain down my spine.

I scream. "No!"

Will lets out an animalistic grunt. His breath reeks of whiskey—I should've known there wasn't coffee in that cup—but his movements are sharp, and his eyes bulge with terrifying focus. As he lunges, I channel all my Muay Thai training, planting my feet and swinging my knee toward his midsection.

He anticipates the move, twisting to the side and catching my knee in his massive hands. With a savage roar, he hurls me against the oven. Pain explodes in my shoulder, but another jolt of adrenaline surges through me.

I rebound off the oven, turning the momentum into a desperate crawl to the other side of the island. Every instinct screams at me to keep moving, keep fighting, even as panic floods my veins.

"I know it was you!" I'm standing again, eyes darting for something I can use as protection. "You raped Amanda! You used that phone to talk to her!"

My eyes land on the pans hanging from the rack above the island. I grab one and throw it at him. He swats it away with a resounding clang as he advances on me, scowling.

"You killed Madeline, too, didn't you? And Regina Smith! Admit it!"

Will shrugs. "You can't expect me to remember their names. There've been so many."

How can that be?

I have to know something before I die. "What about me, Will? Were you part of my attack?"

Will scoffs so dismissively, my eyes nearly explode from my skull.

"Admit it. You were there. A killer never forgets the names of his victims. Kylie Boyd. Regina Smith. Madeline Miller."

"Might recall a 'Regina,' now that you mention it."

I snatch another pan and hurl it before making a run for it. My hand is on the screen door—my mind already racing through the forest—when Will grabs my shoulders and tosses me back onto the kitchen floor.

"That bitch deserved what happened to her. Barely gave us a choice."

I slide backward until my back is pressed against the center island. Will's bloated face consumes my field of vision, and the stench of his liquor-soaked body turns my stomach. But those last words he said linger in my ears.

I look up into his cold, dead eyes. "What do you mean by 'us?'"

CHAPTER
FIFTY-TWO

Will brushes past my question with a sneer. "That girl from a couple days ago had to die no matter what. Just so you know."

"How did you know anything about her?"

"She had big-ass mouth and was telling people she was on the verge of discovering Regina Smith's body. Once she said she was close...she had to go." He points his sawed-off at me with a trained, steady hand. "You've all done something to deserve it."

My world stops. In that moment, facing down my death, all the fear leaves my body. "So you admit you attacked me?"

Will shrugs. He almost looks proud.

I've waited my entire adult life to learn the identity of my attackers. I'd always thought it would be gratifying. "Why'd you do it?"

Will's eyes go flat. "You dumped my twin brother to let some gross old man knock you up."

My stomach sinks. *For all these years, I thought my relationship with Mr. Blessed remained a secret. But Will knew. Which means...*

I climb to my feet, bracing myself against the kitchen sink behind me. The steel wash basin is cold and slimy.

I think about the two men who attacked me. The bigger one inflicted most of the pain. The smaller one was gentler. Like he had a soft spot for me, even during the attack.

"Arthur was with you that night." It's a statement, not a question. But Will's too far down memory lane to so much as acknowledge me.

"Imagine my surprise when I heard the rumor about you and a teacher. Disgusting." He spits on the ground, keeping the gun trained on me. "You and Blessed both got what you deserved."

Stammering, I search Will's face for an explanation, and his deadened eyes tell all.

"You're the ones who lit his house on fire."

Will's proud smile broadens. "Told him we'd kill him and his family if he didn't leave right away. You should've seen him cry."

My mind fills with images of Mr. Blessed, cowering under the threat of Will's metal baseball bat, gathering his family and skipping town.

There's a sound outside, and Will's eyes flick away from me, just for a split second. Heart racing, I try to push past him, but the barrel of his gun slams into me.

Directly across the stomach.

With all the force of a baseball bat.

He laughs as I stumble backward against the kitchen island.

And that's when something deep inside me snaps.

My body remembers the pain of the attack I suffered years ago, and decades-old rage surges. I grab a cast-iron skillet from above the island and swing it with all my might.

Like a slugger sailing one over the stadium fence.

The flat of the pan connects with Will's shoulder. He

stumbles, and his shotgun skitters across the floor, disappearing under the couch where Amanda lies unconscious.

"Bitch!"

The momentum of my swing carries me around, leaving me open to Will, who rushes forward. I catch him with the pan on a backswing, hitting him above his ear. He staggers but grabs the pan and twists it from my grip, tossing it aside.

But I've hurt him. He's bleeding.

I don't hesitate, reaching for anything I can use—another pan, a wooden spoon, even—my survival instinct in overdrive. My scrambling fingers close on the cool, smooth hilt of a knife in the block on the counter.

As Will struggles to steady himself, I pull the knife free, the blade ringing against the wood. I lunge with the point aimed at his chest, but he deflects my thrust with the swipe of a backhand and grabs my wrist, twisting until I drop the weapon.

Will forces me to the ground, his weight crushing me—unstoppable against days of exhaustion. The deadness in his eyes promises I'm going to lose.

I'm going to die.

But resolve burns in my gut, stronger than my fatigue. The shotgun is still behind me, under the couch. With a burst of energy, I drive my knee into his groin and dive for the weapon.

My fingers close around the grip. I spin back toward the kitchen just as Will recovers. Now he lunges at me, his face contorted with rage.

Without thinking, I raise the gun, point the barrel, and pull the trigger.

The blast deafens me, and the gun bucks wildly, almost flying from my hands as I fall back on my ass. Will's eyes widen in shock as he stumbles, blood blossoming on his stomach. He staggers backward before hitting the kitchen island and stumbling to the floor.

I sit there. Shaking. Watching as Will bleeds out, his eyelids fluttering. Open and shut. Open and shut.

The shotgun slips from my grasp, and I turn to Amanda, calling her name.

She doesn't stir. I scramble over and kneel on the couch beside her, crying and screaming. "Wake up! Come on, Amanda. We've got to go!"

Will moans from the kitchen, muttering that he's going to kill us both before he starts choking on his own blood.

I glance back. Will is still blinking, slowly, but the rest of his body is very still.

Turning back around, I slap Amanda across the face. "Wake up!"

She does not move, but she has a pulse, so I grab her arms and try to drag her. She's too heavy, and when I pull, I fall backward and slam into the TV across the room, sending it crashing down.

Getting back to my feet, I pull my phone out of my pocket and dial 911. I have no service inside the cabin. But a memory from barbecues at the cabin with the whole family—including the member now bleeding out in the kitchen—reminds me there might be a spot out front to pick up a signal.

"I'll be right back. Okay, Amanda? I'm going to call for help."

She groans like she's suffering indescribable pain, but she does not form any words. Will writhes on the kitchen floor, gurgling. With a deep breath, I push open the door and stumble outside.

My phone screen consumes my field of vision as I desperately look for the signal that could save Amanda's life. But I can't pick up a single bar.

After a full minute spinning in circles with my phone

above my head, I break out into an anguished, frustrated cry, screaming out into the vast nothingness of Putnam.

"Somebody help! Please! Help!"

My voice echoes off the valley floor in the distance and up through the trees around me. There are no other houses—or people—for miles.

I've never been more trapped or felt more helpless. But then...salvation arrives in the form of a beat-up blue Toyota Tacoma.

CHAPTER
FIFTY-THREE

I run toward the familiar truck, waving my arms and screaming for help. My cries are scratchy and wild. I trip halfway there on a tree root, falling hard on my forearms.

The driver's door opens and out step two perfectly clean white sneakers. Ignoring the gravel embedded into the skin of my bleeding arms, I scramble to my feet.

"Jonathan!"

My boss—my friend—hurries toward me and takes me in his arms. "What happened? Are you okay?"

"Will..." I gasp, struggling to catch my breath. "He did it! He impregnated her...Amanda...and..." I swallow hard, the words sticking in my throat. "He killed Regina. And Madeline."

Jonathan's eyes widen, his grip on my shoulders tightening. "Whoa, hold on." He looks toward the cabin, his brow furrowed. "Will's in there? Is he after you? Will Yuen?"

Will's body explodes into my mind—the meaty gash in this chest, dark-red blood pouring onto the hardwood floors. Is he dead yet?

"He...he's shot," I stammer, my voice barely a whisper.

Jonathan pulls me close, keeping his eyes focused on the cabin behind me. "I'm here. It's going to be okay." His throat rises and falls as I feel him swallow one big breath after another. "Is Amanda still inside?"

"Yeah. She...she's all drugged up, though, and I think..." Suddenly, I freeze as a realization hits me, and I take an instinctual step back from Jonathan's embrace. "How do you know Amanda's inside?"

He's gripping something tightly in his right hand. A second step back reveals it's a hunting blade engraved with a swirling, snakelike design.

His eyes are graphite, and mine are shallow pools.

Slowly, the corner of his mouth ticks up. "Therapeutic intuition."

I've never seen this look before, and the danger radiating from his expression is palpable, an invisible force pushing me away.

"Everything's okay, Lizette. I promise."

"Um...I...should go." I can't let Jonathan get into that cabin. So I turn and walk out into the forest, hoping he'll come after me. Hoping I'll lose him and get back to save Amanda before it's too late.

Glancing back, I see him following me with big, confident steps. "Lizette! Wait up."

I run.

Seconds later, I push through a thick wall of brush and glance back. Jonathan advances with a disturbing calm—moving slowly, leisurely—like he has all the time in the world. He steps carefully through the forest, as if he's more concerned with keeping his pristine shoes clean than with catching me.

My heart pounds in my ears as I run. But no matter how fast I go, he closes the distance with unnerving ease.

I never told Jonathan I was coming here.

When I glance back, he's closed the gap by more than half. He's faster than me, stronger, and he's getting closer. But every step toward me is a step farther from Amanda and another chance for her to wake up and get free. I push myself harder, knowing I can't afford to stop, can't afford to let him catch me, even though it feels inevitable that he will.

Jonathan calls after me. "You need to relax, Lizette! You're gonna get hurt."

Adrenaline propels me deeper into the woods. Jonathan's voice carries through the trees, taunting me, but looking back will slow me down. I need to focus on the path ahead, on finding a way to safety, on putting distance between him and that cabin.

I catch my foot on a tree stump and hit the ground. Panting, shaking, I move to stand, but I've fallen through a thicket of bushes, and for just a moment, Jonathan has no idea where I am.

An enormous, hollowed-out tree beckons to me from thirty feet away. A curtain of English ivy mostly obscures the hole, and with the shape I'm in, it's my only hope at salvation.

My bleeding knees and forearms sting as I crawl through the underbrush while Jonathan calls my name.

"We need to talk, Lizette." His voice is measured and calm, just the way it sounds when he pops into my office at the end of a long day. "Whatever you think, you've got it all wrong."

I part the curtain of ivy. Press my body into the tree's hollow. Pull the long vines closed to obscure my hiding spot.

Though I'm shrouded from Jonathan's view, the warmth of the small, dark space is so unwelcoming. Within seconds, the invasive vines are scratching and smothering me.

Jonathan's voice is louder now. A stranger would never notice, but I can tell his patience is being tested. I can tell he's angry, that he's ready and willing to use that knife.

A tendril of ivy brushes against my calf. I squeeze my eyes tight and force myself to hold still.

Jonathan steps through the thicket of bushes that protects my tree from the rest of the forest. A true predator, he stops and smells the air. Then he speaks as he scans the treetops, as though he thinks I might've taken refuge in a branch.

"No idea what you think is going on here, but whatever it is, you're wrong, sweetheart." Vines obscure half his face, but the portion I can see is unfamiliar to me. And I've never heard him call anyone *sweetheart*. Especially not me.

"You think you know what's happening here, but you're blinded by your own ego." Jonathan's laugh echoes through the trees, sending a chill down my spine. "You think of yourself as a savior, but we both know the truth. You're not as selfless as you pretend to be."

Nausea overtakes my body, and hot tears sting the backs of my eyes.

"Come out so we can talk." Jonathan steps closer to my hiding place. "I know you're over here somewhere." He fixes his gaze on the curtain of ivy. "I only came up to the cabin to try to find you, Lizette. I've been worried about you."

His hand reaches for the ivy, and I press myself as far back as I can. The blade of his knife pierces the curtain, slowly pulling it aside.

I squeeze my eyes shut, bracing for the inevitable. Seconds tick by, each one an eternity. Then, silence.

When I open my eyes, I'm face-to-face with Jonathan, his expression unreadable.

Silent tears drop to my feet as I wait for him to make his move. Instead, his lips twitch into a ghost of a smile.

"Hi, Liz."

CHAPTER
FIFTY-FOUR

I'm motionless inside the wet, decaying tree, inches from Jonathan's blade—but my mind's moving a hundred miles an hour. "You're sick, just like Will," I spit out, ignoring the stinging pain shooting through my body. Ignoring the knife inches from my face. "And you were part of it all. Regina. Kylie. Madeline. Everything."

"Lizette." His voice is gentle, like he's talking to an upset toddler. "I kept hoping you'd stay away from Amanda, but you wouldn't leave the situation alone."

"*You're* the father of her baby." My eyes search for an escape, but he consumes my field of view. "Not Will. And when she saw us almost kiss in the office, she blamed Arthur to get back at me."

"You were projecting." He shakes his head as though he's disappointed in me. "Trying to fix your past by making something right in the present. Textbook, really."

The word *textbook* triggers a cascade of memories of when I'd walked in on Jonathan poring over psychology journals. I'd admired how hard he worked to deepen his knowledge, but it seems now he'd been researching cutting-edge ways to manipulate and control teenage girls.

His lips curl into a cruel smile as he reaches out to brush a strand of hair from my face. "Don't be scared. I'm the same guy I always was. Look."

He makes a big show of tucking the hunting knife into a sheath hanging from his belt. Then he steps back several paces with his palms out toward me. "Like I said. I'm here to help you."

The instant Jonathan creates space between us, I lunge out of the hollow, my body coiled with tension. As soon as I'm clear of the tree, I swipe a leg behind him and shove hard against his chest. It's a schoolyard trick I haven't pulled since fifth grade, but it works, and he hits the dirt with a groan.

Stepping on his chest, I race back toward the cabin with wild abandon. There's no way I'm going to outrun Jonathan in the forest. That's clear now. But if I can get to Will's shotgun...

"You bitch!"

He's already closing in on me. I jump over a fallen log and increase my speed.

Jonathan screams a series of expletives.

I'm so out of breath, I'm coughing now, and my chest burns. The cabin is fifty feet away. Forty. Thirty.

Whitley's words ring in my ears. *"Don't tell me Artie never told you how close we were."*

My foot catches on a loose stone, and I stumble forward, struggling to maintain my balance. I can't fall again. If I fall again, I might not make it back up.

Before I can regain my footing, Jonathan grabs my shoulder and spins me.

He strikes me across the jaw with the back of his hand. The force of the blow sends me reeling backward, and I land hard on my elbow. A sickening crunch reverberates in my head, and shooting pain flies up my arm.

I scream as dirt works its way into the wound.

"*You think you're smarter than me?*" Jonathan grabs my shirt and yanks me up. He hits me across the face again. "Yeah, right. You're so stupid, you fell in love with me."

His laugh hurts worse than my elbow, and shame burns in my chest. I hadn't fallen in love with him, but I'd certainly been attracted.

More tears stream down my face as I try to stand then stumble down again. "You're disgusting."

Jonathan kicks dirt at me. I scuttle back on my hands but soon find myself pressed up against a gathering of rocks along a crumbling wall. A loose snakeskin curls around the base of the stones.

"You know this is all happening because of your little paternity test, right? If you weren't such a pain the ass, I would've forced her to give up the baby for adoption. Just like the others."

An intense emotional pain settles over my rib cage. "*Others*? You did this to other girls?"

Will and Jonathan were Whitley's cronies back in high school.

They killed Regina.
They killed Kylie.
And they killed Madeline. She was too close to finding Regina's body.

"It's so easy when your colleague tells you about all her most vulnerable campers." Jonathan laughs to himself. "Every few years, one of them gets pregnant. And I deal with it. It's never hard to get them to do exactly as I say. Speaking of which. Stand up."

I spit on his perfect white shoes.

He grabs my arm and forces me to my feet. I thrash against

his grip, but he's too strong. His fingers dig into my skin as he pulls my body close, his hot breath brushing my ear.

"You're so pretty, Lizette. It's a shame I never got you to cheat. I was so close."

I think of my close calls with Jonathan. I think of Annabelle—his wife and my friend. I scowl. "Yeah, right, you psychopath. You're disgusting."

He shrugs. "I think I'm gonna kill you now."

The words jolt terror through me, but I don't hesitate. Reeling back, I drive a sharp elbow into Jonathan's chest. The blow pushes him back, but he recovers quickly, rage reddening his cheeks.

In a swift motion, I drive my knee up and into the soft spot beneath his rib cage.

Drawing the hunting blade with a snick of steel against leather, he swipes at me, but he's gasping for breath, and I duck away.

He recovers and advances, taking another swing at me, and another. I trip and fall backward, the ground rushing up to meet me. Jonathan wastes no time kneeling on my chest.

Face contorting into a twisted, angry expression, he raises the knife. I squirm out from under him, the blade slicing the air inches from my face. Jonathan's momentum carries him forward, and he lands hard on all fours.

I seize the opportunity and scramble to my feet, my heart racing as I scan my surroundings for a weapon. I'm about to grab a rock when a large copperhead slithers out from the enclosure.

Where there's snakeskin...

In a swift motion, I grab the snake behind its head. Fueled by adrenaline and sheer desperation, I lunge forward and thrust its open mouth toward Jonathan.

The serpent's sharp white fangs find their mark, sinking

into Jonathan's neck. He stumbles backward, screaming and clawing at the snake, his cries echoing through the air.

I have no idea if it was a dry bite or if the fangs hit deep enough. But Jonathan is screaming and tearing at his neck, and that buys me a few precious seconds. Dropping the snake in his lap, I turn and sprint toward the cabin, my heart pounding.

Seconds later, I burst through the screen door, scanning for Will's fallen gun. Urgency mounts with every breath.

If he survives, Jonathan will be coming for me with everything he has.

CHAPTER
FIFTY-FIVE

Amanda's head hangs off the couch like a dog that can't fit on its bed. She looks worse than before, but her chest rises and falls with steady breaths, and she has a faint pulse.

I'm not too late.

"Hey! Wake up." I shake her shoulders. Nothing.

I grab the shotgun off the floor and turn to look out the front window.

There's no sign of Jonathan. Most likely, he passed out from the snakebite. Or he's lurking around the cabin, waiting to attack.

I pat myself down, looking for my car keys, but they're not on me. I must've lost them somewhere in the forest.

Fuck.

Will's in the kitchen—deader than dead—but I'm going to need to search his corpse for the keys to his cruiser.

I move closer to his body—shredded flesh, exposed intestines—and the stench hits me like a fist. The metallic tang of the blood. The loosened bowels. The sickly sweet odor of death.

I need those fucking keys.

Falling into a squat in a pool of his blood, I unclip the carabiner from Will's belt loop with trembling hands.

My feet slip on the slick floor, but I manage to stand and turn back toward Amanda as Jonathan's fist catches me square in the jaw.

I fall on top of Will, the shotgun sliding from my grasp, and for a split second, the room falls silent.

My head spins with all the blows I've taken. Sitting for just a breath, I touch the pain radiating from my jawbone before looking up at Jonathan.

My boss. My friend. Now my would-be killer. His hair stands in every direction, and the snakebite on his neck is oozing and swollen. His chest heaves with labored breaths—another side effect of the venom—and mud clings to his perfect white shoes.

Jonathan doesn't have long until he passes out...I hope. But he won't need much time to kill me or Amanda and call one of his cronies for help.

I stretch toward the shotgun, but Jonathan's faster than me. Before I manage to cover an inch, he grabs me by the hair and drags me through the river of Will's blood out onto the back patio.

It's hot out, and the air is thick with humidity and smoke.

I try to twist out of Jonathan's grasp. "Wake up, Amanda! You gotta wake up!"

"Shut the fuck up!" Jonathan throws me down, and I land hard on my back.

"Get away from me!" I instinctively shift my weight, my Muay Thai training kicking in as I thrust my hips upward and twist, attempting to throw Jonathan off balance. But he's too heavy, too prepared.

Jonathan swats my next kick aside and falls forward, pinning me to the ground with his legs around my hips. I try to bring my elbow up for a strike—a move that felt so effective in training—but Jonathan is faster. He reels back and punches me hard in the face. Sweat drips from the tip of his nose onto my cheek and into my mouth.

He's so close, I swear I can smell the venom rotting the skin around his snakebite.

Desperate, I recall my instructor's words about using an opponent's proximity against them. I jam a finger into Jonathan's eye socket, aiming for the pressure point we'd practiced. For a moment, I think it's working, but Jonathan recovers quickly. He elbows me across the face and dislodges my thumb. In a flash, he rips the knife off his belt again.

As he grunts over me, I finally see Jonathan as the animal he's always been. He could kill me with the shotgun I dropped, but that would be too civilized.

The man is operating on primal instincts. And he wants to smell my fear as I take my last breath.

Jonathan shoves the knife against my neck. "Look at me. Now!"

The steel blade is cold, and it cuts me as I turn my head away. Jonathan's knees dig into my stomach, and he uses his free arm to pin my wrists to the ground.

I'm desperate to continue the fight, but each movement brings the blade closer to me. I stop struggling and lie still. Jonathan's inches away, but instead of looking at his face, I focus on the blue skies above.

This image of nature is my version of life flashing before my eyes. But I don't see my tragedies or traumas. I see crisp, bright blue. The same blue sky that's always been there and will always be.

Every sound in my tiny universe falls into the muted distance, swallowed by the silence of these last moments. I'm alone with that patch of blue, suspended between this world and the next.

Then, out of nowhere, a gunshot shatters the stillness.

Jonathan screams, his body jerking back from the impact. He loses his grip on the knife, and the blade falls away from my neck. Another shot cracks through the air like thunder, and Jonathan slumps forward, his weight pressing down on me.

Gasping for breath, I struggle against the heavy, bleeding mass pinning me to the ground. My hands are slick with Jonathan's blood as I shove him off with all my remaining strength. He crashes onto the patio beside me, choking and gurgling, the life draining out of him as he bleeds into the unforgiving concrete.

CHAPTER
FIFTY-SIX

Arthur tucks his handgun into his waistband and falls to his knees beside me.

I have no words as he brushes my hair from my face, cups my cheeks, and kisses me square on the mouth.

He's so clean. Unmarred by blood, unmarred by the elements. And that familiar smell of Old Spice makes me feel, just for a moment, that this is a day like any other.

After a second kiss, he pulls back, still holding my head in his hands. "I'm so sorry, Lizette." His eyes are wide and vulnerable. "I should've told you the truth about everything before we got married. Never should've lied."

The cognitive dissonance of this moment short-circuits my brain. Jonathan's dead body is beside me. Will's corpse is inside the cabin. Amanda's passed out on the couch, hopefully not dying.

And my husband is looking at me with more love than he has in months.

"It all started in high school, hanging around Whitley's place with Jonathan and my brother. I thought it was all over. Then...I mean...all this." He pulls me closer to him. "But I need you to know, I never wanted any of this to happen. And I'm sorry for all of it."

I prop myself up, hissing as my wounded elbow scrapes against the concrete and pain shoots up my arm. Arthur helps me sit up the rest of the way.

"I never cheated on you." He tucks a strand of hair behind my ear. "You believe me, right? I didn't get that girl pregnant."

He squeezes my hand. I don't pull it away. "I know."

I think I must be in shock, because I can barely remember calling the police on Arthur or having him carted away. But I do remember being convinced he was evil in the worst way.

Now that he's killed Jonathan...does that make him better or worse?

And what about me?

"Did you help Will kill Madeline Miller?" I ask, glancing at Jonathan's crumpled body.

Arthur flinches, whether from my question or the gruesome scene, I can't tell. "No, no, no," he says, shaking his head rapidly. His voice cracks. "Of course not."

"What about Regina Smith?" I force myself to look at my husband, even though the bloody carnage spreading across the patio fights for my focus.

Arthur's eyes move to Jonathan's body, too, then back to me. "Lizette, we can talk about this stuff later. Right now, we need to help Amanda, right?" His hand trembles as he reaches for mine.

"What about Regina Smith?" I shift my weight, and my body instantly tallies every punch and fall, the pain flashing across my consciousness like a brutal scoreboard.

He turns away, his body tensing. "Jonathan...he got rough with Regina one night. Me and Will..." He trails off with his face turned toward the patio.

"What happened?"

Arthur closes his eyes for a long moment. When he opens

them, they're brimming with tears. "We helped bury her out in Putnam."

It's Madeline's theory, almost to the word.

It seems Arthur thinks these confessions will endear me to him. And I need him to continue believing that. Otherwise, there's no way I'm escaping this cabin.

"Tell me about Kylie." My voice sounds hollow, even to my own ears, but this is the best version of calm I can muster.

Arthur wipes his face, leaving a streak of dirt across his forehead. "She was with Jonathan. Then she...she cheated on him. At first, he was okay with it, but then—"

A branch snaps in the forest, and we both freeze.

After a tense moment, I guide Arthur back. "But then what, Arthur?"

He hangs his head. "Jonathan tried, but he couldn't let the cheating go. So, he, uh, he used his dark psychology or whatever. He convinced her to kill herself. While he watched."

My jaw hardens. *That's the story Jonathan told me of his "biggest failure," twisted into the truth.*

Arthur looks away, his shoulders bunching toward his ears, and he lets out a loud sob. He brings a hand to his face and swipes the tears away angrily, but that does nothing to stop them. "I just wish none of this shit ever happened. I want my life back. Want to be young again and not screw up like this."

My heart softens—*don't we all?*—but then I remind myself that the man before me is a liar and a killer. He shot his oldest friend three times and then immediately began trying to win me back with this emotional display.

"Those guys were always going crazy, and I was just stuck with them, standing in the back, wishing I was dead. I'm telling you, Liz. It was never me. But it's just...it's followed me forever."

He wipes his tears with so much aggression, it looks like he might peel his skin off.

"I'm telling you, I never cheated on you. That...that phone...Jonathan gave one to me and Will so we could talk about what was going on with Madeline. He was afraid if she found Regina..."

Is Arthur telling the truth about any of this? Is he just guilty of hanging out with the wrong crowd?

"Let's just...let's go home, Liz." Arthur reaches for my hand, and I flinch involuntarily.

He pulls back, hurt flashing across his face. "We can still be together. We can adopt a kid, the cutest little baby in the world."

Arthur's shirt is now smeared with the blood of his brother and best friend from helping me sit up. My stomach churns.

"I'll never hurt you again." His voice weakens. "We can have a new beginning."

His words echo in my head. I sit taller, biting through the pain and looking only toward the future. "Give me your handgun, Arthur."

He pulls away a few inches. "Why?"

"Because Amanda Holland knows too much. And if we're going to start again, we have to kill her."

He studies me.

I take a deep breath. "She told me you got her pregnant. She lied. She ruined my life and almost made me ruin yours too." I put my hand out, waiting for the gun. "I want to be the one to do it."

CHAPTER
FIFTY-SEVEN

"I'll give it to you inside." Arthur turns toward the cabin, keeping the handgun tucked into his waistband. I lag, and he turns back. "Come on."

I do not trust this man. But I'm going to have to if I want to pull this off. A fraction of a smile flickers on my face, and I soften my eyes.

"Sorry. Uh. More than a little wounded over here."

He looks at me like I'm a toddler who dropped her ice cream cone, when, in fact, I'm a bruised mess, covered in dirt and leaves and lots of blood that mostly isn't mine. "Poor girl. You look…yeah. We're gonna have to get you cleaned up."

Crossing back over to me, Arthur extends his hand. I take it, and he gives it a squeeze. It reminds me of how he squeezed my hand just before we walked down the aisle on our wedding day.

Like he's trying to tell me we're in this together, no matter what.

I squeeze back.

When Arthur pushes the screen door open, the hinges

creak. Will's blood glistens on the floor just beyond the door, and I pull Arthur back before he enters.

"Wait."

Turning back, he cocks his head and narrows his eyes. "What?"

"Um...your brother's in there."

Arthur blinks several times in rapid succession. "He's hurt?"

I fight to keep a neutral expression, maybe to hide my vulnerability, or perhaps to protect what's left of his. Arthur reads the tragedy etched on my face nonetheless, and his eyes fall.

Letting go of my hand, he storms into the house. I stay back.

There's something horribly wrong about consoling someone for the death of a person you killed yourself...

Arthur's feet slap against the blood-wet floors. The stink of death has turned sour now. I clasp my lips tight to avoid an audible gag.

Sobs ring out from inside, mixed with the sad sound of Arthur calling out his brother's name, urging him to rise from the dead.

A deep sadness compels me to run into the forest and never come back. *I can build a shelter. I can survive. I can avoid humankind for the rest of my life.*

But Amanda is inside that cabin, and I need to take care of her.

Arthur calls my name in anguish. I take a big breath to try to steady my shaking limbs and enter the cabin.

My husband looks up at me from over his brother's gutted body. His eyes are deep red, and blood covers his hands and arms. For a moment, tragedy does enough talking for the two of us.

How do I explain what happened here? How do I seek absolution for killing my husband's brother?

Soon, Arthur's expression turns from grief into hardened, determined hatred. His eyes might as well glow red as he addresses me in a shaking voice.

"Jonathan did this?"

I force my lying mouth to say, "Yes."

"Then he deserved to die. And I'm glad I was the one to do it."

I close my eyes tight and then open them again. This is a misunderstanding I'm going to have to live with for the rest of my life. "I'm sorry I didn't tell you sooner. Jonathan just… unloaded."

"The police won't ask a single question when they see this scene. But we'll explain it anyway." Arthur looks past me, and I can almost watch him processing the chaos. "Jonathan drugged Amanda. You and Will came to help her. But Jonathan killed Will. And he would've killed you, too, if I hadn't shown up."

Will Yuen does not deserve to die a hero. But I'm not going to get killed on that hill.

A low moan jerks my head across the room. Amanda's awake and struggling to get to her feet. She whines like an anxious dog seized by disorientation.

She locks eyes with me and reaches out with a sickly pale arm. "Ms. Silva."

Tears stream down her face. I see a once-innocent girl who fell for my psychopath boss. I see a version of myself I've always hated. I see an opportunity to erase the past and start fresh.

"There's no use crying, Ms. Holland." My voice is practiced and cold. "You know what happens next."

Arthur removes the handgun from his waistband as Amanda cries out, "No!" I grab his arm as he draws back the slide and checks the chamber.

"I told you. I want to do it."

His chest rises and falls, and he stands half an inch taller. This is a look I've never seen from my husband before. At first, I can't peg it. But then I realize...it's respect.

He presents the handgun to me like a ring bearer. "You can have one shot. Then I take over."

I point the weapon at Amanda, and she slides to the edge of the couch.

The gun stays steady as I aim it right between Amanda's eyes. "You're a dumb slut, you know that?"

She blinks her big blue eyes. Hatred boils up within me. "Please don't."

"You're dumb enough to think these men love you. But you're nothing but an empty body for them. A brain to control. A weak, pathetic person for them to push around however the fuck they want. You know that, and you let it happen anyway. Because you want it. You love when people treat you as worthless as you know you are."

Amanda's eyes well with tears.

Searing pain rushes through me. "Bitch! Idiot! *Isn't this what you wanted*? The danger? The excitement?"

Amanda's more cogent now, most likely from the adrenaline released by my threats. She tries to stand, and I push her back down.

"You had every opportunity in the world, and you ruined it by falling for an older man."

She's crying now.

"Stupid, horny slut! What do you do, fuck every man who gives you a compliment?"

"Ms. Sil...Ms. Silva...please, stop..." She can barely speak.

"Bitch. How could you be so stupid? How could you sacrifice your body like that?"

After saying everything I needed to say, to myself, I turn away from Amanda and aim the gun at Arthur.

My hands are wrapped so tight around the grip that the cold metal has warmed. The barrel remains steady as my tears clear and my eyes widen.

"You attacked me that night." I widen my stance. "You knew about Mr. Blessed, and you almost killed me for it. Beat me half to death, then showed up with flowers at the hospital."

"You're…you're obviously confused." Arthur's eyes dart around the room. I don't know if he's clocking the exits or looking for something to hurt me with. "You need to give me that gun, Lizette."

I laugh. In my periphery, I spot the fallen shotgun—barely visible behind the kitchen island—but thankfully, Arthur has no idea it's there.

"I shot my best friend for you, Lizette. You're…you're stressed out. Hormonal. You don't know what you're saying."

With my free hand, I toss Amanda my phone. "Call 911. There should be enough signal about two hundred feet down the path in. Can you do that?"

She's got the hiccups from all the crying, but her response is clear. "Yes."

"Don't do that, Amanda!" Arthur's face reddens. "Ms. Silva's confused. She was just threatening to kill you, remember."

"That was just to get the gun out of your hands," I explain. "I'm done letting you control me, Arthur. Don't tell me what to do. Not now. Not ever again."

Amanda stands to go, but Arthur shakes his head and starts muttering to himself. He begins pacing back and forth, blocking the way. I have the gun, but I don't want to use it unless it's necessary, and I'm not sure how to react to his behavior.

I'm about to call out for Arthur to stand still when he lunges at me.

Time slows. I see the rage in his eyes and the tension in his muscles as he propels himself forward.

His body slams into mine as I reach out to stop him, driving the barrel of the handgun under his chin. The impact knocks the breath from my lungs as my finger tightens on the trigger and the gun goes off.

The blast rings in my ears as the top of Arthur's head erupts in blood and gore.

He falls backward, away from me, his blood and brains raining down on my face.

I've just shot my husband. The man I loved. The man I'd planned to spend the rest of my life with. The man who betrayed me.

Amanda is screaming. That's registering somewhere in my mind. But the screams sound far away, almost like they're under water.

Arthur's gun slips from my grasp, my legs give out, and I sink to the floor. The room spins as the reality of what I've done sets in.

My husband's brains are spattered all over the ceiling because of me.

A laugh escapes me, twisting into a sob. I've ended the threat, but with it, the life Arthur and I built. Our shared dreams are shattered, leaving only the painful truth I'll have to face every day.

My hands shake violently, sticky with the blood of three men.

Taking a deep, shuddering breath, I force myself to stand. There will be time to process this later. Right now, Amanda needs me.

I collapse on the couch beside her. "Amanda. I'm...I'm so sorry for what I said. I had to make it convincing."

Tears stream down Amanda's cheeks. "I know."

She hugs me, and as we embrace, my years of self-hatred

float away. A small voice whispers words of comfort only I can hear.

You broke the cycle.

CHAPTER
FIFTY-EIGHT

"No need to move the plants, I've got 'em!" I hurry to catch up with one of the burly mover guys as he trudges toward his truck with a box of plants in hand.

He hands me the box—with the orchid I'd purchased from Maggie sitting proudly in the center—and gives me a look that says, *Okay, crazy plant lady*.

Smiling, I rush toward my Outlander with the plants clutched to my chest. I call back out to him as I gingerly place the box in the back seat beside a dozen others.

"The plants ride with me so they can get light through the sunroof." *And so I don't get separation anxiety on the ride to my parents' place.*

A *Sold* sign protrudes from my manicured front lawn, and my wind chimes ring gently on the porch. Their music is a quiet reminder of the past I'm leaving behind and a gentle push toward my new future.

My phone rings with a video call from Amanda. I smile and answer.

"Hey, sweetie."

"Hi!"

I lean into the car and straighten up the plants in back. "Baby born yet?"

"Still no. But Mr. and Mrs. Tallman are here, and they are so sweet." Her smile is soft and caring. "You were right. Mrs. Tallman is so happy I said she could be with me for the birth."

"Good." The plants are perfectly straight now, each in their own little pot, ready for their journey. "But you need to get some rest, so get off the phone and call me after. Okay?"

Amanda pouts. "If you move to Denver, you're never going to come back."

"Amanda. That's—"

"All-or-nothing thinking, I know. Chapter one of the handbook."

She holds up a copy of my CBT bible—*The Feeling Good Handbook*—and I laugh. "You might be the only teen mom in history to do therapy homework on her due date."

Joining my laughter, Amanda gives me a gentle goodbye and disconnects. I'm still for a moment after she goes.

She's so lucky the baby is fine after everything that happened to her. And here's hoping the kid's luck keeps building from here.

Part of me wants to stay in Wildfire to keep helping girls like Amanda. But with all that's happened, I'm not ready to help others heal. After years of genuine—some might say pathological—avoidance, it's time for me to heal myself.

The movers leave, and I do one last walk-through of the house, promising I'll be a few minutes behind them out on I-60 West. Trailing my hand along the kitchen counters, I can't avoid thinking back to my perfect-on-the-outside suburban life.

There's Arthur at the stove, cooking my favorite meal. There we are laughing over a game of Scrabble, joking about how I always win and he never tries. There's the dog we fostered for six months, devouring my purse like it's a T-bone steak.

There's the bloodstain on the ceiling of the cabin as Arthur's faceless body falls away from mine.

I miss him every day, despite the lies, despite everything he did. Might even still love him. Pretty sure part of me always will.

Arthur's basement office is empty. There are green stains on the wall, and I think of the eucalyptus that used to grow there. It had been so fussy, but I'd kept it alive because Arthur loved it, and I loved him.

My chest burns with anxiety, regret, and at least a little bit of hope as I turn off the light and start back up the stairs. But I double back and look twice at the wall plate surrounding the light switch.

It's looks much newer than the others. And the bottom screw appears loose, which would've seriously grated Arthur's perfectionist brain.

I try to tighten the screw with my manicured nail—recently painted, thank you very much—but it falls right out.

"Hmm."

In less than five minutes, I've gone out to the shed, grabbed a rusty screwdriver, and returned to the basement.

Instead of putting the bottom screw back in place, I remove the top one, and the wall plate releases into my palm. There, shoved beside the outlet box, is a familiar smartphone.

"Son of a bitch. The burner."

I remove it from the wall.

Do I turn it into the police? Or do I take one last crack at getting it open?

Last time, every code I'd tried failed. Though there was one number I'd never punched in...the date Arthur and Will attacked me.

For me, it was one of the unluckiest days of my life. But

for Arthur...the attack had brought us together when nothing else could.

I take the stairs to the kitchen two at a time. My phone charger is the only item from that room I've yet to pack, and I need it now more than ever.

After a few minutes of impatient toe-tapping, the phone powers on. I try the six-digit date from the attack. A wheel spins.

The phone unlocks.

At first glance, the phone has only the standard apps. I don't care about the weather or the stopwatch, and I'm not trying to use the calculator. So I click into the messaging app to see what I find.

After a brief delay, the screen populates with hundreds of messages between Jonathan, Arthur, and Will.

My eyes narrow as I scroll, trying to get to the first message sent. But I roll back over a year, and the phone keeps adding more messages to the list.

"They were talking every single day."

I click a random message from half a year ago. It's a link to a golf course Will wants to check out somewhere in Hawaii. Not what I'm looking for.

Next, I scroll forward to midsummer, when Madeline Miller went missing. There are dozens of messages between the three of them. More evidence than the police would ever need.

These guys were so arrogant—so sure they were above the law—the messages are shockingly bold.

In one message, Arthur asks, *Where is she buried?*

In the next, he gets—and receives—confirmation that Madeline is *just a little way from R.S. Basically in the same spot though.*

I remember the coyote feasting on Madeline's insides. *Must've been a shallow grave.*

This is more than a smoking gun. This is a gun covered in fingerprints, with a confession note taped to it, found in the home of the killer.

"But why did Arthur keep this? Why did any of them?"

Then it hits me—insurance.

This phone contains proof of everything these monsters have done. They've been controlling each other with blackmail, trapped in a web of distrust and paranoia.

If only I'd gotten the phone to open and turned it into the police, Madeline might still be alive.

There's no use thinking that way, and it's a classic example of what my CBT handbook would call "crystal ball thinking." But the pain of the tragic thought pulls my eyes closed for a long, quiet moment.

When I open them again, I pull down the search bar in the messages app and look up my name. "Lizette" pops up in dozens of messages over the past few months, but it's the most recent exchange that catches my eye.

Jonathan reports that I've taken an interest in Amanda and says I'm about to ruin everything.

Will suggests *taking care of her, as hard as that might sound*, and he gets full support from Jonathan. But Arthur pushes back. He promises that he has me *under control* and says he'll get me out of town for a week to put some distance between me and *the Holland girl*.

My heart aches as I remember how Arthur tried to drag me to the beach while all this was going down. I don't know if I'm grateful to him or furious with him for protecting Jonathan from my prying eyes.

I hate that he thought he controlled me. I hate even more that in some ways he was right.

Arthur had claimed he'd been an unwilling bystander in the horrible crimes the others committed. I believed he'd never truly wanted to be there, and that none of it had been his idea.

But at what point does that stop mattering? "You were there," I say aloud. "More than guilty by association."

I text Chief Prentice to let him know I'm leaving the burner behind. Then I drop the phone onto the counter as tears pool in my eyes.

I miss my husband. And I'm tempted to take pity on myself, to wallow in loneliness, and play the victim.

But the truth is I have always been alone, just like we all are. That's not a bad thing. And now that I've accepted it, I can finally live free.

I'm truly, deeply grateful to Arthur. He saved my life. But what about Regina, Kylie, and Madeline? What about the girls he never thought were worth saving?

All I'd ever wanted was to be special, and he'd made me feel like that, for a while.

But I need to find the meaning in my suffering—the good hidden inside my pain. That means I have to accept the pain, feel it, and simply allow it to pass. No more stories. No more drama. Just life.

With a deep breath, I gather my bag and step out onto the porch. Warm, late-afternoon sunlight washes over my face, and each step I take toward my car feels light, as if my feet barely touch the ground.

The drive from the house out to the interstate takes only a few minutes, but it feels like a journey from one life to another. Just before I reach the highway, I spot something on the side of the road that brings a tiny smile to my face.

A copperhead is sunning itself on a fallen tree.

I pull to the shoulder and watch. The copperhead rests undisturbed. *Happy, even.*

Closure, noun
The process of finding resolution and peace after a

significant life event, often marked by acceptance and the quiet realization that it's time to move forward. Not to be confused with forgetting—because some things, like snakes and old memories, stick with you. See also, the peace that comes from no longer living a lie.

The End

ACKNOWLEDGMENTS

How does one adequately express gratitude to all those who have transformed a shared dream into a stunning reality? Let us attempt to do just that.

First and foremost, our families deserve our deepest thanks. Their unwavering support and encouragement have been our bedrock, allowing us the time and energy to translate our collective imagination into the words that fill these pages. Their belief in our vision has been a constant source of strength and inspiration.

As coauthors, our journey has been uniquely collaborative and rewarding. Now, with Mary also embracing the additional role of publisher, our adventure has taken on an exciting new dimension. This transition from solely writing to also publishing has been both a challenge and a joy, opening doors to share our work more directly with you, our readers.

We are immensely grateful to the entire team at Mary Stone Publishing — a group who believed in our potential from the very beginning. Their commitment extends beyond editing our words; it encompasses the tireless efforts of designers, marketers, and support staff, all dedicated to bringing our stories to life. Their expertise, creativity, and passion have been vital in capturing the essence of our tales and sharing them with the world.

However, our greatest appreciation is reserved for you, our beloved readers. You took a chance on our book, generously sharing your most precious asset—your time. It is our fervent hope that the pages of this book have rewarded that generosity, offering you a journey worth taking and memories that linger.

With all our love and heartfelt appreciation,

Mary & Matt

ABOUT THE AUTHOR

MARY STONE

Nestled in the tranquil Blue Ridge Mountains of East Tennessee, Mary Stone has transformed her peaceful home, once bustling with her sons, into a creative haven. As her family grew, so did her writing career, evolving from childhood fears to a deep understanding of real-life villains. Her stories, centered around strong, unconventional heroines, weave themes of courage and intrigue.

Mary's journey from a solitary writer to establishing her own publishing house marks a significant evolution, showcasing her commitment to the literary world. Through her writing and publishing endeavors, she continues to captivate and inspire, honoring her lifelong fascination with the mysterious and the courageous.

Connect with Mary online

facebook.com/authormarystone
x.com/MaryStoneAuthor
goodreads.com/AuthorMaryStone
bookbub.com/authors/mary-stone
pinterest.com/MaryStoneAuthor
instagram.com/marystoneauthor

Discover more about Mary Stone on her website.
www.authormarystone.com

MATT GIEGERICH

Matt is a USA Today bestselling author of mysteries and psychological thrillers. A graduate of Duke University and a member of the Writers Guild of America, Matt blends suspense with cinematic flair in his storytelling. He lives in Brooklyn, NY with his dog, Gopher.

Discover more about Matt Giegerich on his website.
www.mattgiegerich.com